LiTTLE DEE
AND THE PENGUiN

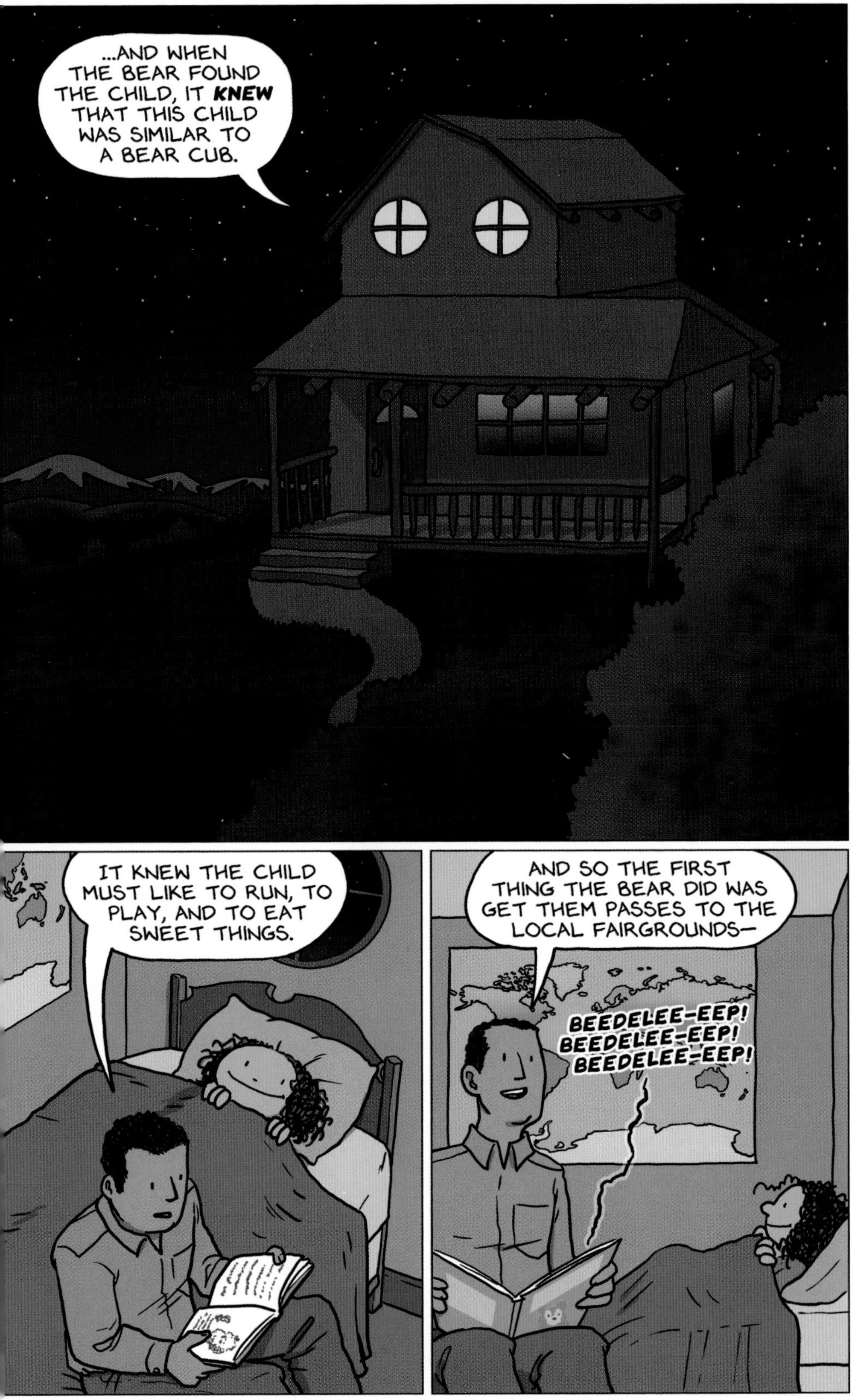
...AND WHEN THE BEAR FOUND THE CHILD, IT **KNEW** THAT THIS CHILD WAS SIMILAR TO A BEAR CUB.
IT KNEW THE CHILD MUST LIKE TO RUN, TO PLAY, AND TO EAT SWEET THINGS.
AND SO THE FIRST THING THE BEAR DID WAS GET THEM PASSES TO THE LOCAL FAIRGROUNDS—
BEEDELEE-EEP! BEEDELEE-EEP! BEEDELEE-EEP!

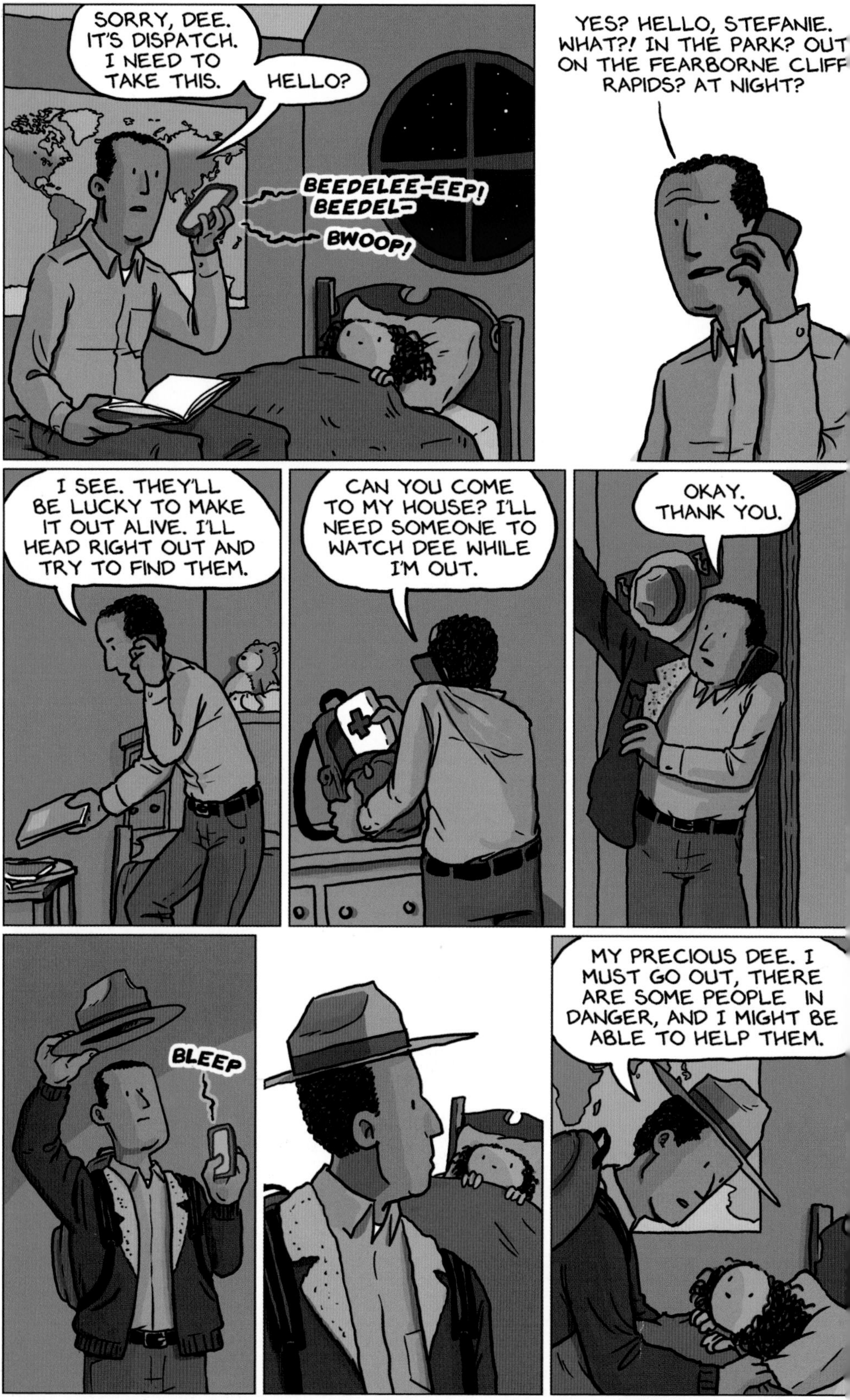
SORRY, DEE. IT'S DISPATCH. I NEED TO TAKE THIS.
HELLO?
BEEDELEE-EEP! BEEDEL-
BWOOP!
YES? HELLO, STEFANIE. WHAT?! IN THE PARK? OUT ON THE FEARBORNE CLIFF RAPIDS? AT NIGHT?
I SEE. THEY'LL BE LUCKY TO MAKE IT OUT ALIVE. I'LL HEAD RIGHT OUT AND TRY TO FIND THEM.
CAN YOU COME TO MY HOUSE? I'LL NEED SOMEONE TO WATCH DEE WHILE I'M OUT.
OKAY. THANK YOU.
BLEEP
MY PRECIOUS DEE. I MUST GO OUT, THERE ARE SOME PEOPLE IN DANGER, AND I MIGHT BE ABLE TO HELP THEM.

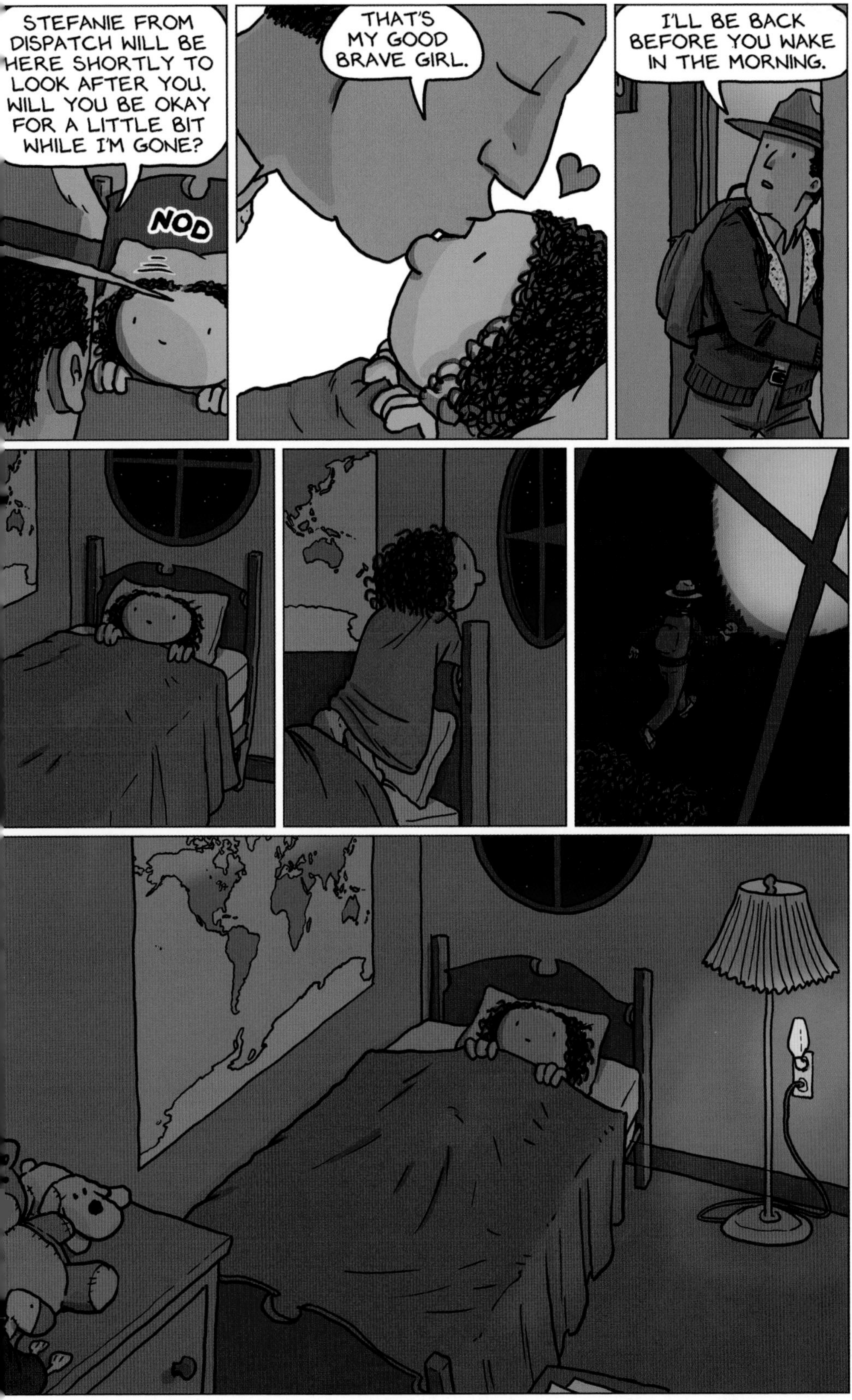
STEFANIE FROM DISPATCH WILL BE HERE SHORTLY TO LOOK AFTER YOU. WILL YOU BE OKAY FOR A LITTLE BIT WHILE I'M GONE?
NOD
THAT'S MY GOOD BRAVE GIRL.
I'LL BE BACK BEFORE YOU WAKE IN THE MORNING.

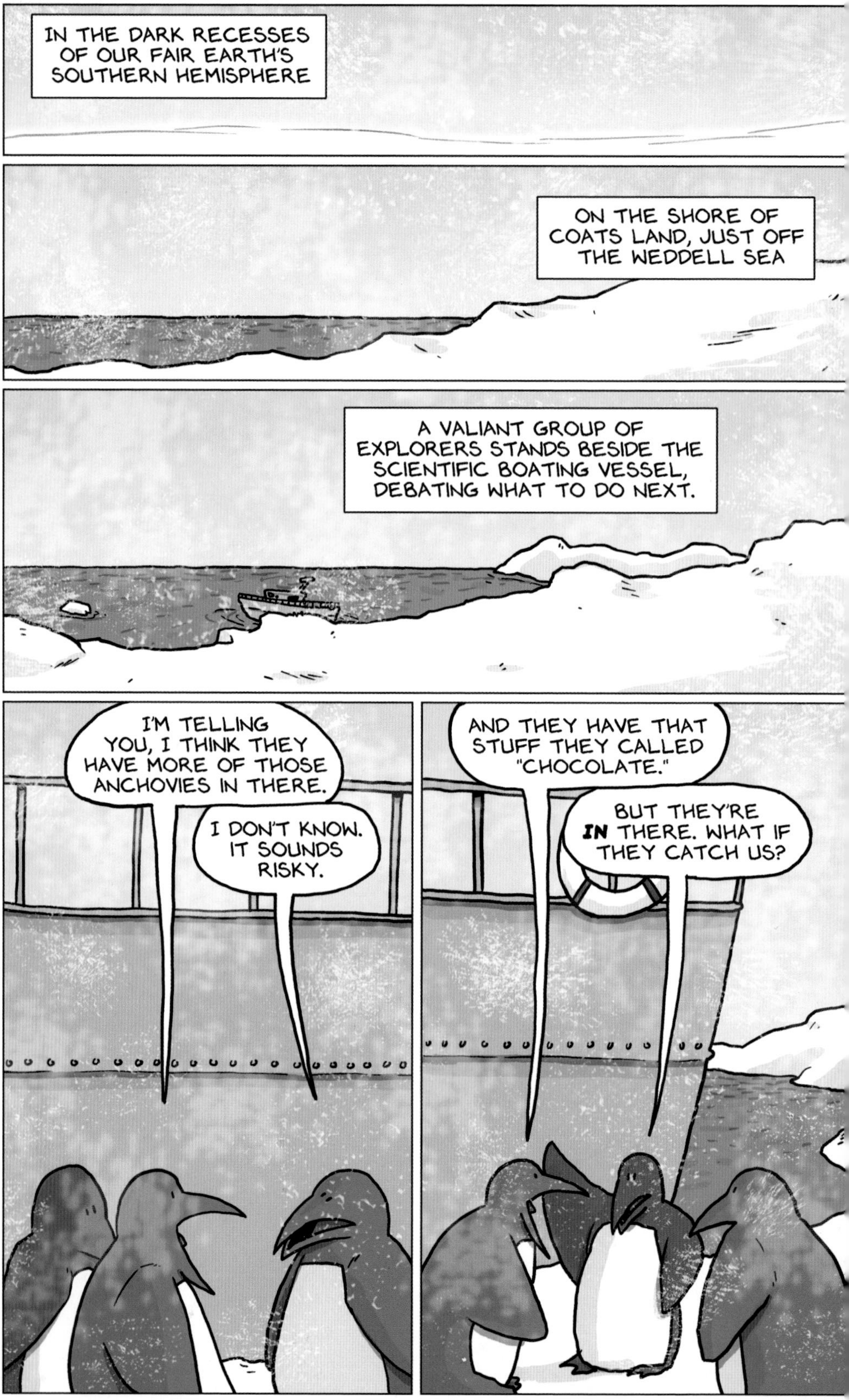
IN THE DARK RECESSES OF OUR FAIR EARTH'S SOUTHERN HEMISPHERE
ON THE SHORE OF COATS LAND, JUST OFF THE WEDDELL SEA
A VALIANT GROUP OF EXPLORERS STANDS BESIDE THE SCIENTIFIC BOATING VESSEL, DEBATING WHAT TO DO NEXT.
I'M TELLING YOU, I THINK THEY HAVE MORE OF THOSE ANCHOVIES IN THERE.
I DON'T KNOW. IT SOUNDS RISKY.
AND THEY HAVE THAT STUFF THEY CALLED "CHOCOLATE."
BUT THEY'RE **IN** THERE. WHAT IF THEY CATCH US?

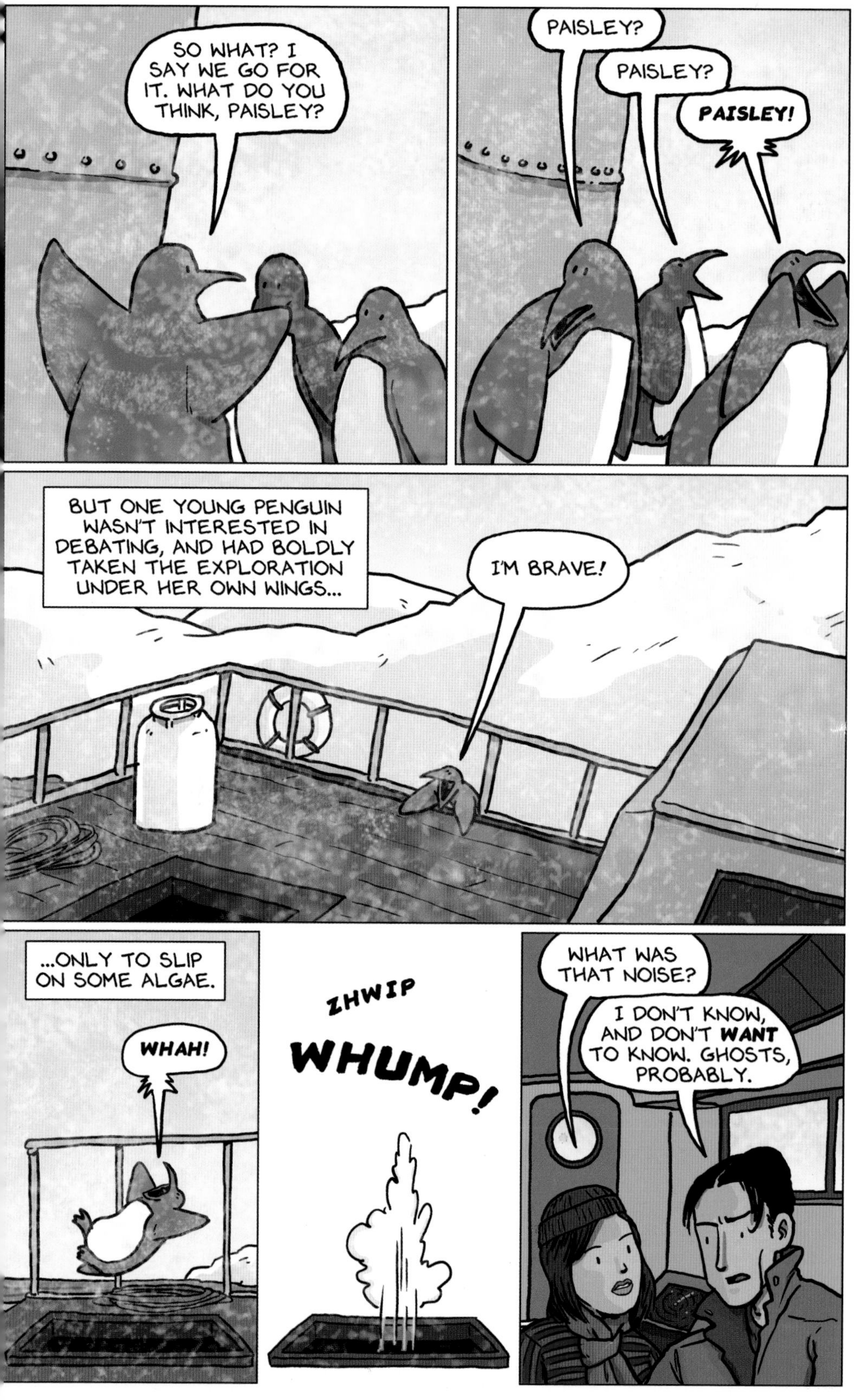
SO WHAT? I SAY WE GO FOR IT. WHAT DO YOU THINK, PAISLEY?
PAISLEY?
PAISLEY?
PAISLEY!
BUT ONE YOUNG PENGUIN WASN'T INTERESTED IN DEBATING, AND HAD BOLDLY TAKEN THE EXPLORATION UNDER HER OWN WINGS...
I'M BRAVE!
...ONLY TO SLIP ON SOME ALGAE.
WHAH!
ZHWIP
WHUMP!
WHAT WAS THAT NOISE?
I DON'T KNOW, AND DON'T WANT TO KNOW. GHOSTS, PROBABLY.

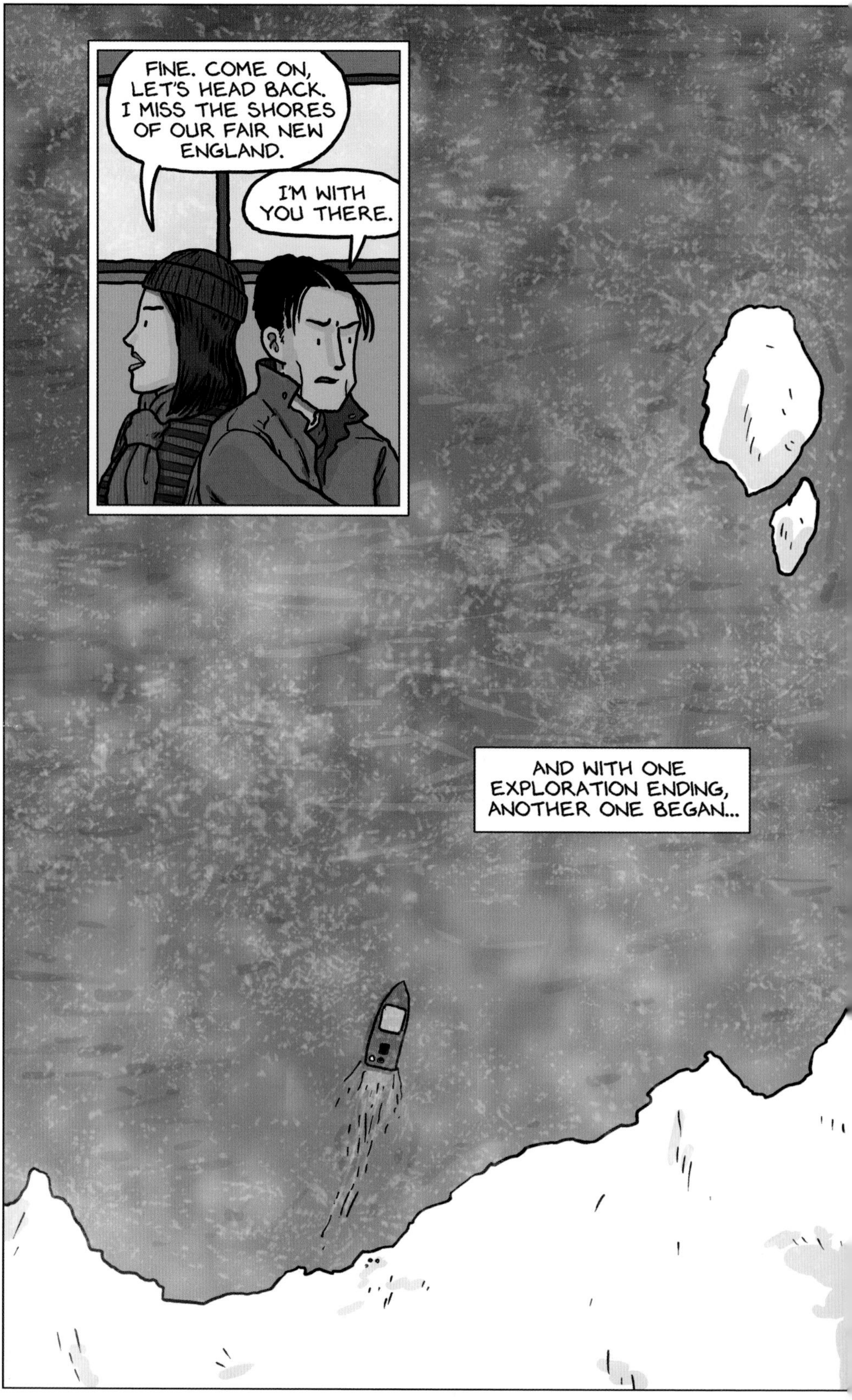
FINE. COME ON, LET'S HEAD BACK. I MISS THE SHORES OF OUR FAIR NEW ENGLAND.
I'M WITH YOU THERE.
AND WITH ONE EXPLORATION ENDING, ANOTHER ONE BEGAN...

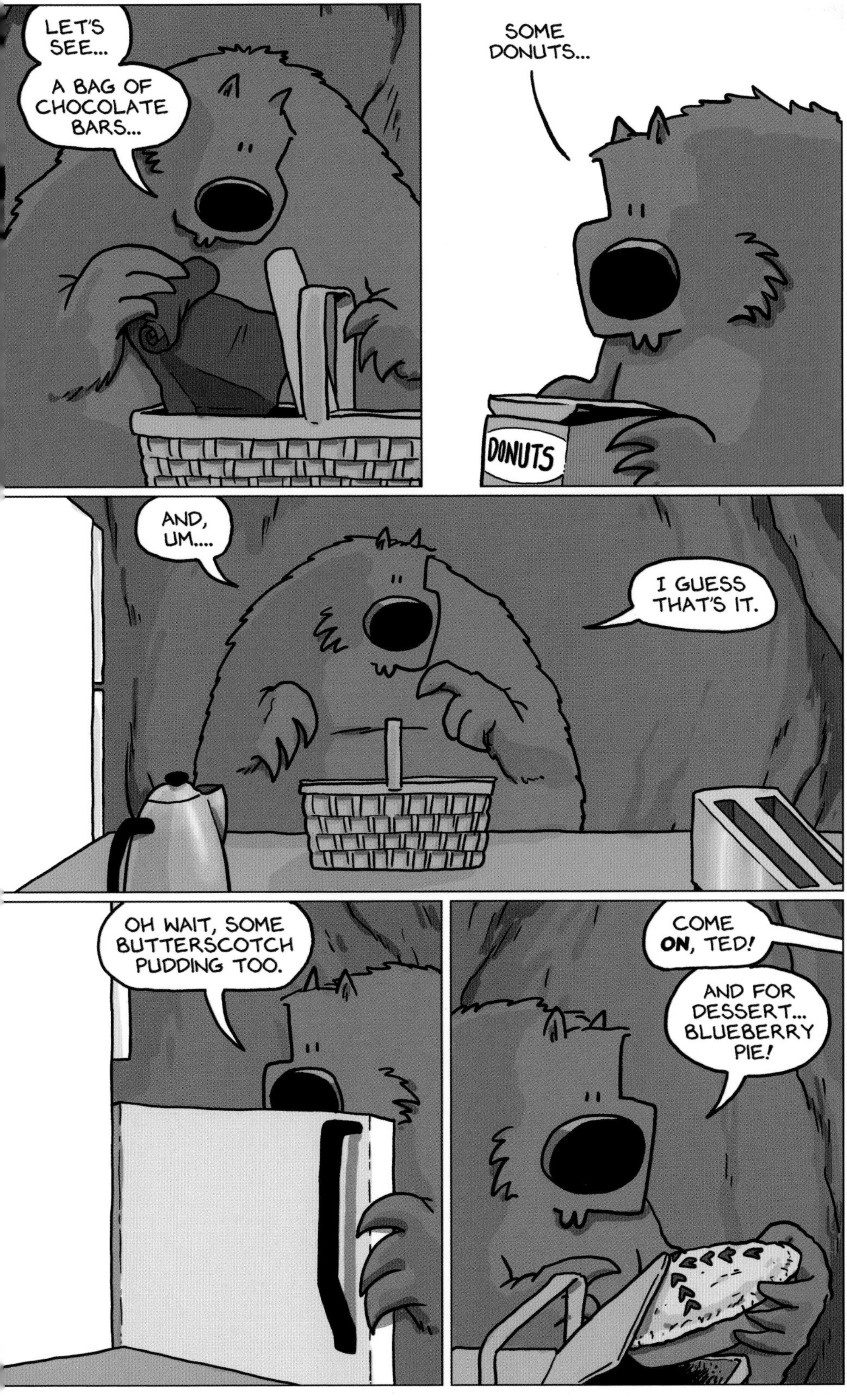
LET'S SEE...
A BAG OF CHOCOLATE BARS...
SOME DONUTS...
DONUTS
AND, UM....
I GUESS THAT'S IT.
OH WAIT, SOME BUTTERSCOTCH PUDDING TOO.
COME **ON**, TED!
AND FOR DESSERT... BLUEBERRY PIE!

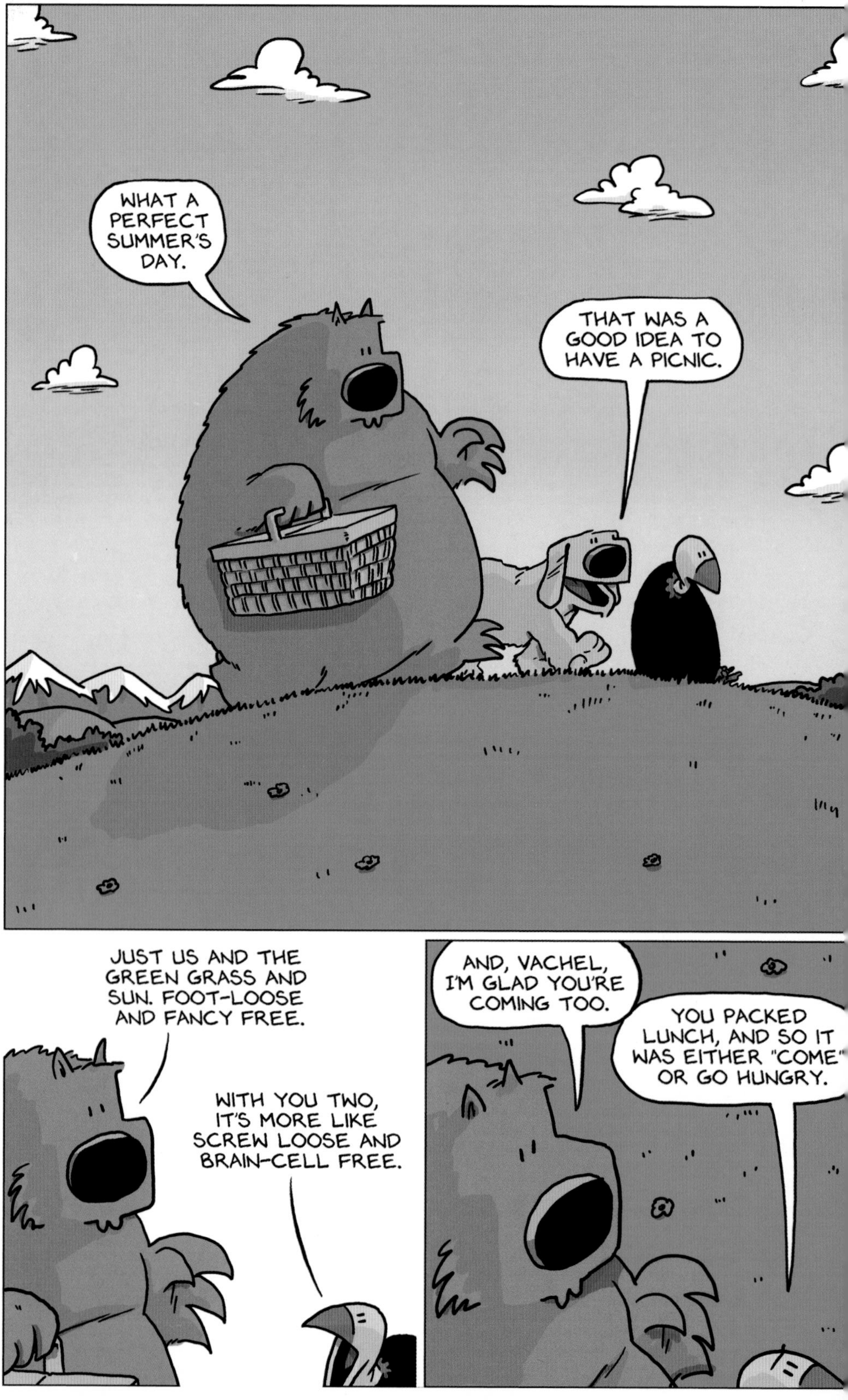
WHAT A PERFECT SUMMER'S DAY.
THAT WAS A GOOD IDEA TO HAVE A PICNIC.
JUST US AND THE GREEN GRASS AND SUN. FOOT-LOOSE AND FANCY FREE.
WITH YOU TWO, IT'S MORE LIKE SCREW LOOSE AND BRAIN-CELL FREE.
AND, VACHEL, I'M GLAD YOU'RE COMING TOO.
YOU PACKED LUNCH, AND SO IT WAS EITHER "COME" OR GO HUNGRY.

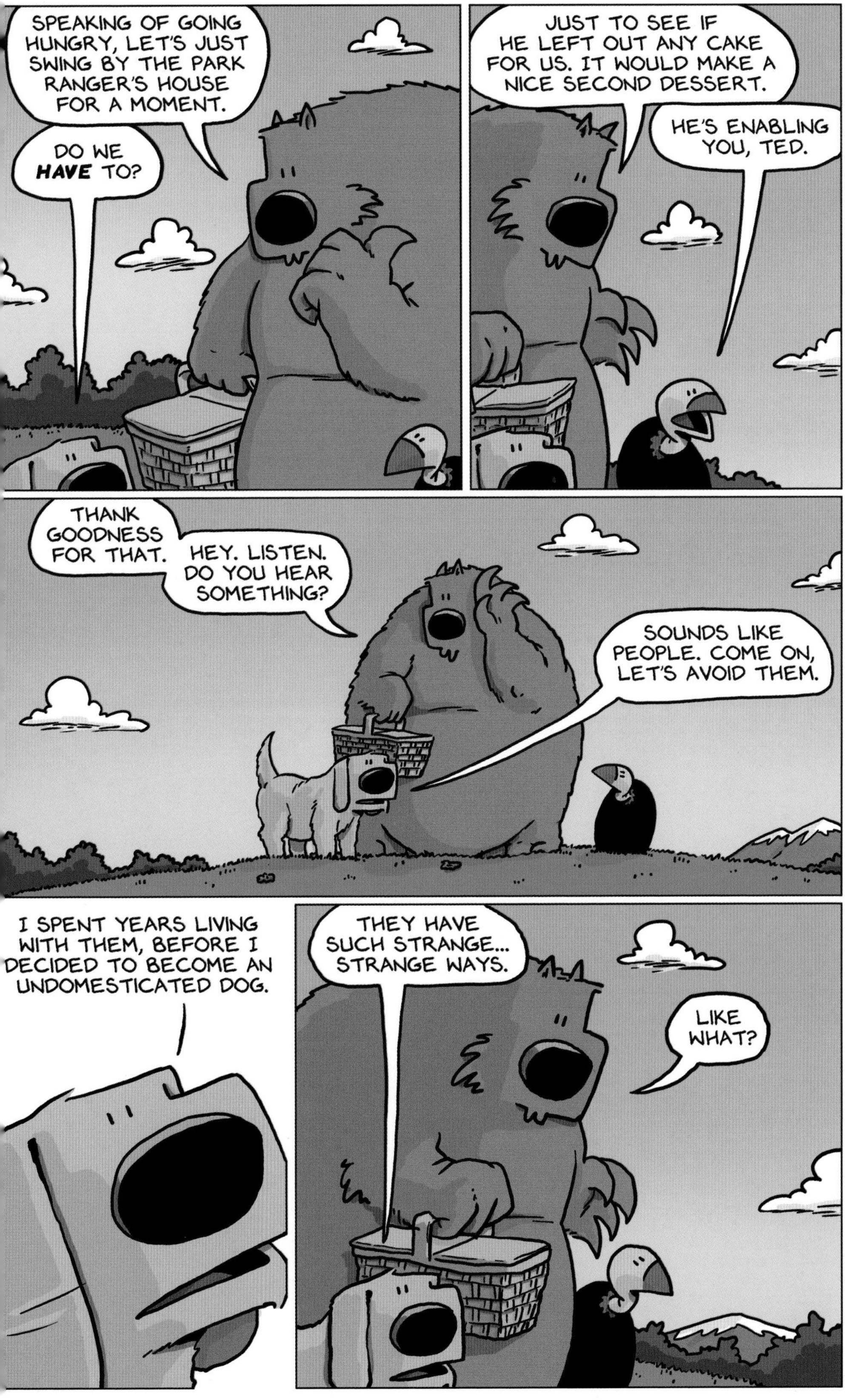
SPEAKING OF GOING HUNGRY, LET'S JUST SWING BY THE PARK RANGER'S HOUSE FOR A MOMENT.
DO WE **HAVE** TO?
JUST TO SEE IF HE LEFT OUT ANY CAKE FOR US. IT WOULD MAKE A NICE SECOND DESSERT.
HE'S ENABLING YOU, TED.
THANK GOODNESS FOR THAT.
HEY. LISTEN. DO YOU HEAR SOMETHING?
SOUNDS LIKE PEOPLE. COME ON, LET'S AVOID THEM.
I SPENT YEARS LIVING WITH THEM, BEFORE I DECIDED TO BECOME AN UNDOMESTICATED DOG.
THEY HAVE SUCH STRANGE... STRANGE WAYS.
LIKE WHAT?

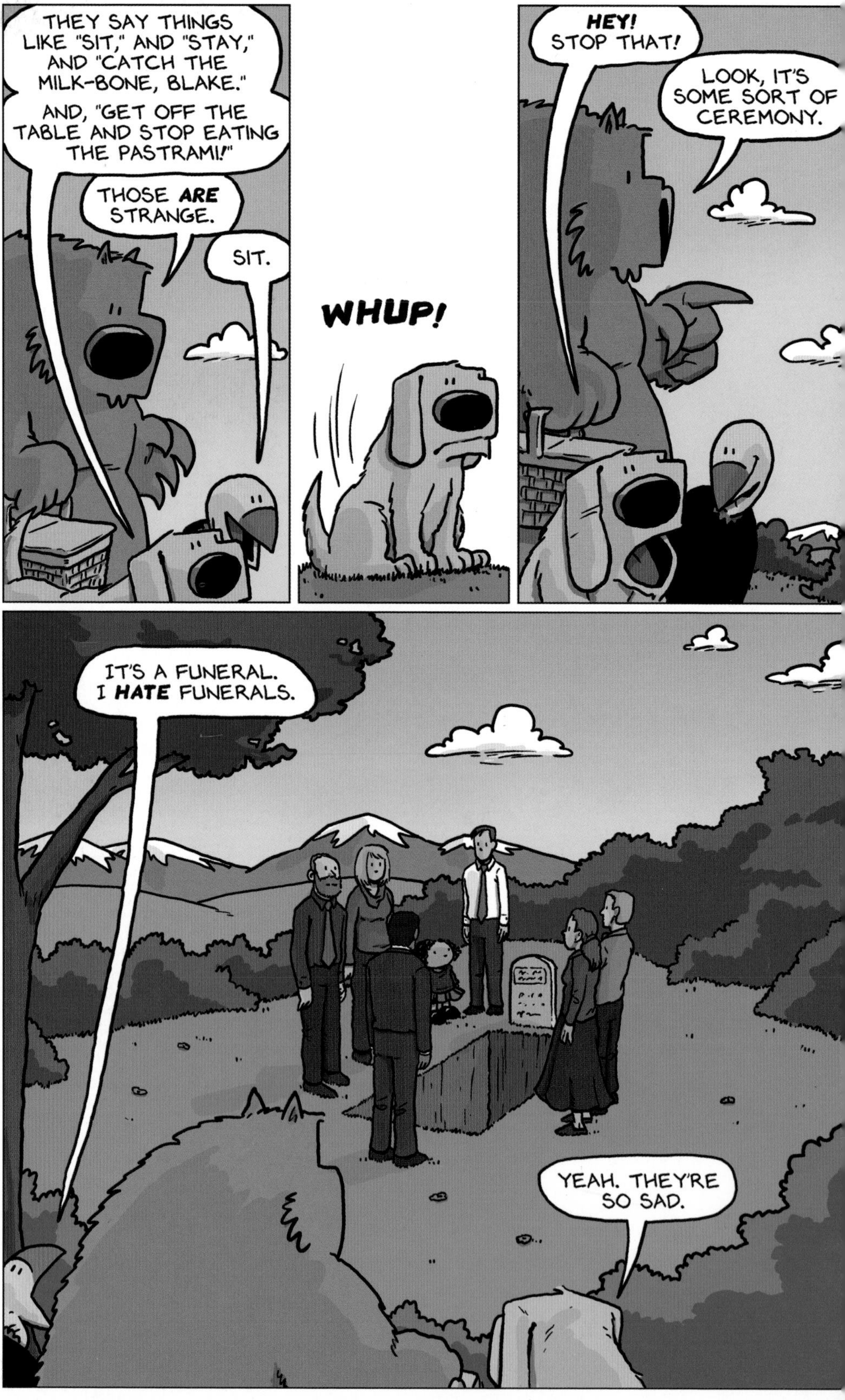
THEY SAY THINGS LIKE "SIT," AND "STAY," AND "CATCH THE MILK-BONE, BLAKE."
AND, "GET OFF THE TABLE AND STOP EATING THE PASTRAMI!"
THOSE **ARE** STRANGE.
SIT.
WHUP!
HEY! STOP THAT!
LOOK, IT'S SOME SORT OF CEREMONY.
IT'S A FUNERAL. I **HATE** FUNERALS.
YEAH. THEY'RE SO SAD.

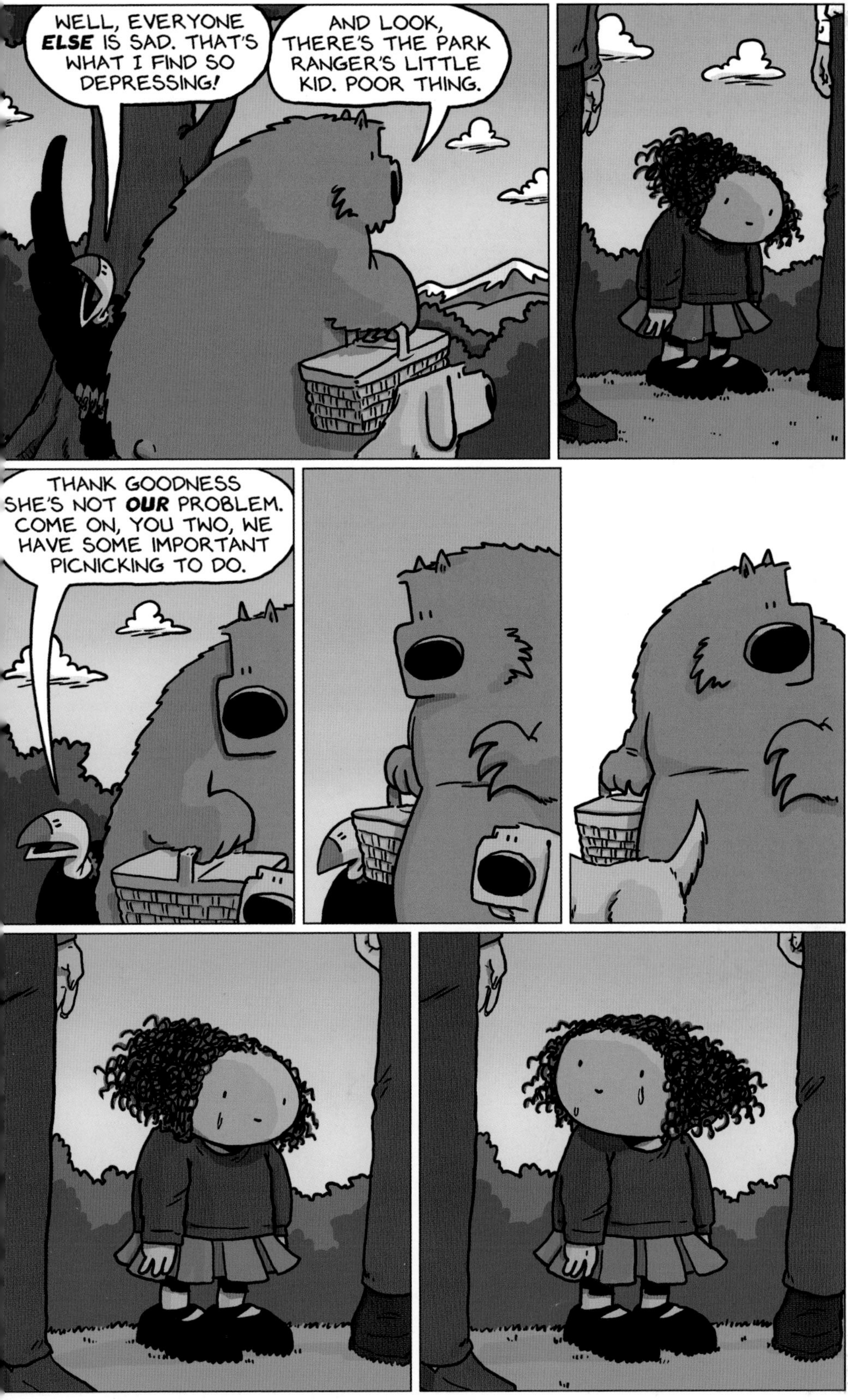
WELL, EVERYONE ELSE IS SAD. THAT'S WHAT I FIND SO DEPRESSING!
AND LOOK, THERE'S THE PARK RANGER'S LITTLE KID. POOR THING.
THANK GOODNESS SHE'S NOT OUR PROBLEM. COME ON, YOU TWO, WE HAVE SOME IMPORTANT PICNICKING TO DO.

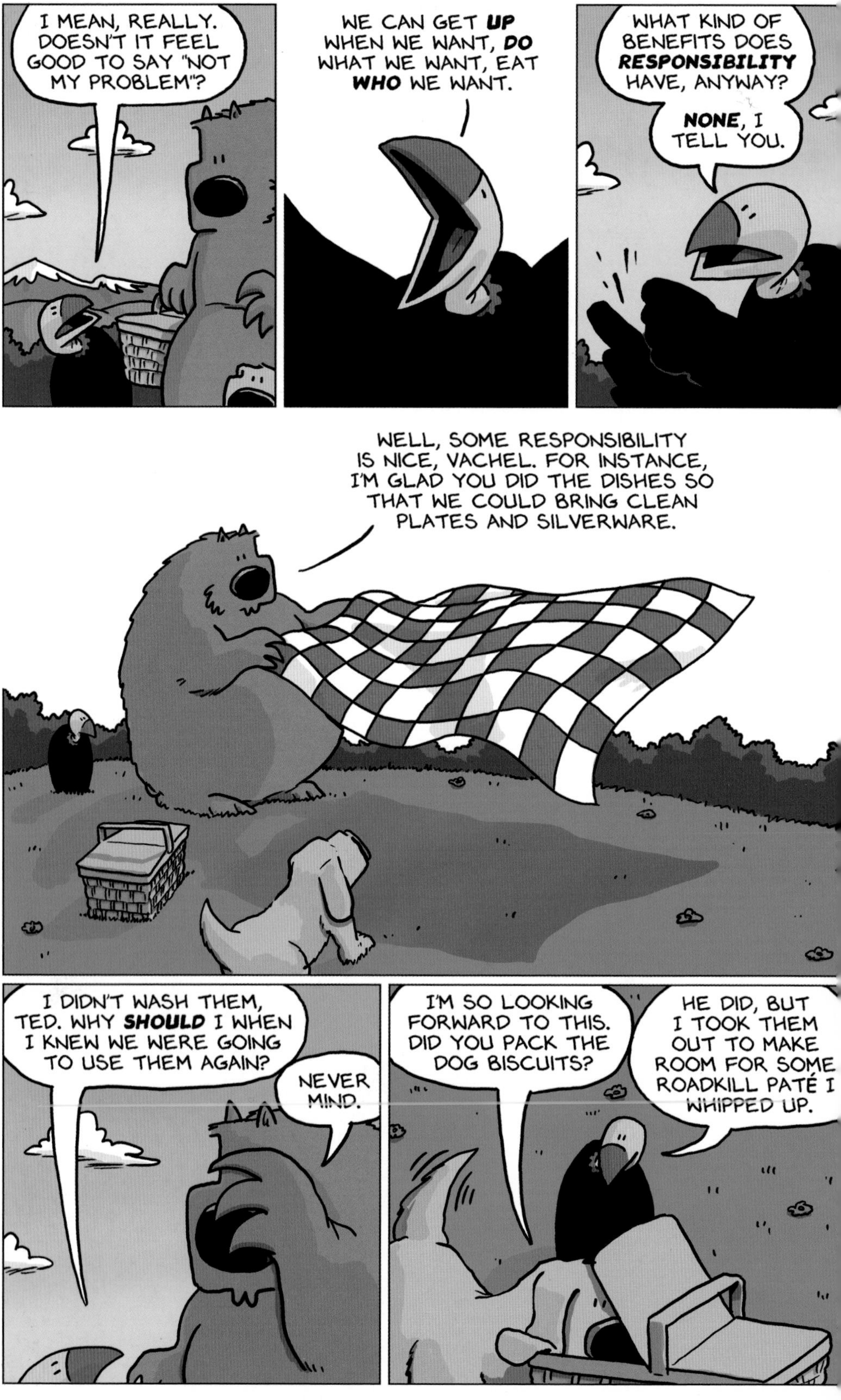
I MEAN, REALLY. DOESN'T IT FEEL GOOD TO SAY "NOT MY PROBLEM"?
WE CAN GET **UP** WHEN WE WANT, **DO** WHAT WE WANT, EAT **WHO** WE WANT.
WHAT KIND OF BENEFITS DOES **RESPONSIBILITY** HAVE, ANYWAY?
NONE, I TELL YOU.
WELL, SOME RESPONSIBILITY IS NICE, VACHEL. FOR INSTANCE, I'M GLAD YOU DID THE DISHES SO THAT WE COULD BRING CLEAN PLATES AND SILVERWARE.
I DIDN'T WASH THEM, TED. WHY **SHOULD** I WHEN I KNEW WE WERE GOING TO USE THEM AGAIN?
NEVER MIND.
I'M SO LOOKING FORWARD TO THIS. DID YOU PACK THE DOG BISCUITS?
HE DID, BUT I TOOK THEM OUT TO MAKE ROOM FOR SOME ROADKILL PATÉ I WHIPPED UP.

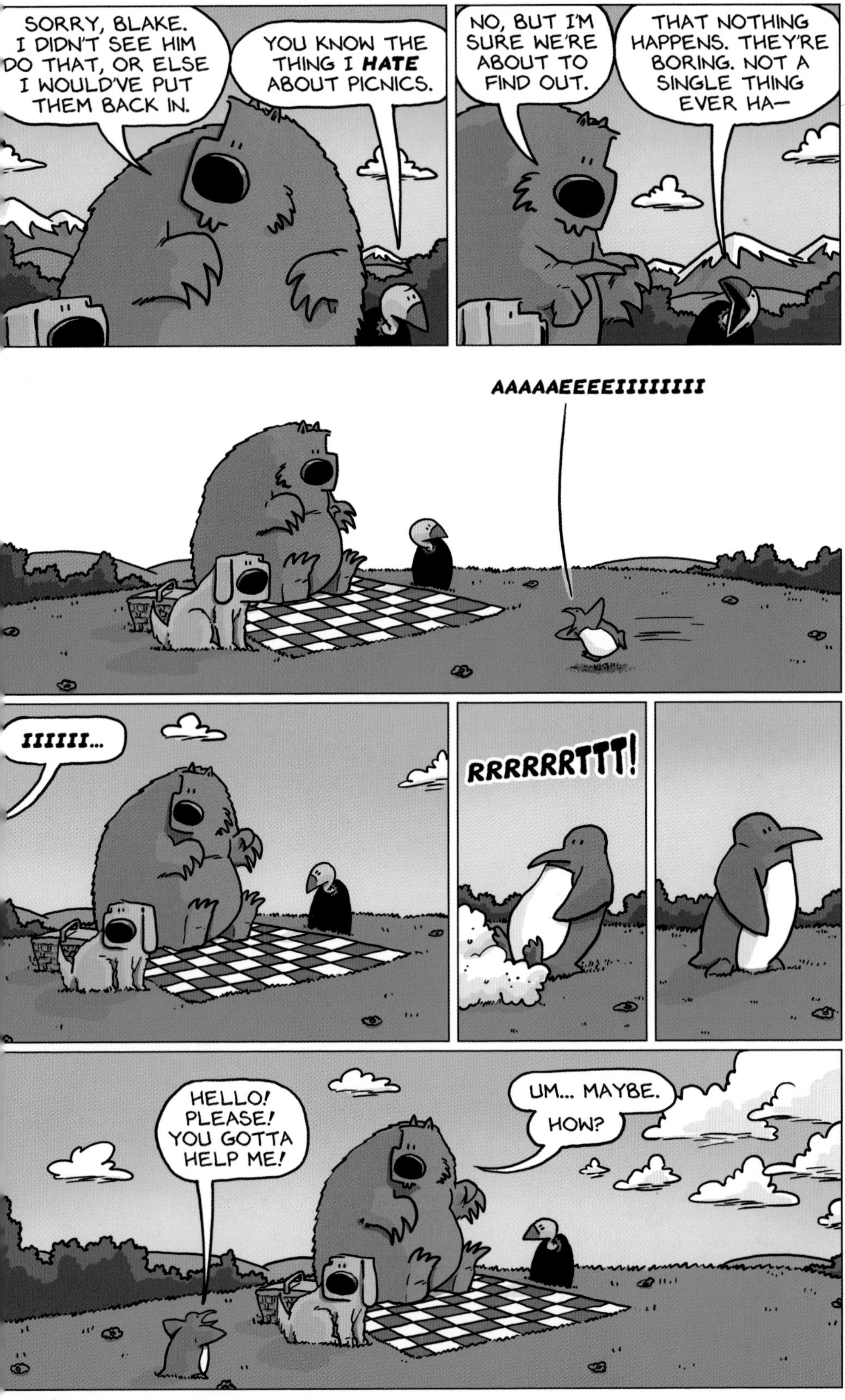
SORRY, BLAKE. I DIDN'T SEE HIM DO THAT, OR ELSE I WOULD'VE PUT THEM BACK IN.
YOU KNOW THE THING I **HATE** ABOUT PICNICS.
NO, BUT I'M SURE WE'RE ABOUT TO FIND OUT.
THAT NOTHING HAPPENS. THEY'RE BORING. NOT A SINGLE THING EVER HA—
AAAAAEEEEIIIIIIII
IIIIII...
RRRRRRTTT!
HELLO! PLEASE! YOU GOTTA HELP ME!
UM... MAYBE.
HOW?

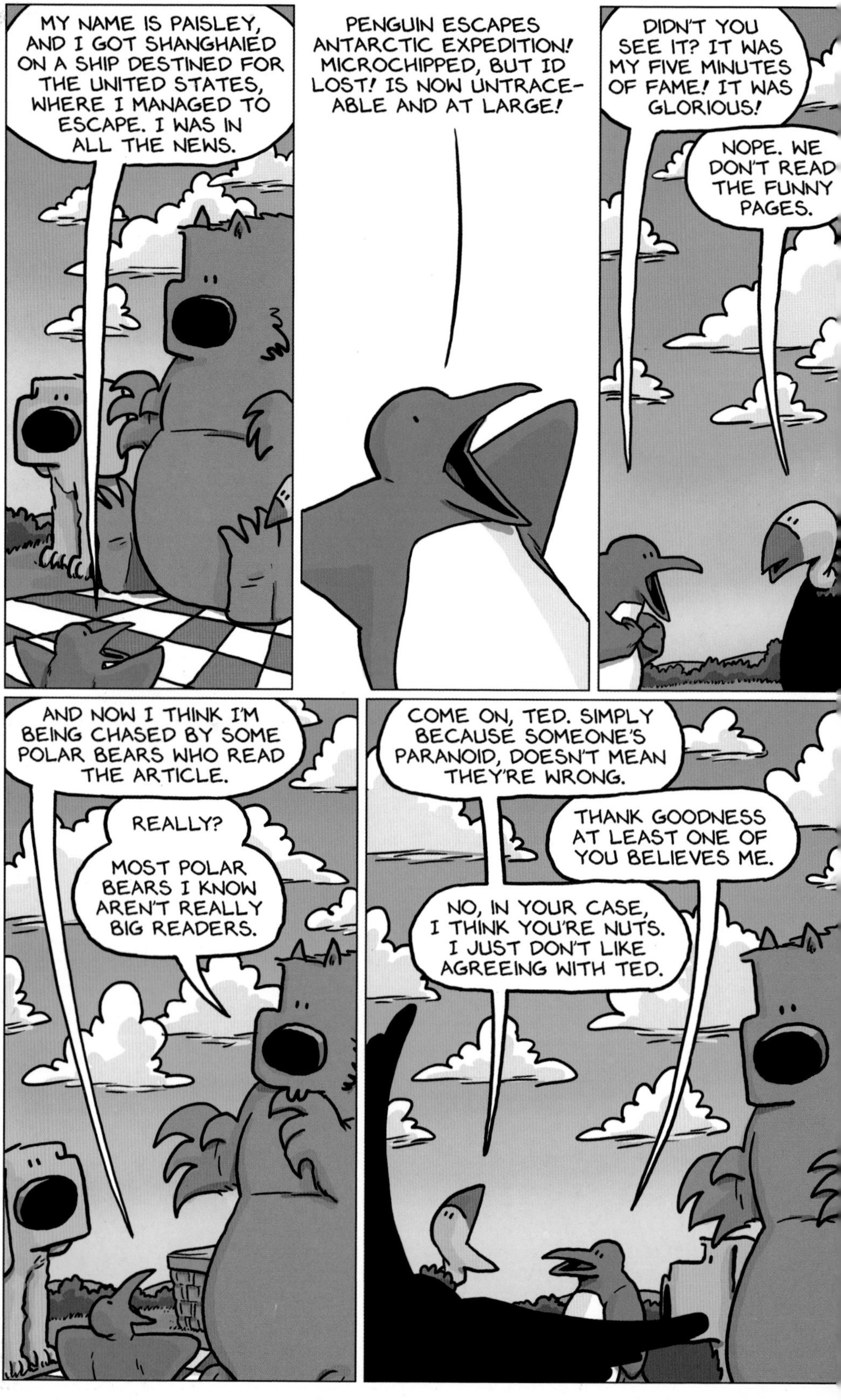
MY NAME IS PAISLEY, AND I GOT SHANGHAIED ON A SHIP DESTINED FOR THE UNITED STATES, WHERE I MANAGED TO ESCAPE. I WAS IN ALL THE NEWS.
PENGUIN ESCAPES ANTARCTIC EXPEDITION! MICROCHIPPED, BUT ID LOST! IS NOW UNTRACE-ABLE AND AT LARGE!
DIDN'T YOU SEE IT? IT WAS MY FIVE MINUTES OF FAME! IT WAS GLORIOUS!
NOPE. WE DON'T READ THE FUNNY PAGES.
AND NOW I THINK I'M BEING CHASED BY SOME POLAR BEARS WHO READ THE ARTICLE.
REALLY?
MOST POLAR BEARS I KNOW AREN'T REALLY BIG READERS.
COME ON, TED. SIMPLY BECAUSE SOMEONE'S PARANOID, DOESN'T MEAN THEY'RE WRONG.
THANK GOODNESS AT LEAST ONE OF YOU BELIEVES ME.
NO, IN YOUR CASE, I THINK YOU'RE NUTS. I JUST DON'T LIKE AGREEING WITH TED.

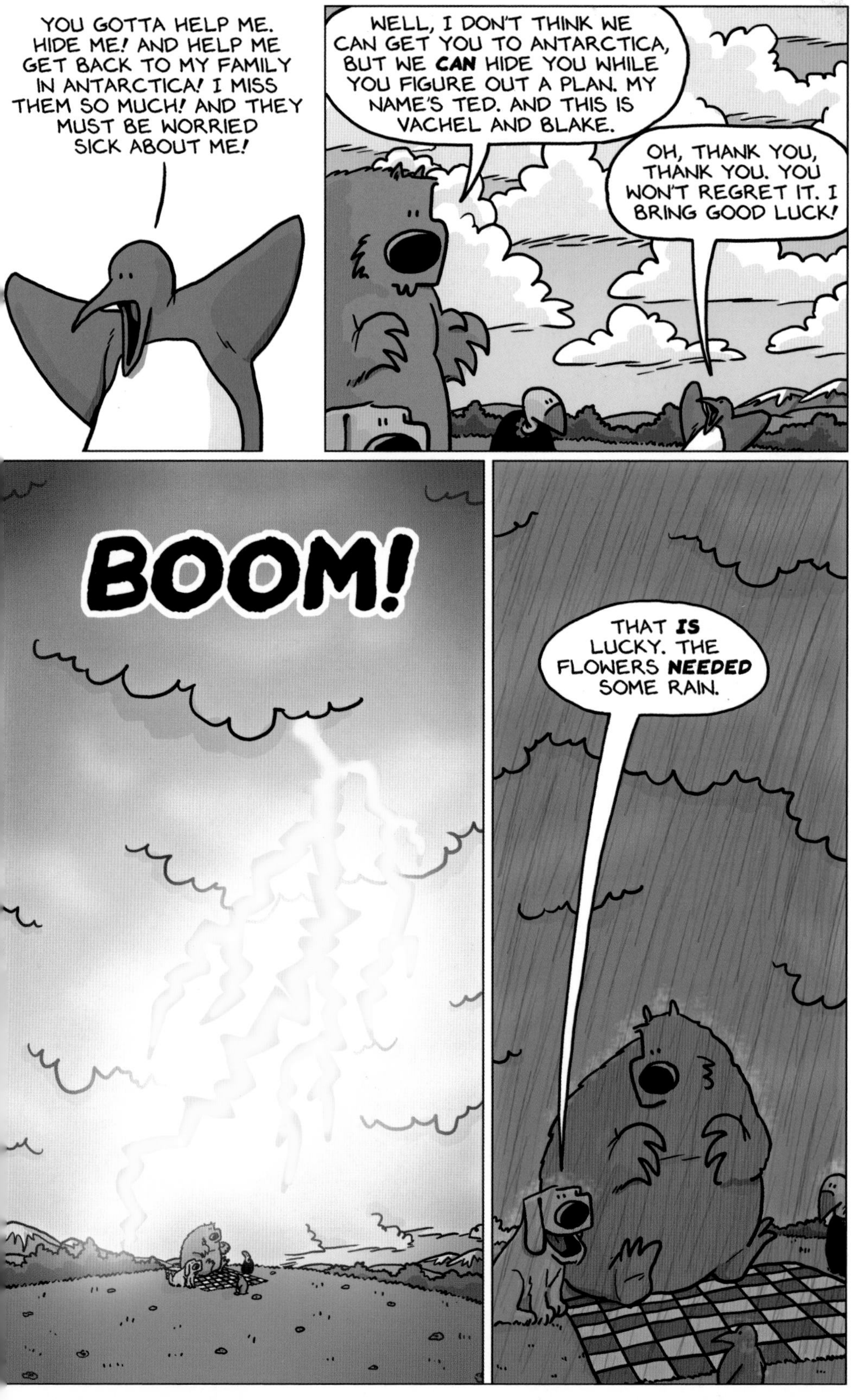
YOU GOTTA HELP ME. HIDE ME! AND HELP ME GET BACK TO MY FAMILY IN ANTARCTICA! I MISS THEM SO MUCH! AND THEY MUST BE WORRIED SICK ABOUT ME!
WELL, I DON'T THINK WE CAN GET YOU TO ANTARCTICA, BUT WE **CAN** HIDE YOU WHILE YOU FIGURE OUT A PLAN. MY NAME'S TED. AND THIS IS VACHEL AND BLAKE.
OH, THANK YOU, THANK YOU. YOU WON'T REGRET IT. I BRING GOOD LUCK!
BOOM!
THAT **IS** LUCKY. THE FLOWERS **NEEDED** SOME RAIN.

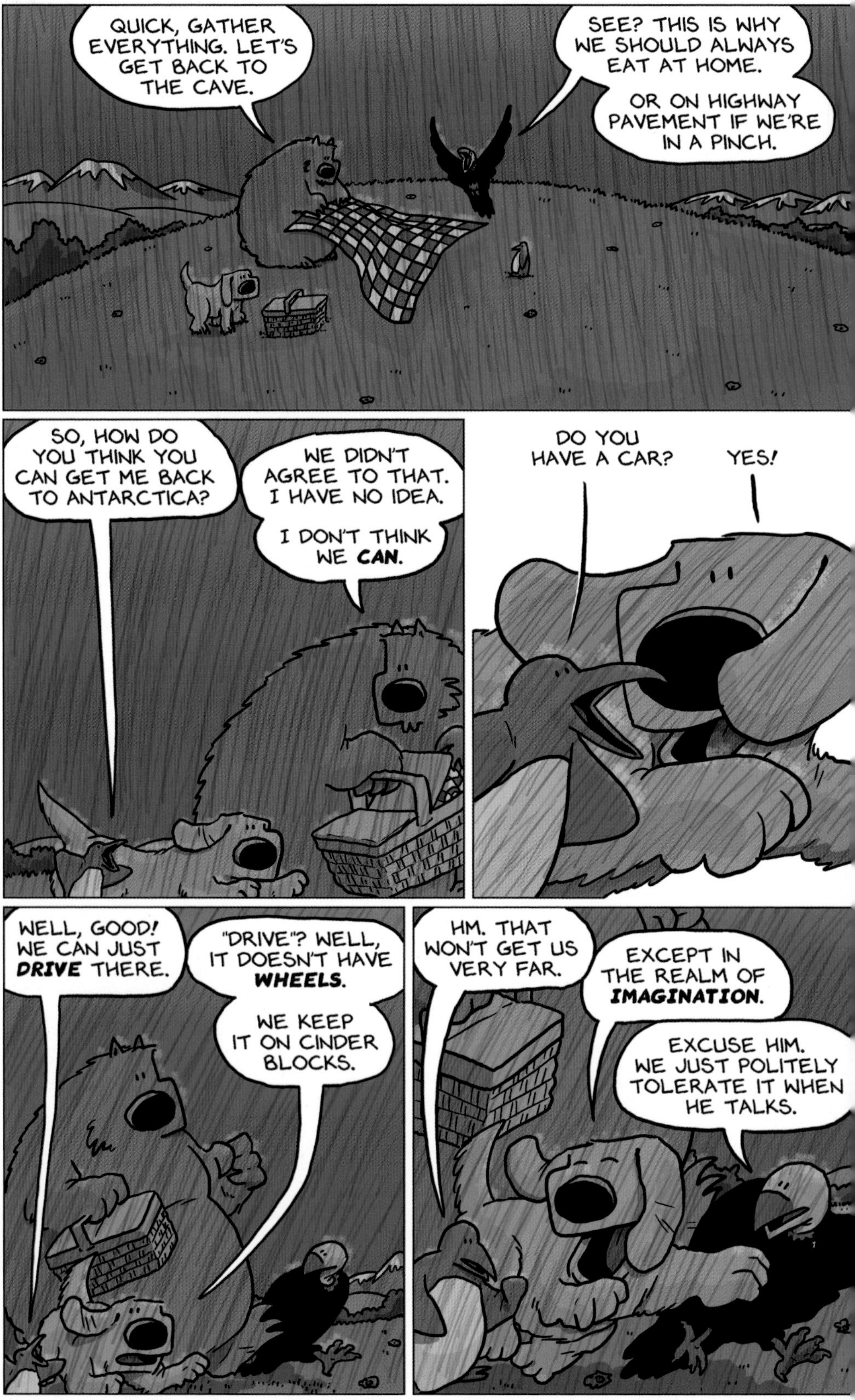
QUICK, GATHER EVERYTHING. LET'S GET BACK TO THE CAVE.
SEE? THIS IS WHY WE SHOULD ALWAYS EAT AT HOME.
OR ON HIGHWAY PAVEMENT IF WE'RE IN A PINCH.
SO, HOW DO YOU THINK YOU CAN GET ME BACK TO ANTARCTICA?
WE DIDN'T AGREE TO THAT. I HAVE NO IDEA.
I DON'T THINK WE CAN.
DO YOU HAVE A CAR?
YES!
WELL, GOOD! WE CAN JUST DRIVE THERE.
"DRIVE"? WELL, IT DOESN'T HAVE WHEELS.
WE KEEP IT ON CINDER BLOCKS.
HM. THAT WON'T GET US VERY FAR.
EXCEPT IN THE REALM OF IMAGINATION.
EXCUSE HIM. WE JUST POLITELY TOLERATE IT WHEN HE TALKS.

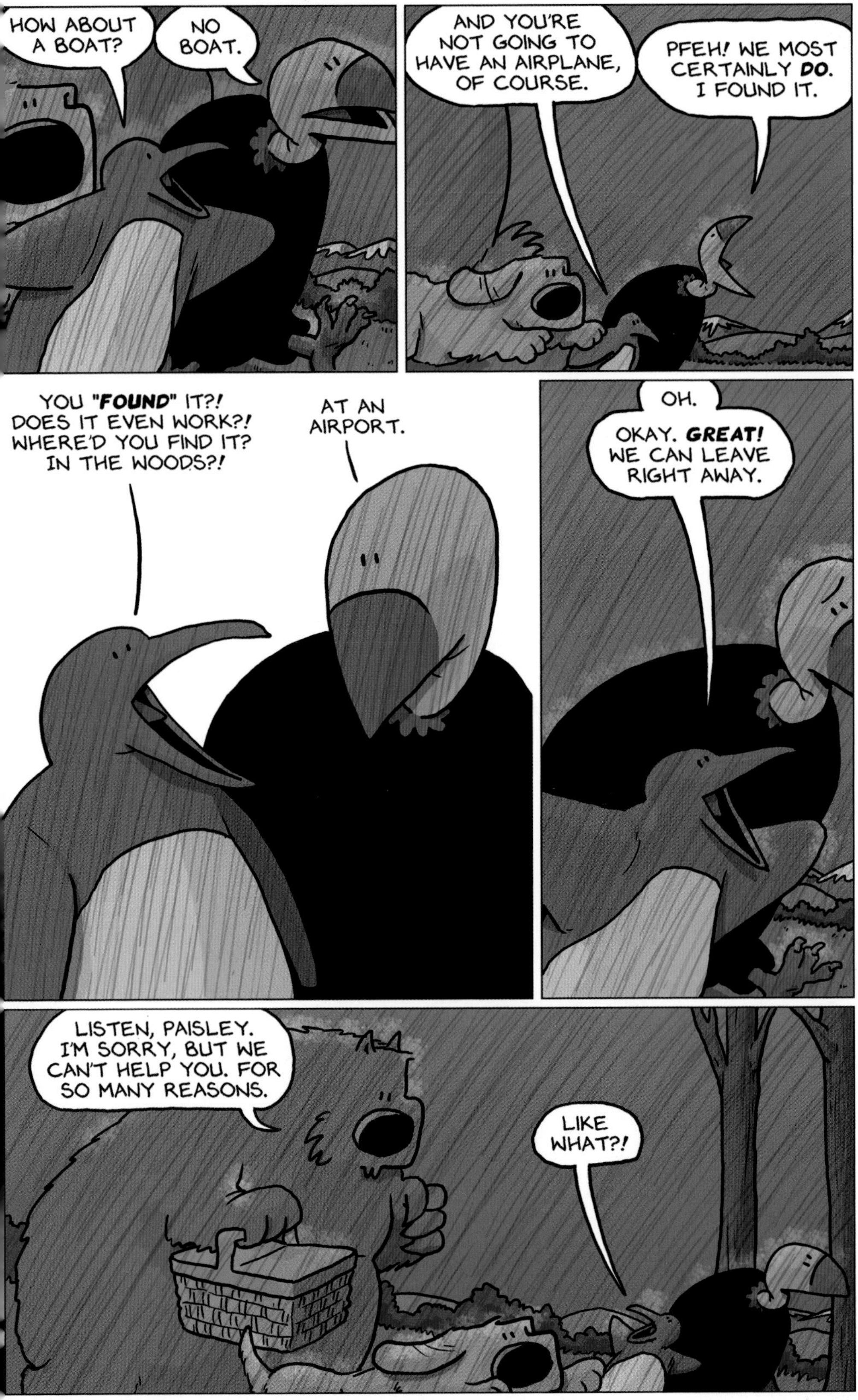

HOW ABOUT A BOAT?
NO BOAT.
AND YOU'RE NOT GOING TO HAVE AN AIRPLANE, OF COURSE.
PFEH! WE MOST CERTAINLY **DO**. I FOUND IT.
YOU "**FOUND**" IT?! DOES IT EVEN WORK?! WHERE'D YOU FIND IT? IN THE WOODS?!
AT AN AIRPORT.
OH.
OKAY. **GREAT!** WE CAN LEAVE RIGHT AWAY.
LISTEN, PAISLEY. I'M SORRY, BUT WE CAN'T HELP YOU. FOR SO MANY REASONS.
LIKE WHAT?!

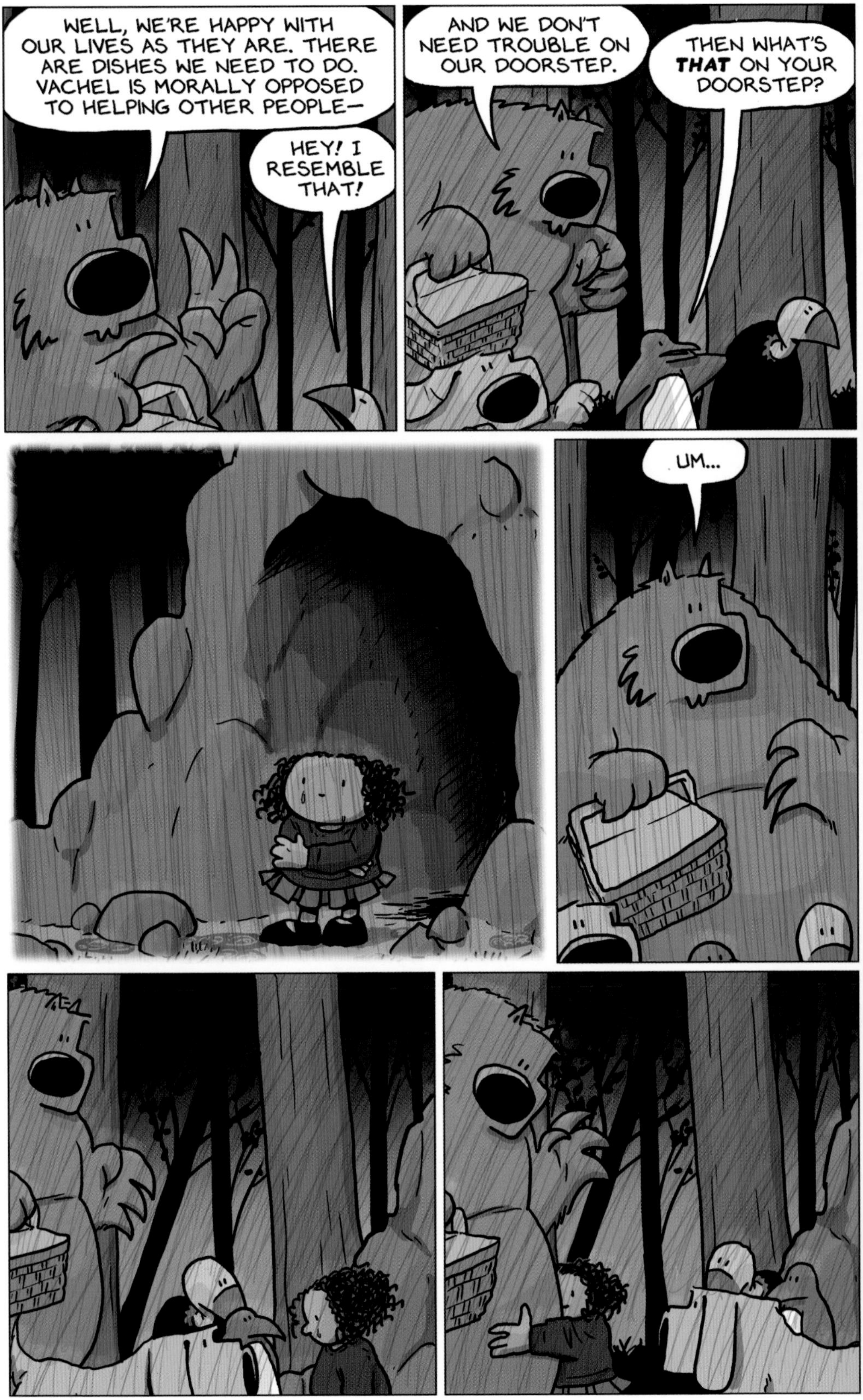
WELL, WE'RE HAPPY WITH OUR LIVES AS THEY ARE. THERE ARE DISHES WE NEED TO DO. VACHEL IS MORALLY OPPOSED TO HELPING OTHER PEOPLE—
HEY! I RESEMBLE THAT!
AND WE DON'T NEED TROUBLE ON OUR DOORSTEP.
THEN WHAT'S **THAT** ON YOUR DOORSTEP?
UM...

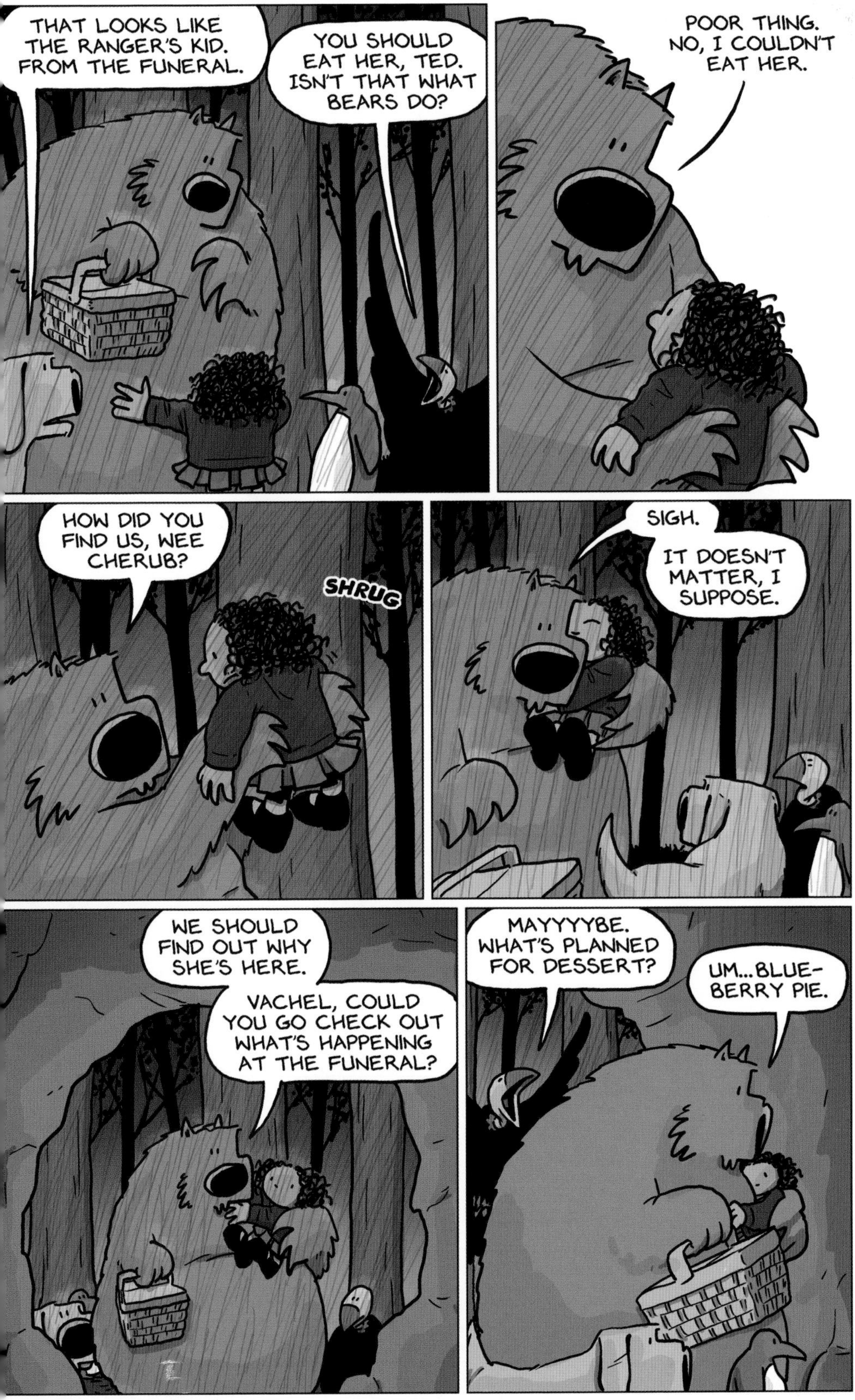
THAT LOOKS LIKE THE RANGER'S KID. FROM THE FUNERAL.
YOU SHOULD EAT HER, TED. ISN'T THAT WHAT BEARS DO?
POOR THING. NO, I COULDN'T EAT HER.
HOW DID YOU FIND US, WEE CHERUB?
SHRUG
SIGH.
IT DOESN'T MATTER, I SUPPOSE.
WE SHOULD FIND OUT WHY SHE'S HERE.
VACHEL, COULD YOU GO CHECK OUT WHAT'S HAPPENING AT THE FUNERAL?
MAYYYYBE. WHAT'S PLANNED FOR DESSERT?
UM...BLUE-BERRY PIE.

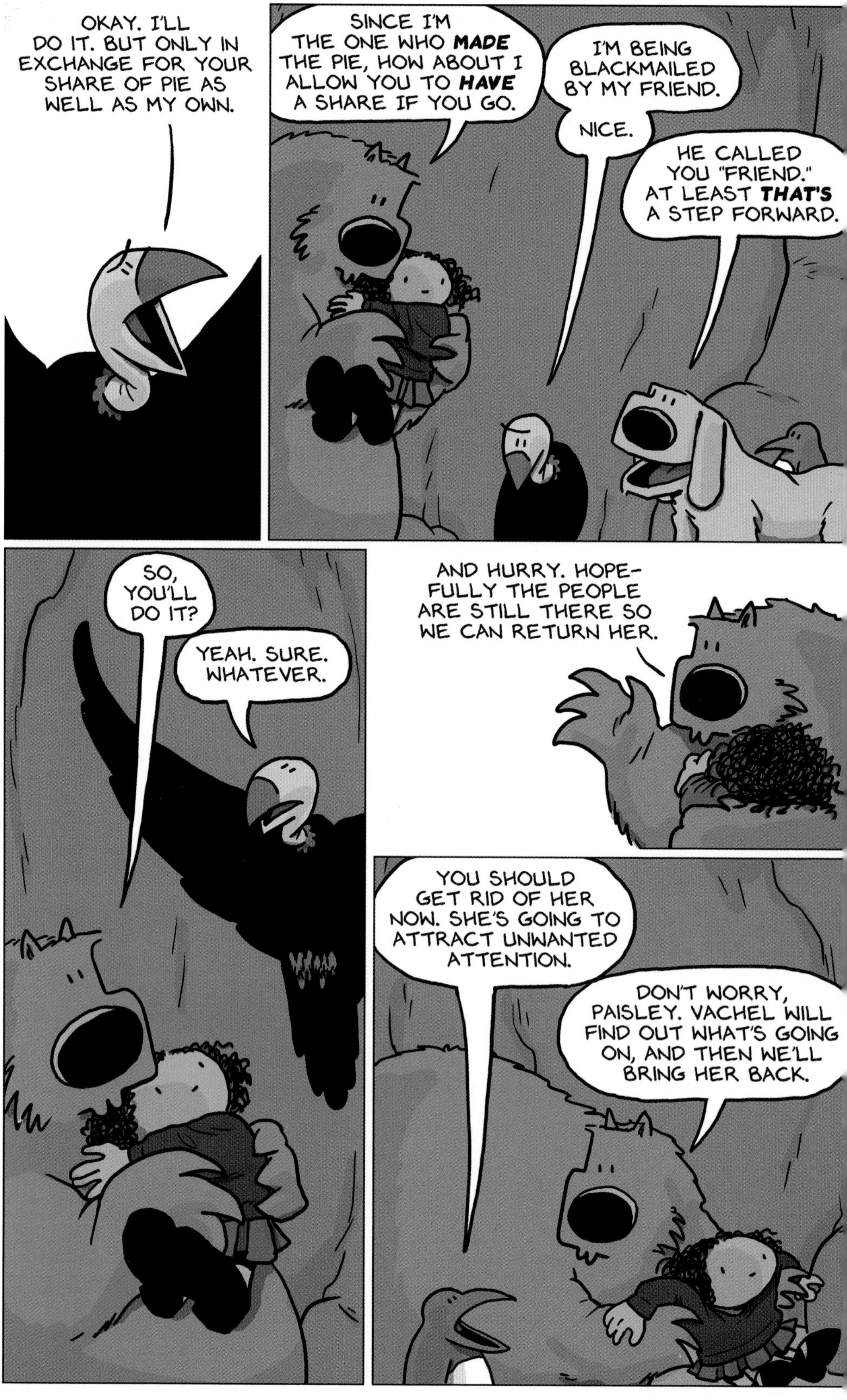
OKAY. I'LL DO IT. BUT ONLY IN EXCHANGE FOR YOUR SHARE OF PIE AS WELL AS MY OWN.
SINCE I'M THE ONE WHO **MADE** THE PIE, HOW ABOUT I ALLOW YOU TO **HAVE** A SHARE IF YOU GO.
I'M BEING BLACKMAILED BY MY FRIEND.
NICE.
HE CALLED YOU "FRIEND." AT LEAST **THAT'S** A STEP FORWARD.
SO, YOU'LL DO IT?
YEAH. SURE. WHATEVER.
AND HURRY. HOPE-FULLY THE PEOPLE ARE STILL THERE SO WE CAN RETURN HER.
YOU SHOULD GET RID OF HER NOW. SHE'S GOING TO ATTRACT UNWANTED ATTENTION.
DON'T WORRY, PAISLEY. VACHEL WILL FIND OUT WHAT'S GOING ON, AND THEN WE'LL BRING HER BACK.

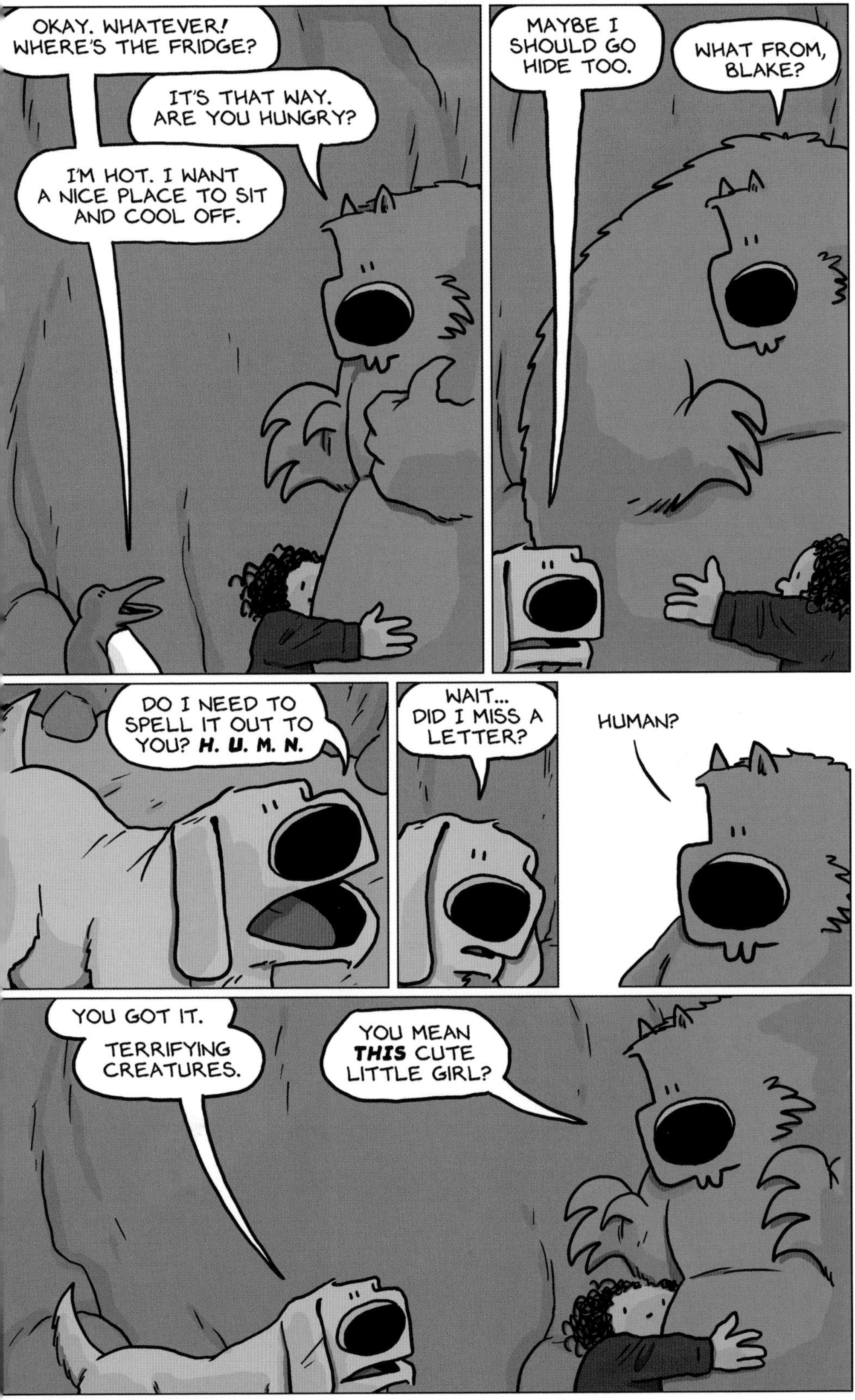
OKAY. WHATEVER! WHERE'S THE FRIDGE?
IT'S THAT WAY. ARE YOU HUNGRY?
I'M HOT. I WANT A NICE PLACE TO SIT AND COOL OFF.
MAYBE I SHOULD GO HIDE TOO.
WHAT FROM, BLAKE?
DO I NEED TO SPELL IT OUT TO YOU? ***H. U. M. N.***
WAIT... DID I MISS A LETTER?
HUMAN?
YOU GOT IT.
TERRIFYING CREATURES.
YOU MEAN ***THIS*** CUTE LITTLE GIRL?

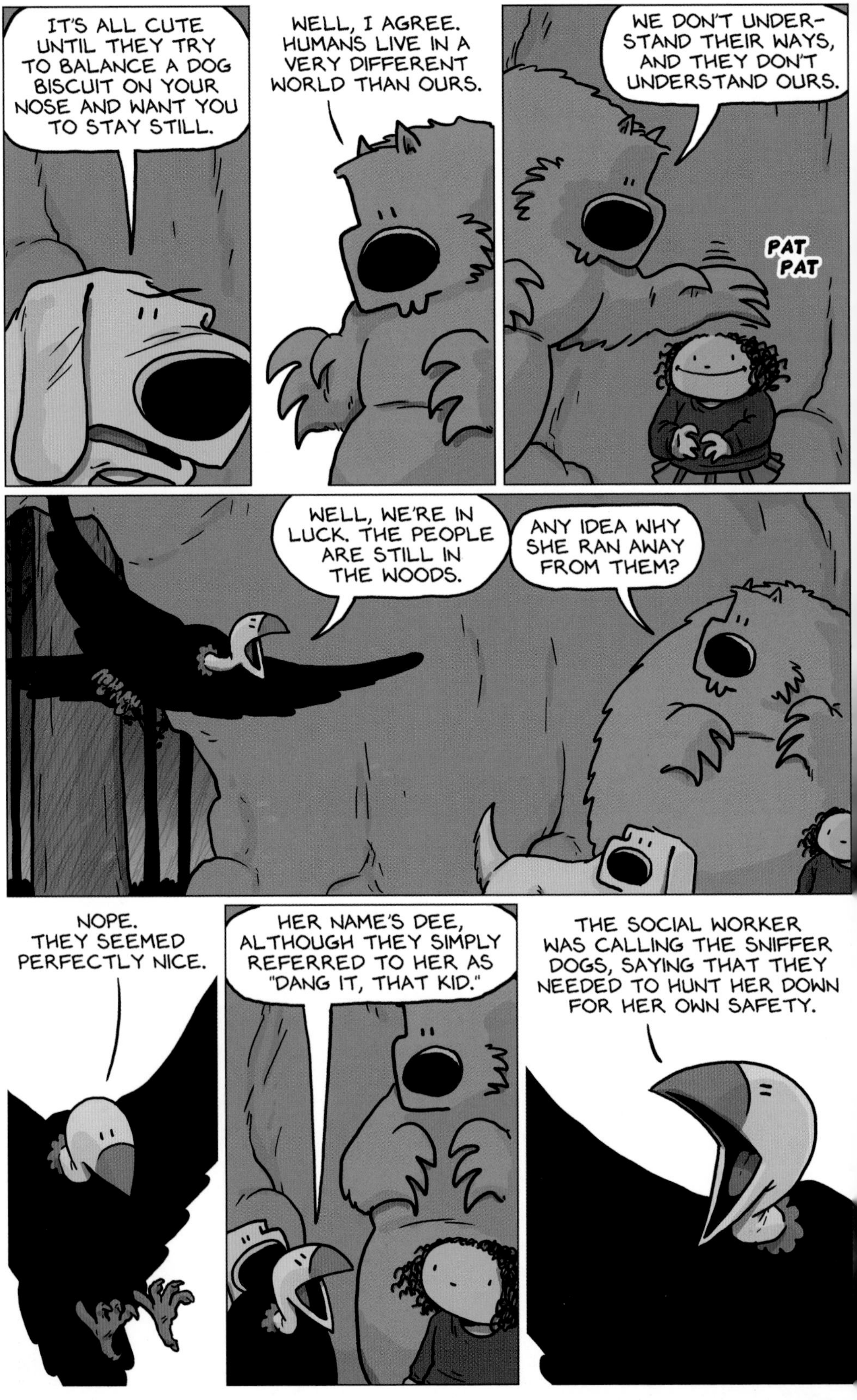
IT'S ALL CUTE UNTIL THEY TRY TO BALANCE A DOG BISCUIT ON YOUR NOSE AND WANT YOU TO STAY STILL.
WELL, I AGREE. HUMANS LIVE IN A VERY DIFFERENT WORLD THAN OURS.
WE DON'T UNDER-STAND THEIR WAYS, AND THEY DON'T UNDERSTAND OURS.
PAT PAT
WELL, WE'RE IN LUCK. THE PEOPLE ARE STILL IN THE WOODS.
ANY IDEA WHY SHE RAN AWAY FROM THEM?
NOPE. THEY SEEMED PERFECTLY NICE.
HER NAME'S DEE, ALTHOUGH THEY SIMPLY REFERRED TO HER AS "DANG IT, THAT KID."
THE SOCIAL WORKER WAS CALLING THE SNIFFER DOGS, SAYING THAT THEY NEEDED TO HUNT HER DOWN FOR HER OWN SAFETY.

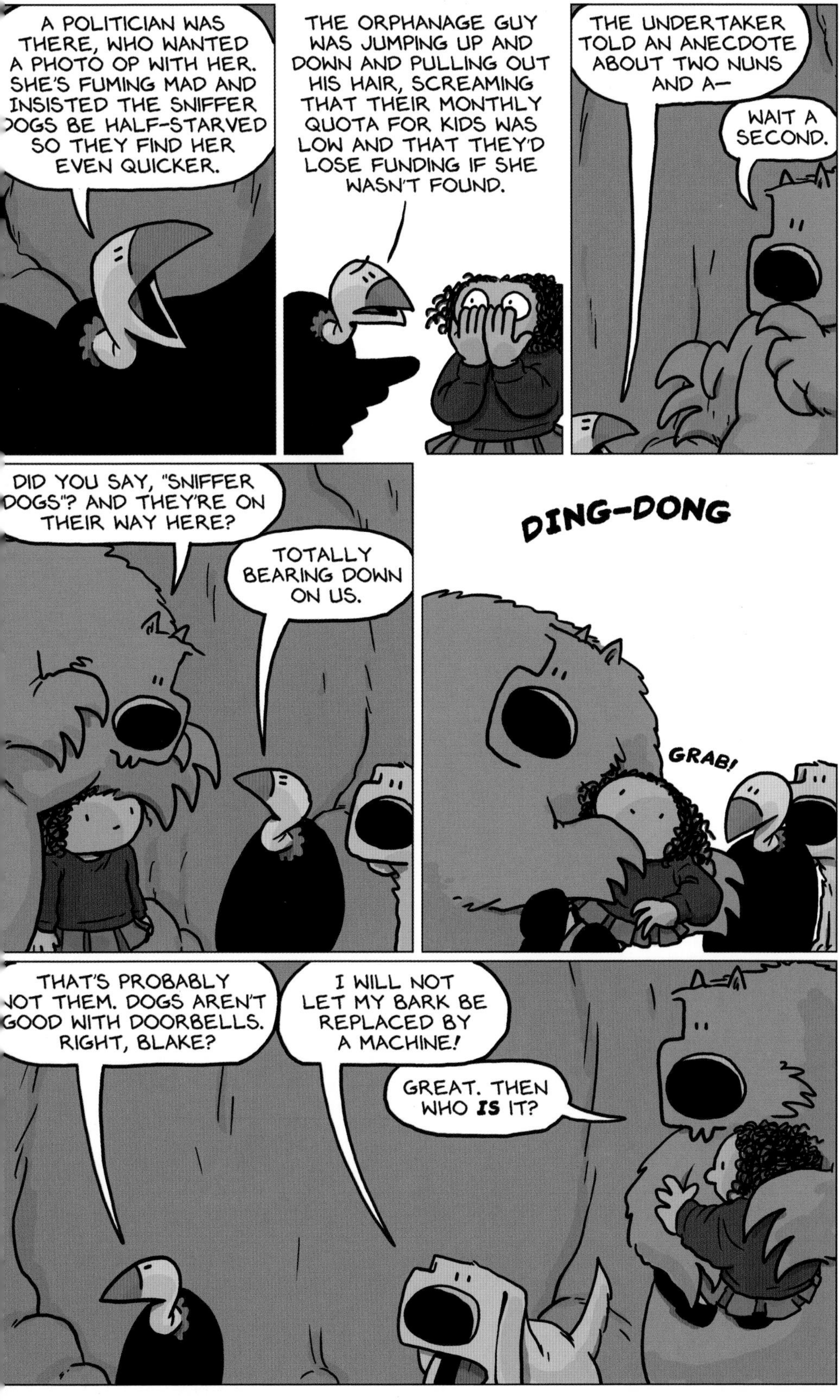
A POLITICIAN WAS THERE, WHO WANTED A PHOTO OP WITH HER. SHE'S FUMING MAD AND INSISTED THE SNIFFER DOGS BE HALF-STARVED SO THEY FIND HER EVEN QUICKER.
THE ORPHANAGE GUY WAS JUMPING UP AND DOWN AND PULLING OUT HIS HAIR, SCREAMING THAT THEIR MONTHLY QUOTA FOR KIDS WAS LOW AND THAT THEY'D LOSE FUNDING IF SHE WASN'T FOUND.
THE UNDERTAKER TOLD AN ANECDOTE ABOUT TWO NUNS AND A—
WAIT A SECOND.
DID YOU SAY, "SNIFFER DOGS"? AND THEY'RE ON THEIR WAY HERE?
TOTALLY BEARING DOWN ON US.
DING-DONG
GRAB!
THAT'S PROBABLY NOT THEM. DOGS AREN'T GOOD WITH DOORBELLS. RIGHT, BLAKE?
I WILL NOT LET MY BARK BE REPLACED BY A MACHINE!
GREAT. THEN WHO **IS** IT?

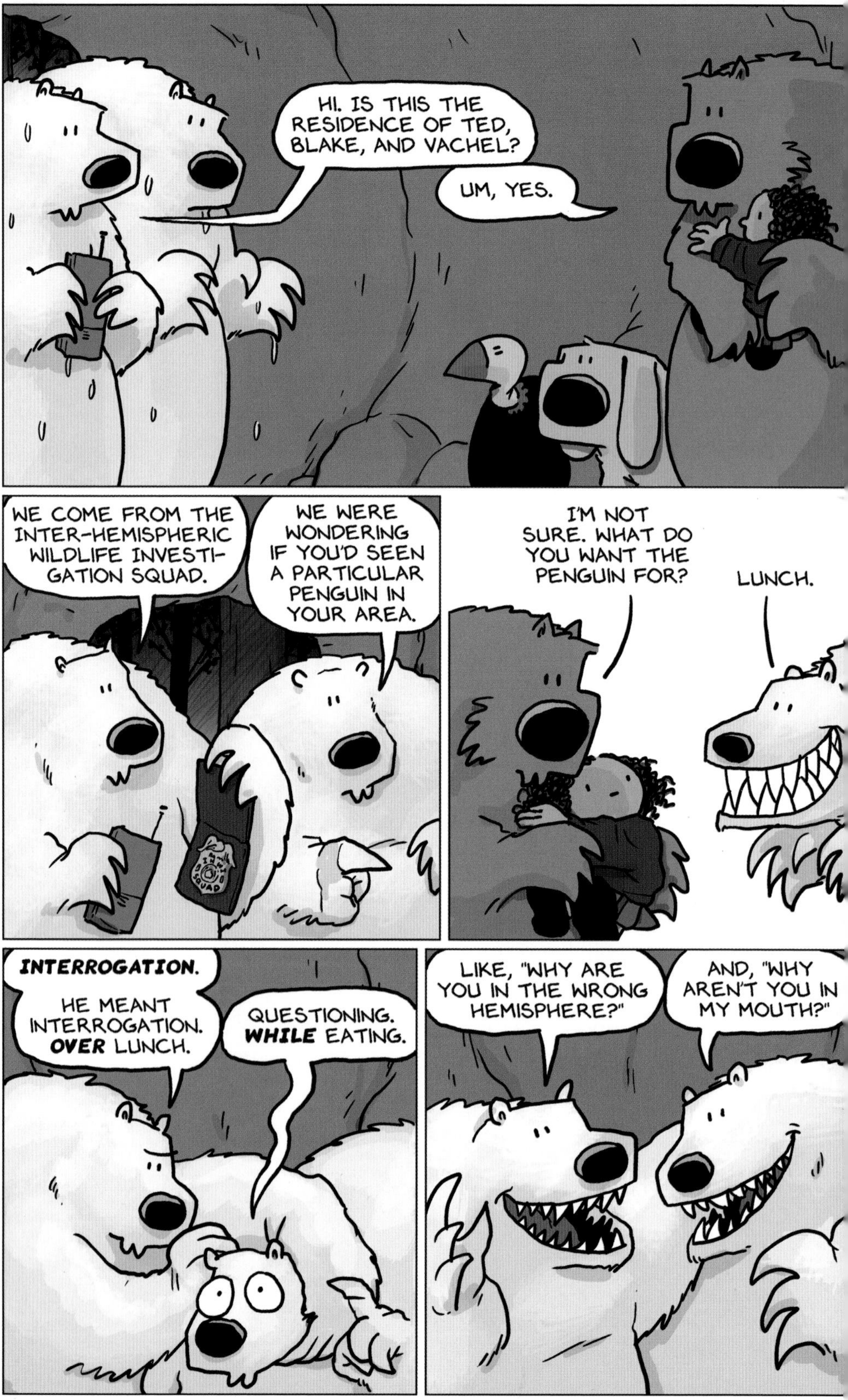
HI. IS THIS THE RESIDENCE OF TED, BLAKE, AND VACHEL?
UM, YES.
WE COME FROM THE INTER-HEMISPHERIC WILDLIFE INVESTIGATION SQUAD.
WE WERE WONDERING IF YOU'D SEEN A PARTICULAR PENGUIN IN YOUR AREA.
I'M NOT SURE. WHAT DO YOU WANT THE PENGUIN FOR?
LUNCH.
INTERROGATION.
HE MEANT INTERROGATION. **OVER** LUNCH.
QUESTIONING. **WHILE** EATING.
LIKE, "WHY ARE YOU IN THE WRONG HEMISPHERE?"
AND, "WHY AREN'T YOU IN MY MOUTH?"

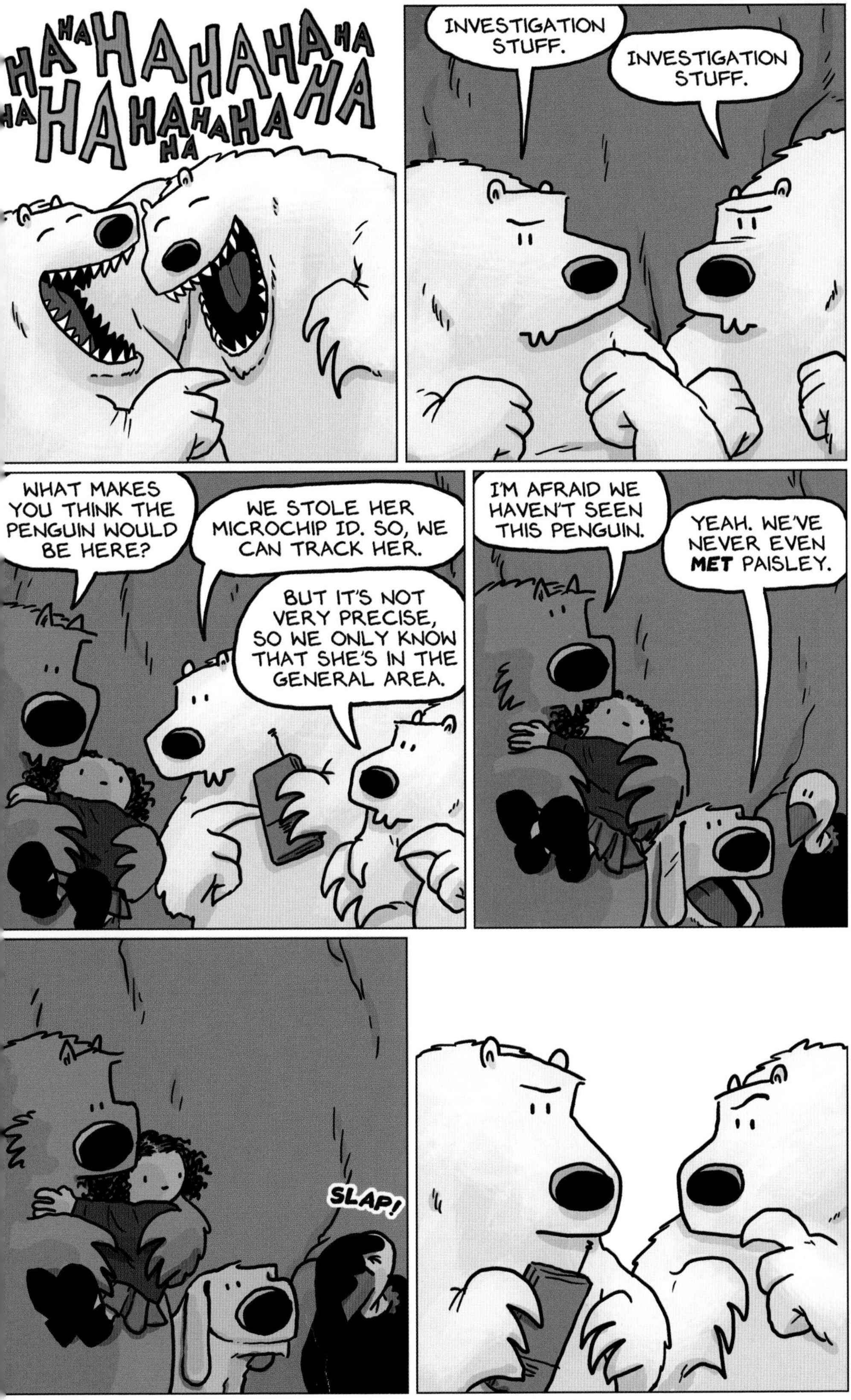
HAHAHAHAHAHAHA HAHAHAHAHAHAHA
INVESTIGATION STUFF.
INVESTIGATION STUFF.
WHAT MAKES YOU THINK THE PENGUIN WOULD BE HERE?
WE STOLE HER MICROCHIP ID. SO, WE CAN TRACK HER.
BUT IT'S NOT VERY PRECISE, SO WE ONLY KNOW THAT SHE'S IN THE GENERAL AREA.
I'M AFRAID WE HAVEN'T SEEN THIS PENGUIN.
YEAH. WE'VE NEVER EVEN **MET** PAISLEY.
SLAP!

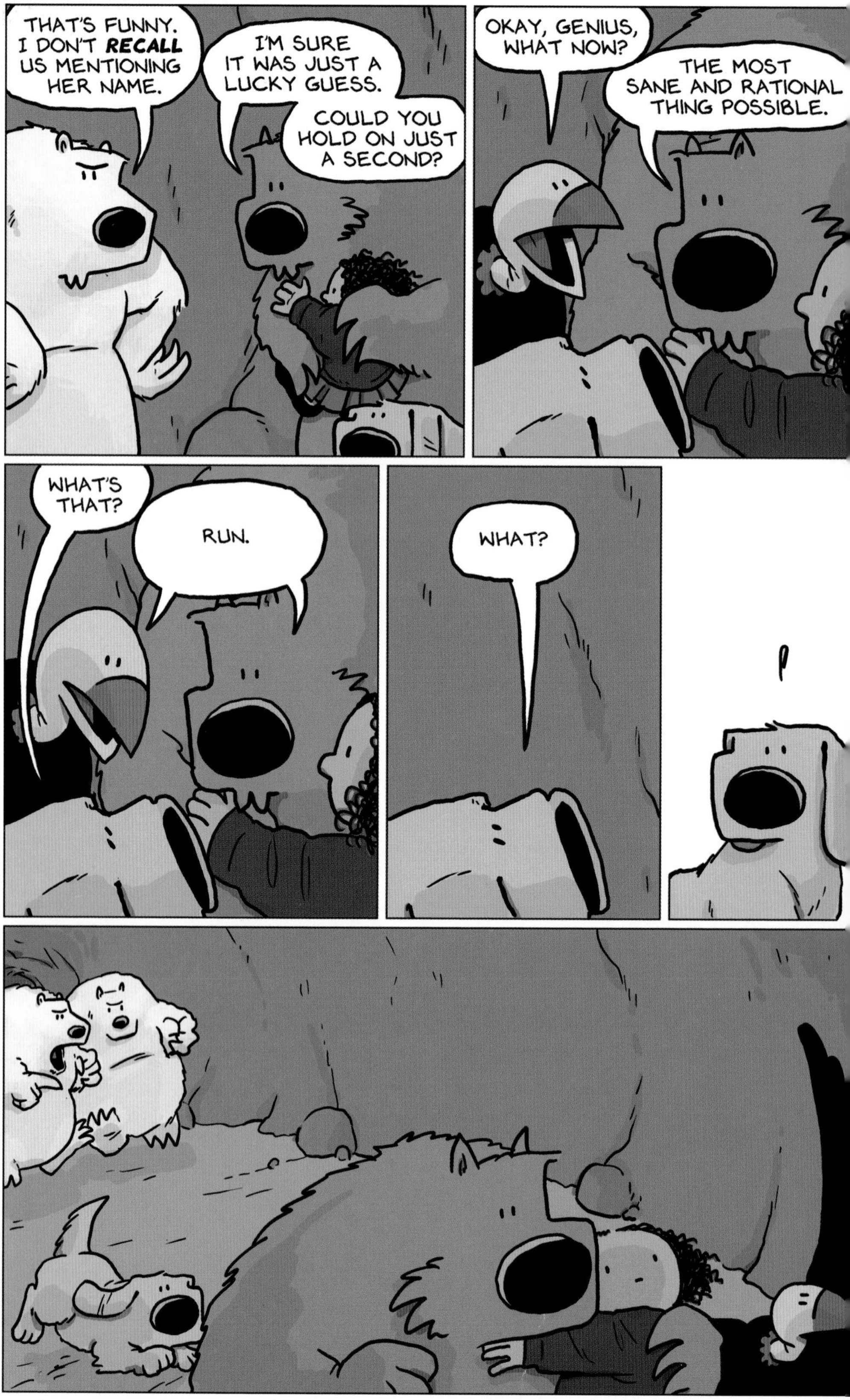
THAT'S FUNNY. I DON'T RECALL US MENTIONING HER NAME.
I'M SURE IT WAS JUST A LUCKY GUESS.
COULD YOU HOLD ON JUST A SECOND?
OKAY, GENIUS, WHAT NOW?
THE MOST SANE AND RATIONAL THING POSSIBLE.
WHAT'S THAT?
RUN.
WHAT?

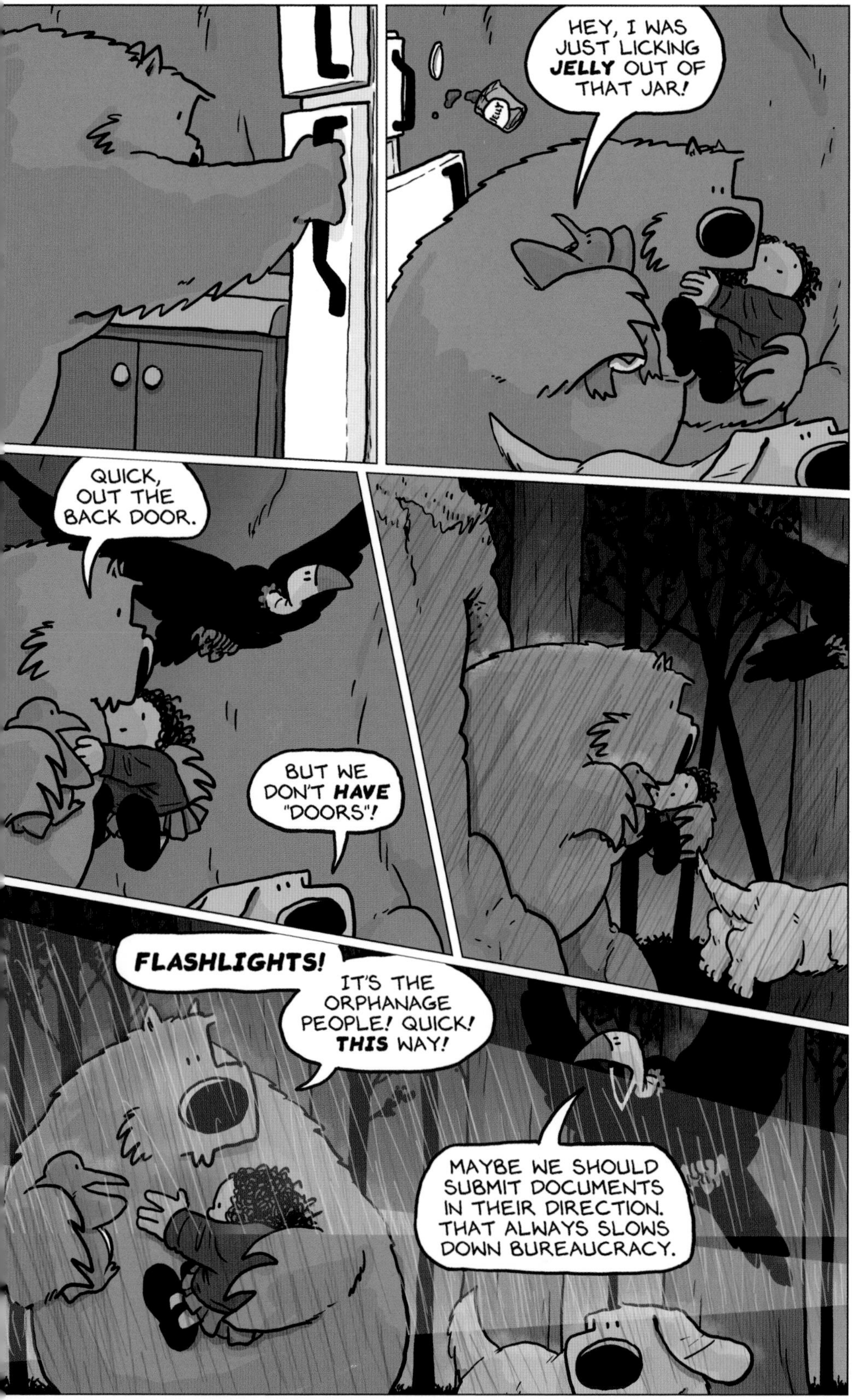
HEY, I WAS JUST LICKING JELLY OUT OF THAT JAR!
JELLY
QUICK, OUT THE BACK DOOR.
BUT WE DON'T HAVE "DOORS"!
FLASHLIGHTS!
IT'S THE ORPHANAGE PEOPLE! QUICK! THIS WAY!
MAYBE WE SHOULD SUBMIT DOCUMENTS IN THEIR DIRECTION. THAT ALWAYS SLOWS DOWN BUREAUCRACY.

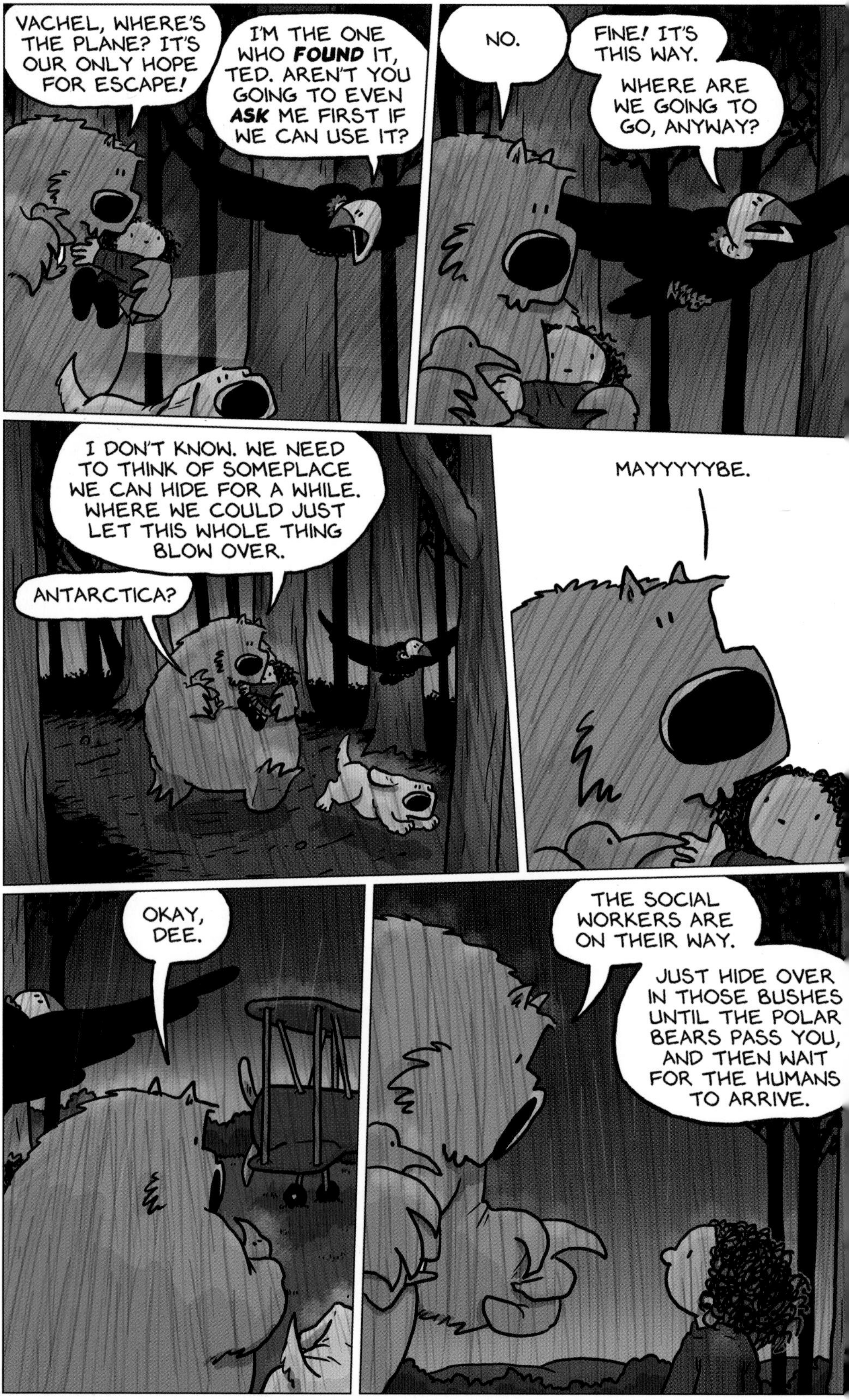
VACHEL, WHERE'S THE PLANE? IT'S OUR ONLY HOPE FOR ESCAPE!
I'M THE ONE WHO **FOUND** IT, TED. AREN'T YOU GOING TO EVEN **ASK** ME FIRST IF WE CAN USE IT?
NO.
FINE! IT'S THIS WAY.
WHERE ARE WE GOING TO GO, ANYWAY?
I DON'T KNOW. WE NEED TO THINK OF SOMEPLACE WE CAN HIDE FOR A WHILE. WHERE WE COULD JUST LET THIS WHOLE THING BLOW OVER.
ANTARCTICA?
MAYYYYYBE.
OKAY, DEE.
THE SOCIAL WORKERS ARE ON THEIR WAY.
JUST HIDE OVER IN THOSE BUSHES UNTIL THE POLAR BEARS PASS YOU, AND THEN WAIT FOR THE HUMANS TO ARRIVE.

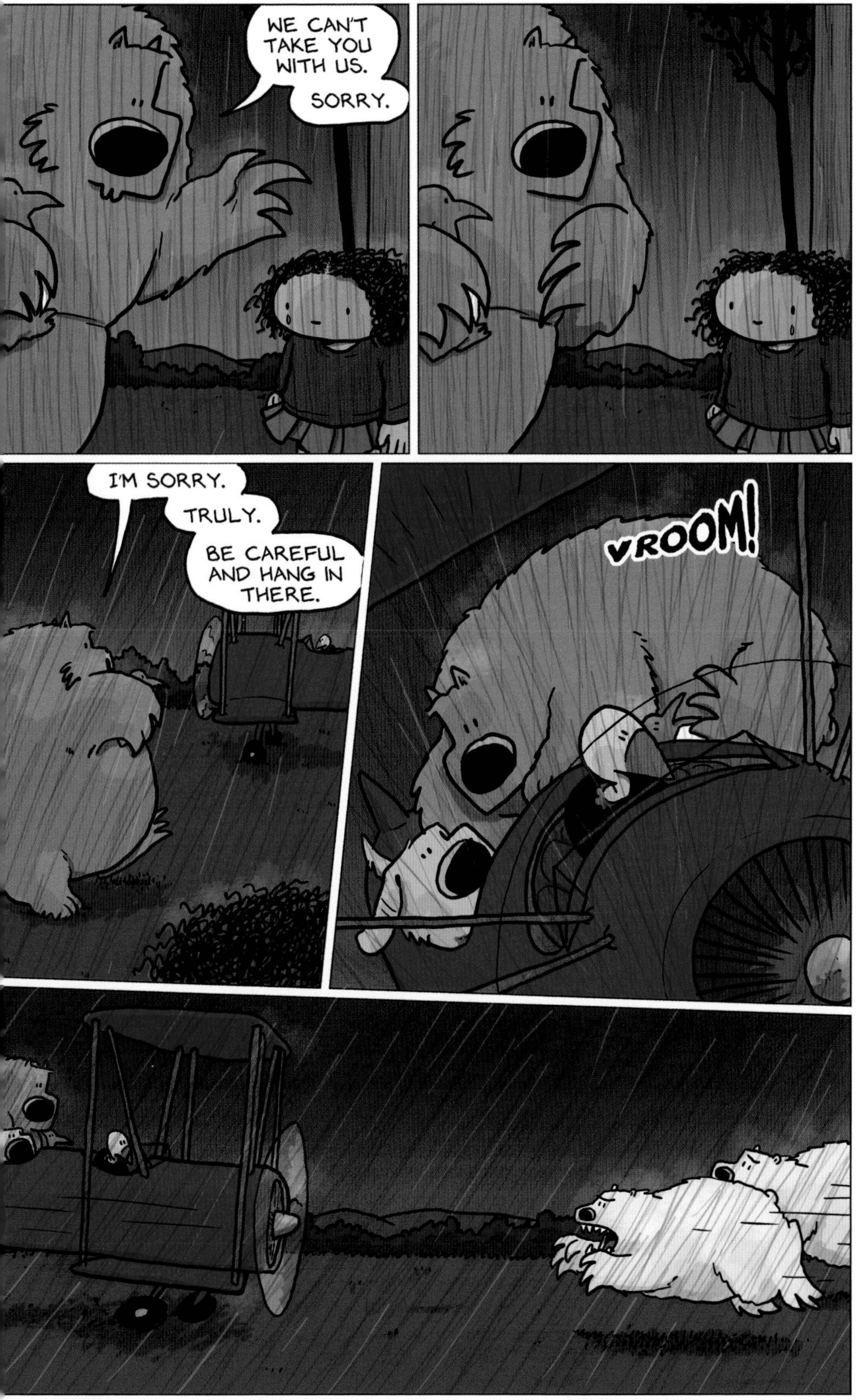
WE CAN'T TAKE YOU WITH US.
SORRY.
I'M SORRY.
TRULY.
BE CAREFUL AND HANG IN THERE.
VROOM!

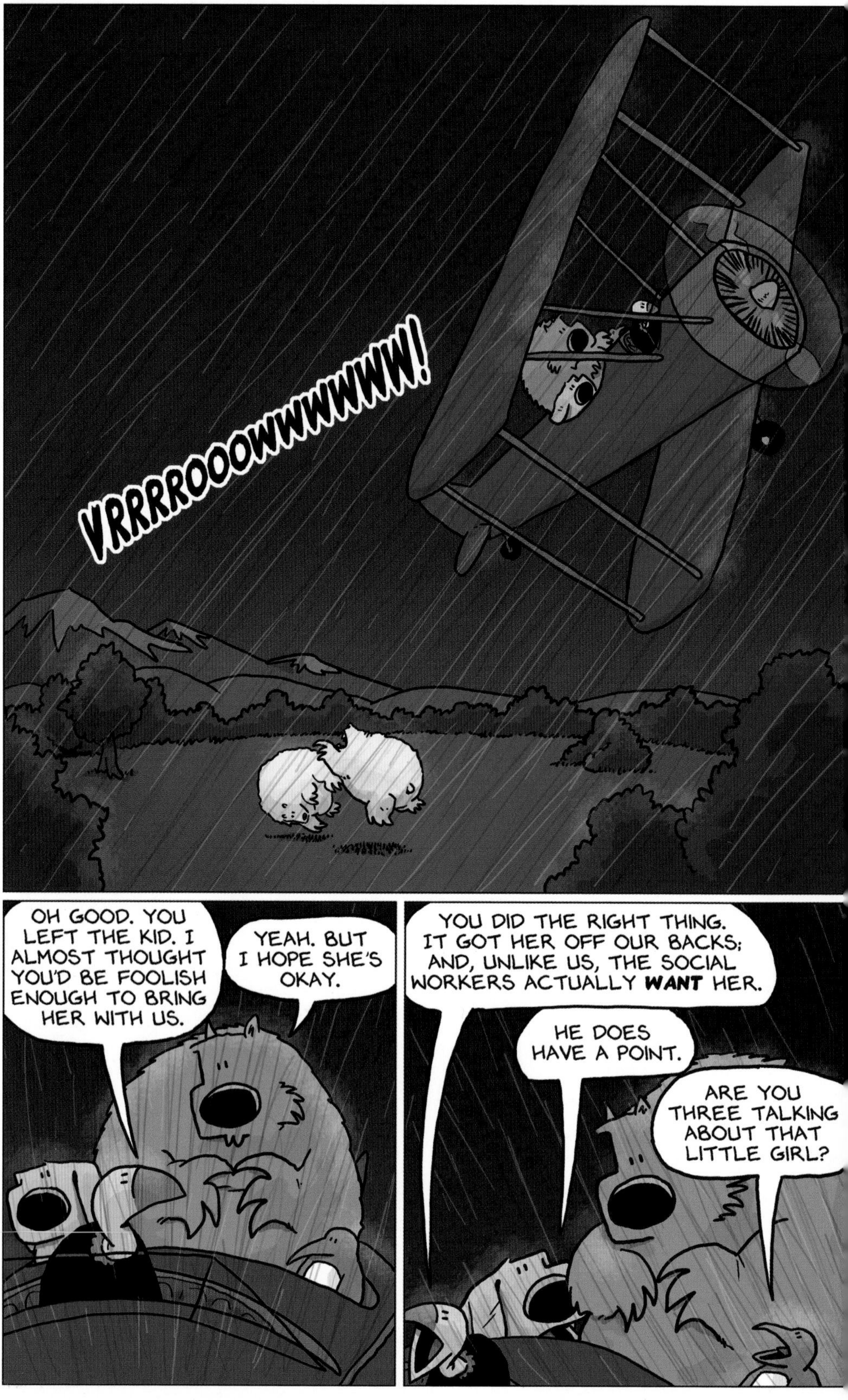
VRRRROOOWWWWWW!
OH GOOD. YOU LEFT THE KID. I ALMOST THOUGHT YOU'D BE FOOLISH ENOUGH TO BRING HER WITH US.
YEAH. BUT I HOPE SHE'S OKAY.
YOU DID THE RIGHT THING. IT GOT HER OFF OUR BACKS; AND, UNLIKE US, THE SOCIAL WORKERS ACTUALLY **WANT** HER.
HE DOES HAVE A POINT.
ARE YOU THREE TALKING ABOUT THAT LITTLE GIRL?

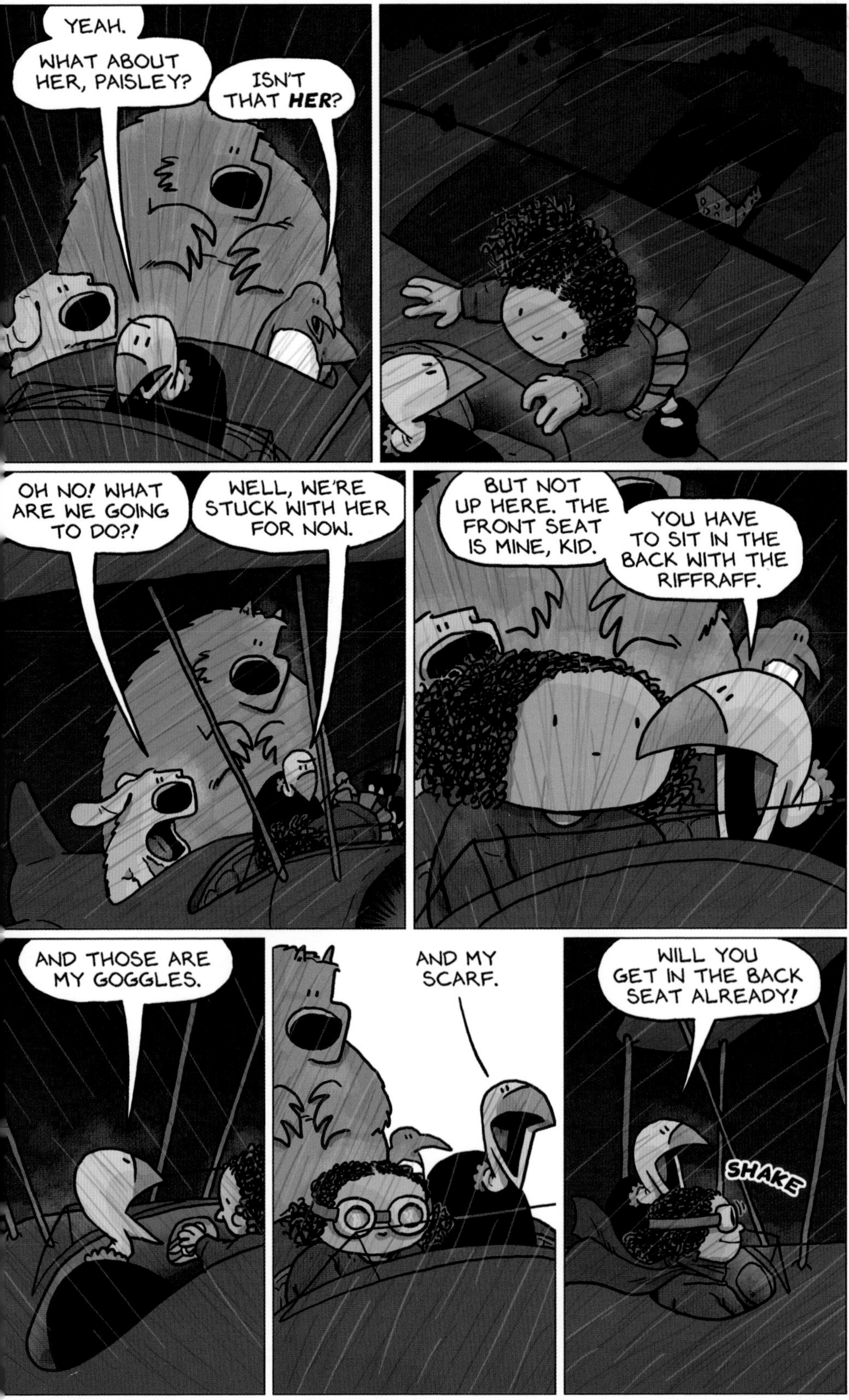
YEAH.
WHAT ABOUT HER, PAISLEY?
ISN'T THAT HER?
OH NO! WHAT ARE WE GOING TO DO?!
WELL, WE'RE STUCK WITH HER FOR NOW.
BUT NOT UP HERE. THE FRONT SEAT IS MINE, KID.
YOU HAVE TO SIT IN THE BACK WITH THE RIFFRAFF.
AND THOSE ARE MY GOGGLES.
AND MY SCARF.
WILL YOU GET IN THE BACK SEAT ALREADY!
SHAKE

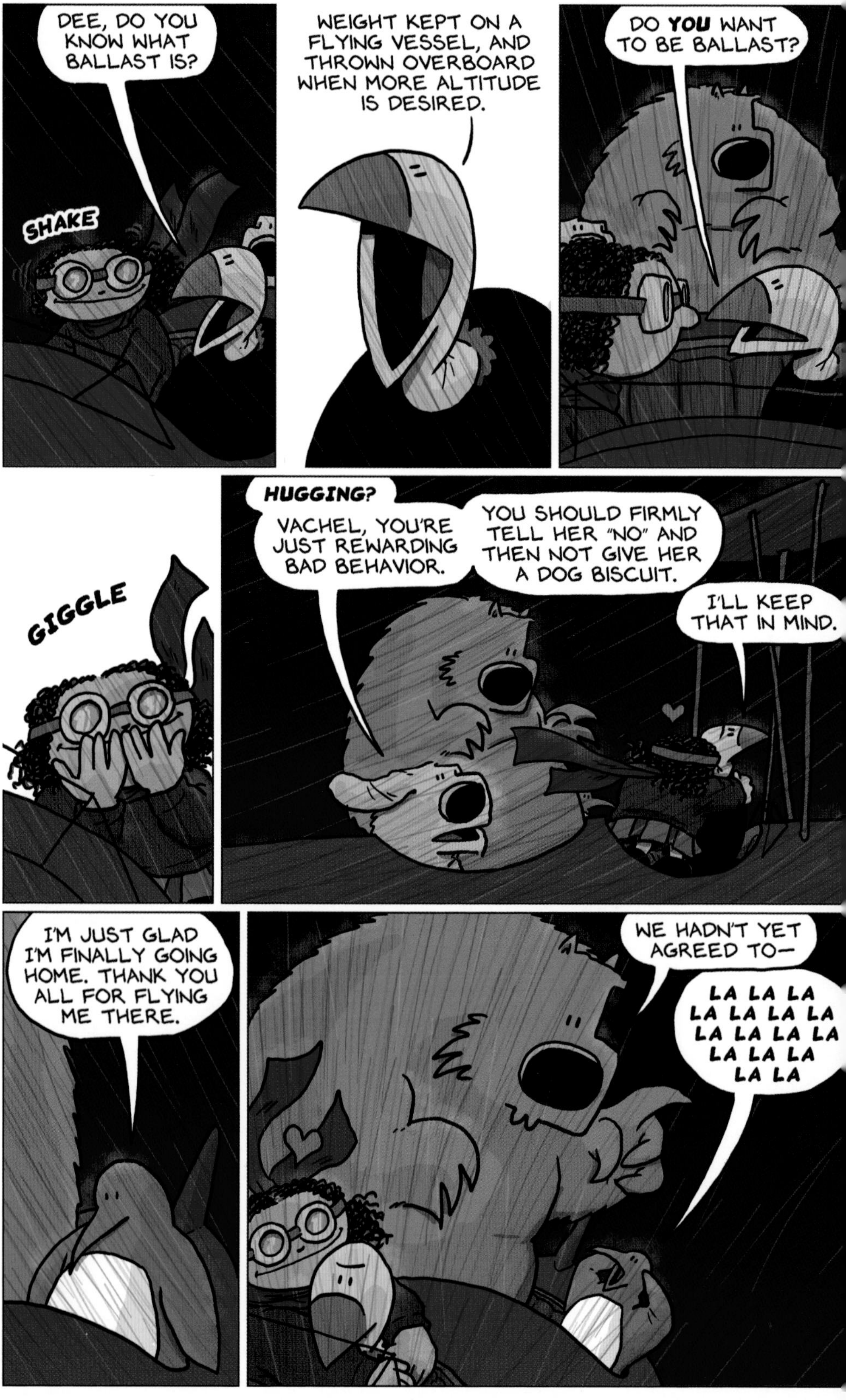
DEE, DO YOU KNOW WHAT BALLAST IS?
SHAKE
WEIGHT KEPT ON A FLYING VESSEL, AND THROWN OVERBOARD WHEN MORE ALTITUDE IS DESIRED.
DO **YOU** WANT TO BE BALLAST?
GIGGLE
HUGGING?
VACHEL, YOU'RE JUST REWARDING BAD BEHAVIOR.
YOU SHOULD FIRMLY TELL HER "NO" AND THEN NOT GIVE HER A DOG BISCUIT.
I'LL KEEP THAT IN MIND.
I'M JUST GLAD I'M FINALLY GOING HOME. THANK YOU ALL FOR FLYING ME THERE.
WE HADN'T YET AGREED TO—
LA LA LA LA LA LA LA LA LA LA LA LA LA LA LA LA

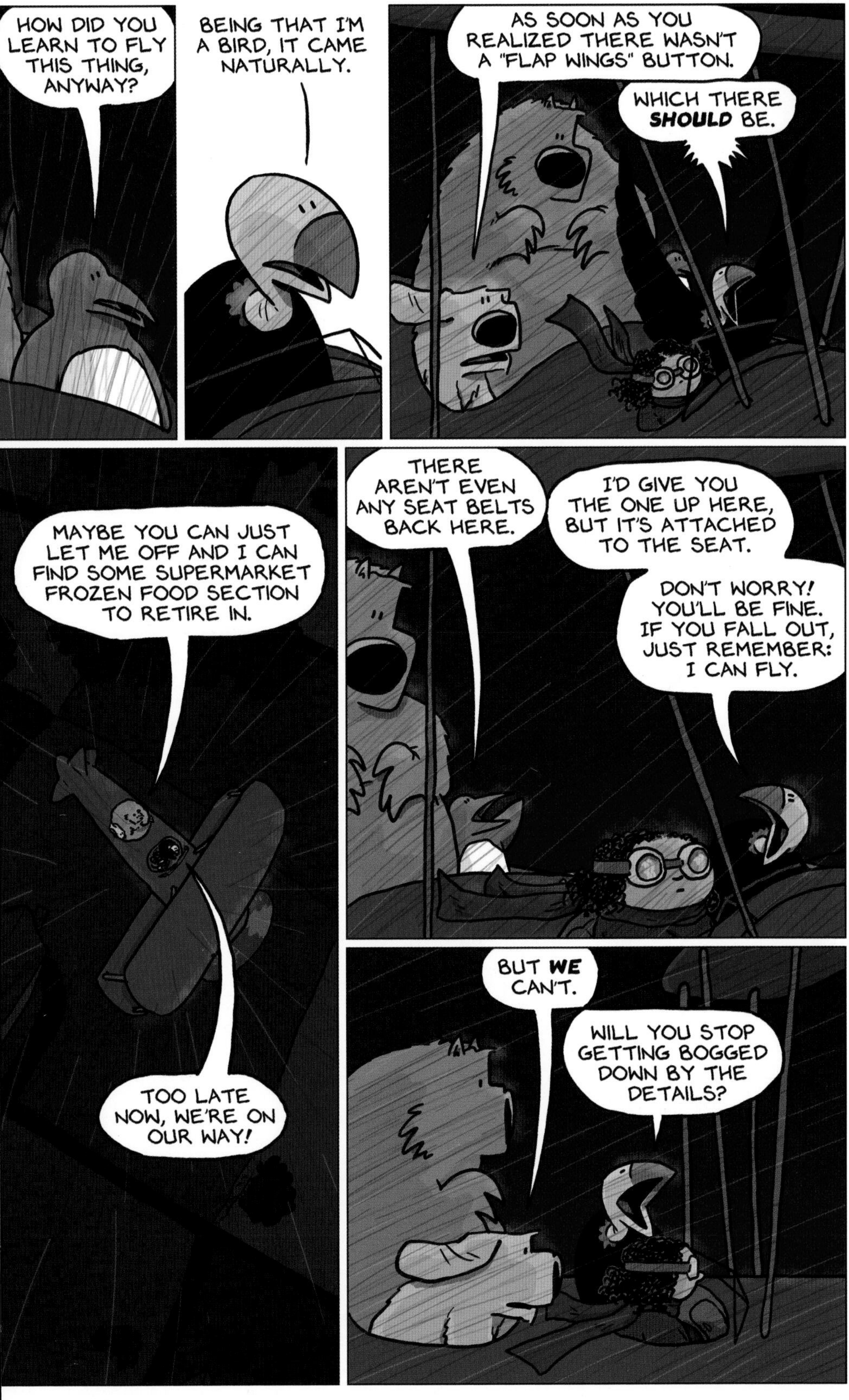
HOW DID YOU LEARN TO FLY THIS THING, ANYWAY?
BEING THAT I'M A BIRD, IT CAME NATURALLY.
AS SOON AS YOU REALIZED THERE WASN'T A "FLAP WINGS" BUTTON.
WHICH THERE **SHOULD** BE.
MAYBE YOU CAN JUST LET ME OFF AND I CAN FIND SOME SUPERMARKET FROZEN FOOD SECTION TO RETIRE IN.
TOO LATE NOW, WE'RE ON OUR WAY!
THERE AREN'T EVEN ANY SEAT BELTS BACK HERE.
I'D GIVE YOU THE ONE UP HERE, BUT IT'S ATTACHED TO THE SEAT.
DON'T WORRY! YOU'LL BE FINE. IF YOU FALL OUT, JUST REMEMBER: I CAN FLY.
BUT **WE** CAN'T.
WILL YOU STOP GETTING BOGGED DOWN BY THE DETAILS?

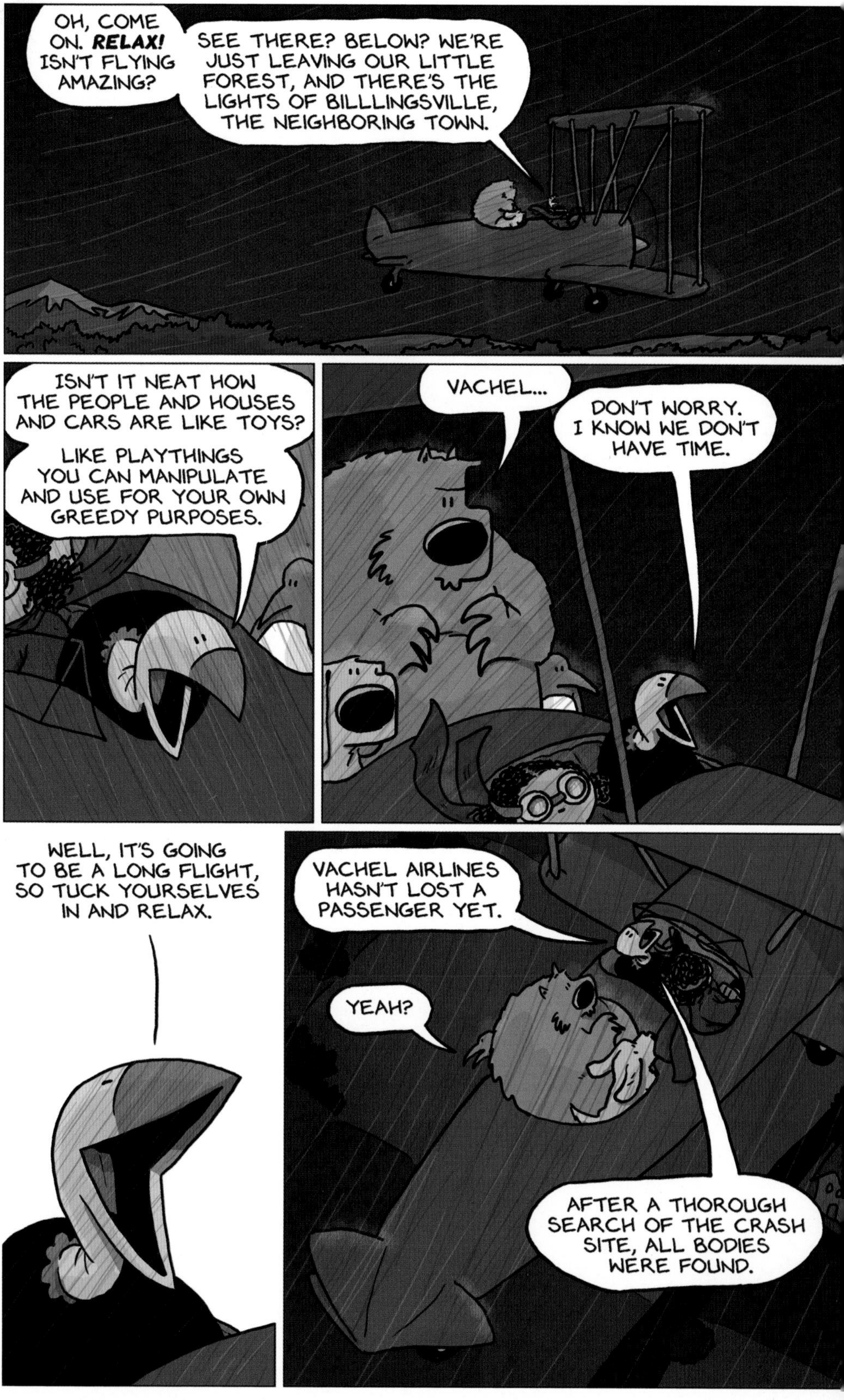
OH, COME ON. **RELAX!** ISN'T FLYING AMAZING?
SEE THERE? BELOW? WE'RE JUST LEAVING OUR LITTLE FOREST, AND THERE'S THE LIGHTS OF BILLLINGSVILLE, THE NEIGHBORING TOWN.
ISN'T IT NEAT HOW THE PEOPLE AND HOUSES AND CARS ARE LIKE TOYS?
LIKE PLAYTHINGS YOU CAN MANIPULATE AND USE FOR YOUR OWN GREEDY PURPOSES.
VACHEL...
DON'T WORRY. I KNOW WE DON'T HAVE TIME.
WELL, IT'S GOING TO BE A LONG FLIGHT, SO TUCK YOURSELVES IN AND RELAX.
VACHEL AIRLINES HASN'T LOST A PASSENGER YET.
YEAH?
AFTER A THOROUGH SEARCH OF THE CRASH SITE, ALL BODIES WERE FOUND.

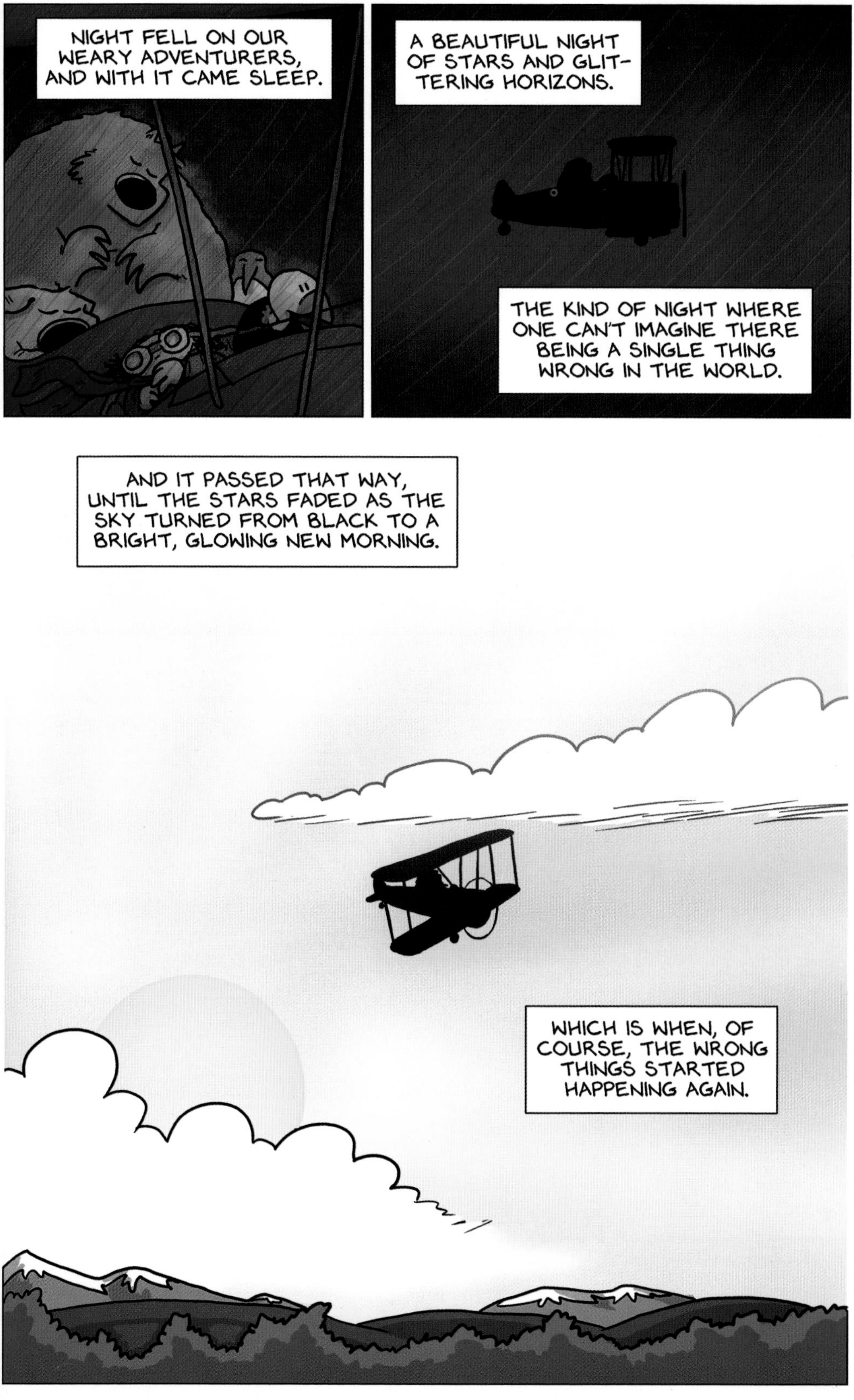
NIGHT FELL ON OUR WEARY ADVENTURERS, AND WITH IT CAME SLEEP.
A BEAUTIFUL NIGHT OF STARS AND GLIT-TERING HORIZONS.
THE KIND OF NIGHT WHERE ONE CAN'T IMAGINE THERE BEING A SINGLE THING WRONG IN THE WORLD.
AND IT PASSED THAT WAY, UNTIL THE STARS FADED AS THE SKY TURNED FROM BLACK TO A BRIGHT, GLOWING NEW MORNING.
WHICH IS WHEN, OF COURSE, THE WRONG THINGS STARTED HAPPENING AGAIN.

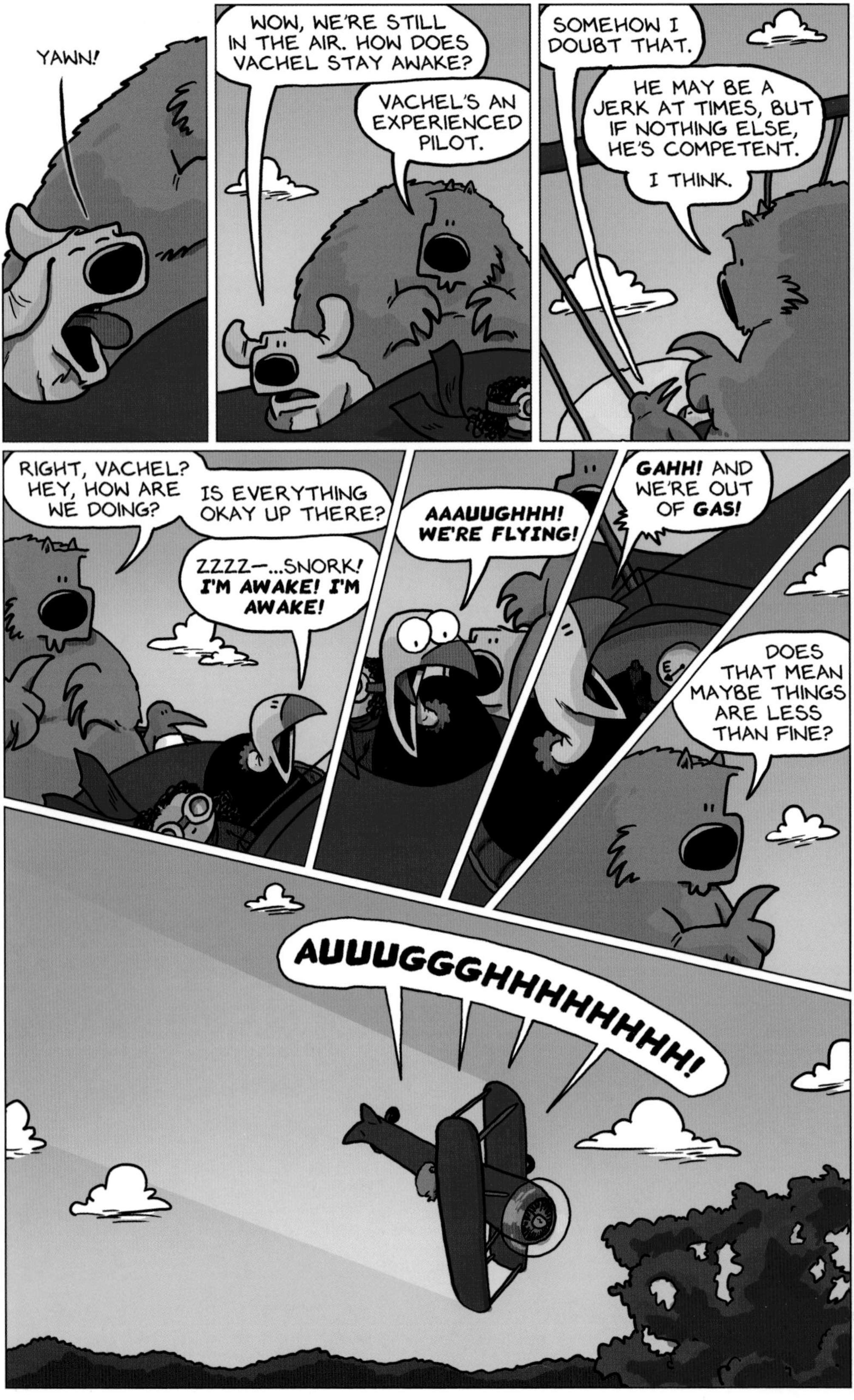
YAWN!
WOW, WE'RE STILL IN THE AIR. HOW DOES VACHEL STAY AWAKE?
VACHEL'S AN EXPERIENCED PILOT.
SOMEHOW I DOUBT THAT.
HE MAY BE A JERK AT TIMES, BUT IF NOTHING ELSE, HE'S COMPETENT.
I THINK.
RIGHT, VACHEL? HEY, HOW ARE WE DOING?
IS EVERYTHING OKAY UP THERE?
ZZZZ—...SNORK! **I'M AWAKE! I'M AWAKE!**
AAAUUGHHH! WE'RE FLYING!
GAHH! AND WE'RE OUT OF **GAS!**
DOES THAT MEAN MAYBE THINGS ARE LESS THAN FINE?
AUUUGGGHHHHHHHH!

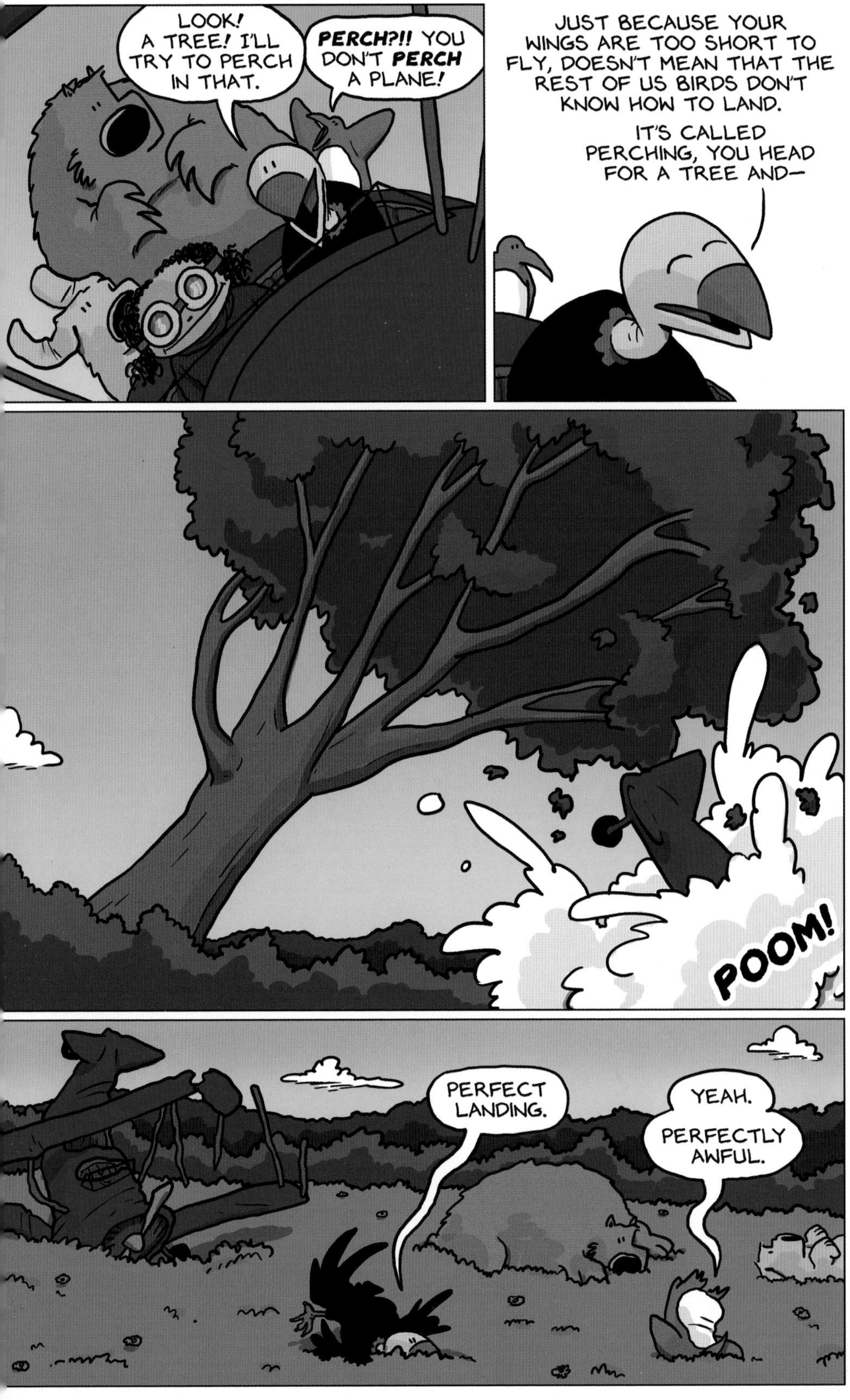

LOOK! A TREE! I'LL TRY TO PERCH IN THAT.
PERCH?!! YOU DON'T **PERCH** A PLANE!
JUST BECAUSE YOUR WINGS ARE TOO SHORT TO FLY, DOESN'T MEAN THAT THE REST OF US BIRDS DON'T KNOW HOW TO LAND.
IT'S CALLED PERCHING, YOU HEAD FOR A TREE AND—
POOM!
PERFECT LANDING.
YEAH.
PERFECTLY AWFUL.

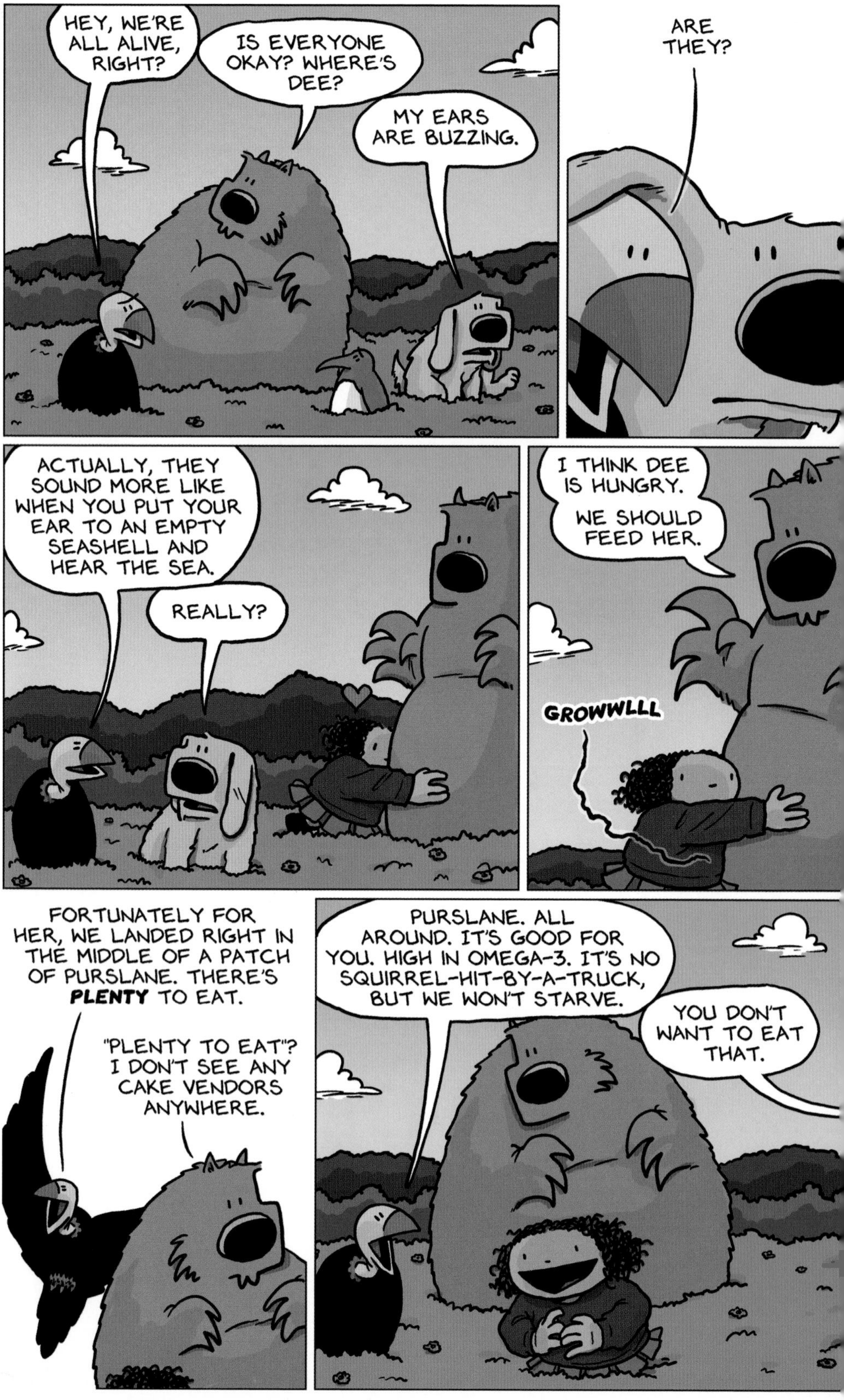
HEY, WE'RE ALL ALIVE, RIGHT?
IS EVERYONE OKAY? WHERE'S DEE?
MY EARS ARE BUZZING.
ARE THEY?
ACTUALLY, THEY SOUND MORE LIKE WHEN YOU PUT YOUR EAR TO AN EMPTY SEASHELL AND HEAR THE SEA.
REALLY?
I THINK DEE IS HUNGRY.
WE SHOULD FEED HER.
GROWWLLL
FORTUNATELY FOR HER, WE LANDED RIGHT IN THE MIDDLE OF A PATCH OF PURSLANE. THERE'S **PLENTY** TO EAT.
"PLENTY TO EAT"? I DON'T SEE ANY CAKE VENDORS ANYWHERE.
PURSLANE. ALL AROUND. IT'S GOOD FOR YOU. HIGH IN OMEGA-3. IT'S NO SQUIRREL-HIT-BY-A-TRUCK, BUT WE WON'T STARVE.
YOU DON'T WANT TO EAT THAT.

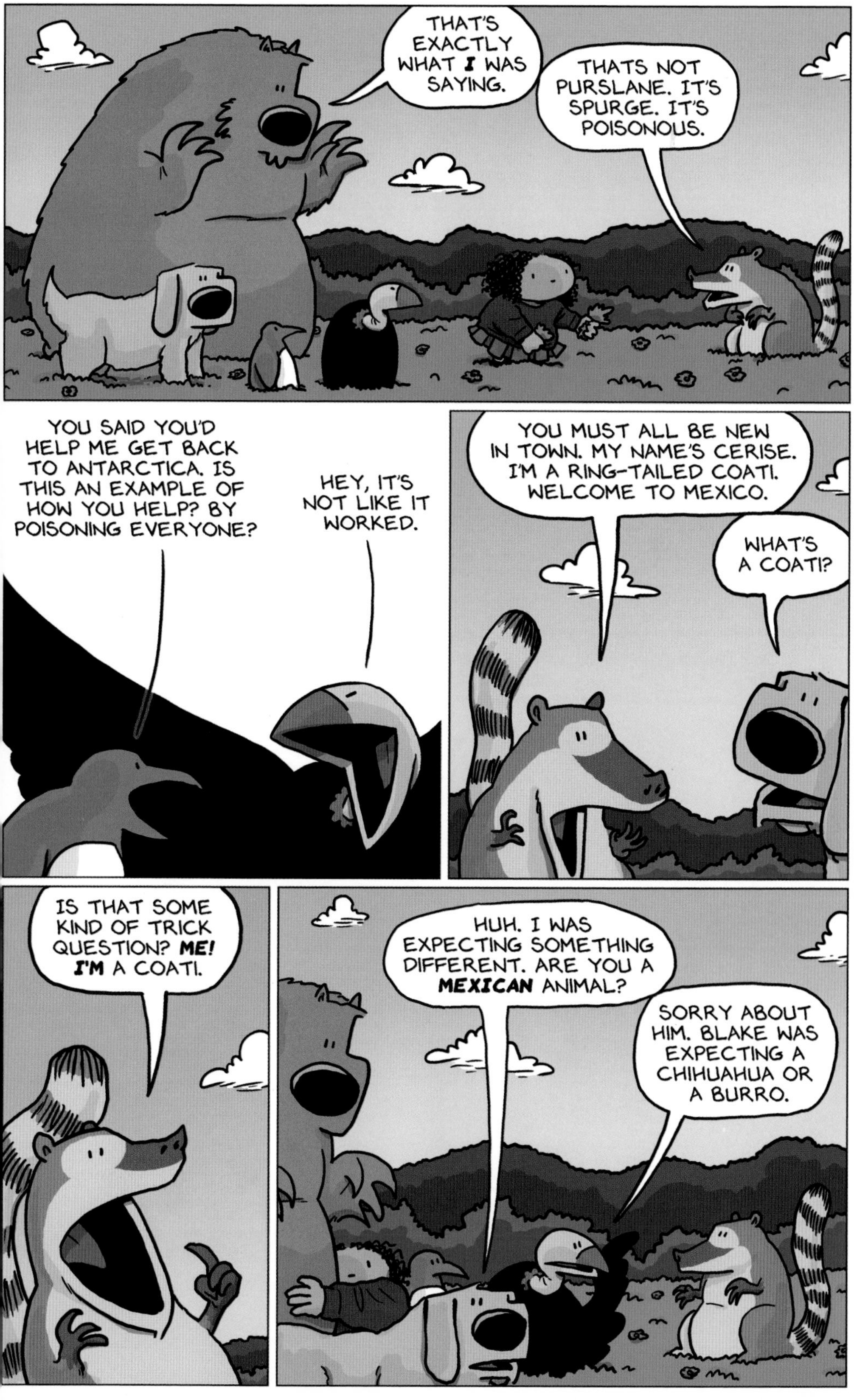
THAT'S EXACTLY WHAT *I* WAS SAYING.
THATS NOT PURSLANE. IT'S SPURGE. IT'S POISONOUS.
YOU SAID YOU'D HELP ME GET BACK TO ANTARCTICA. IS THIS AN EXAMPLE OF HOW YOU HELP? BY POISONING EVERYONE?
HEY, IT'S NOT LIKE IT WORKED.
YOU MUST ALL BE NEW IN TOWN. MY NAME'S CERISE. I'M A RING-TAILED COATI. WELCOME TO MEXICO.
WHAT'S A COATI?
IS THAT SOME KIND OF TRICK QUESTION? **ME! I'M** A COATI.
HUH. I WAS EXPECTING SOMETHING DIFFERENT. ARE YOU A **MEXICAN** ANIMAL?
SORRY ABOUT HIM. BLAKE WAS EXPECTING A CHIHUAHUA OR A BURRO.

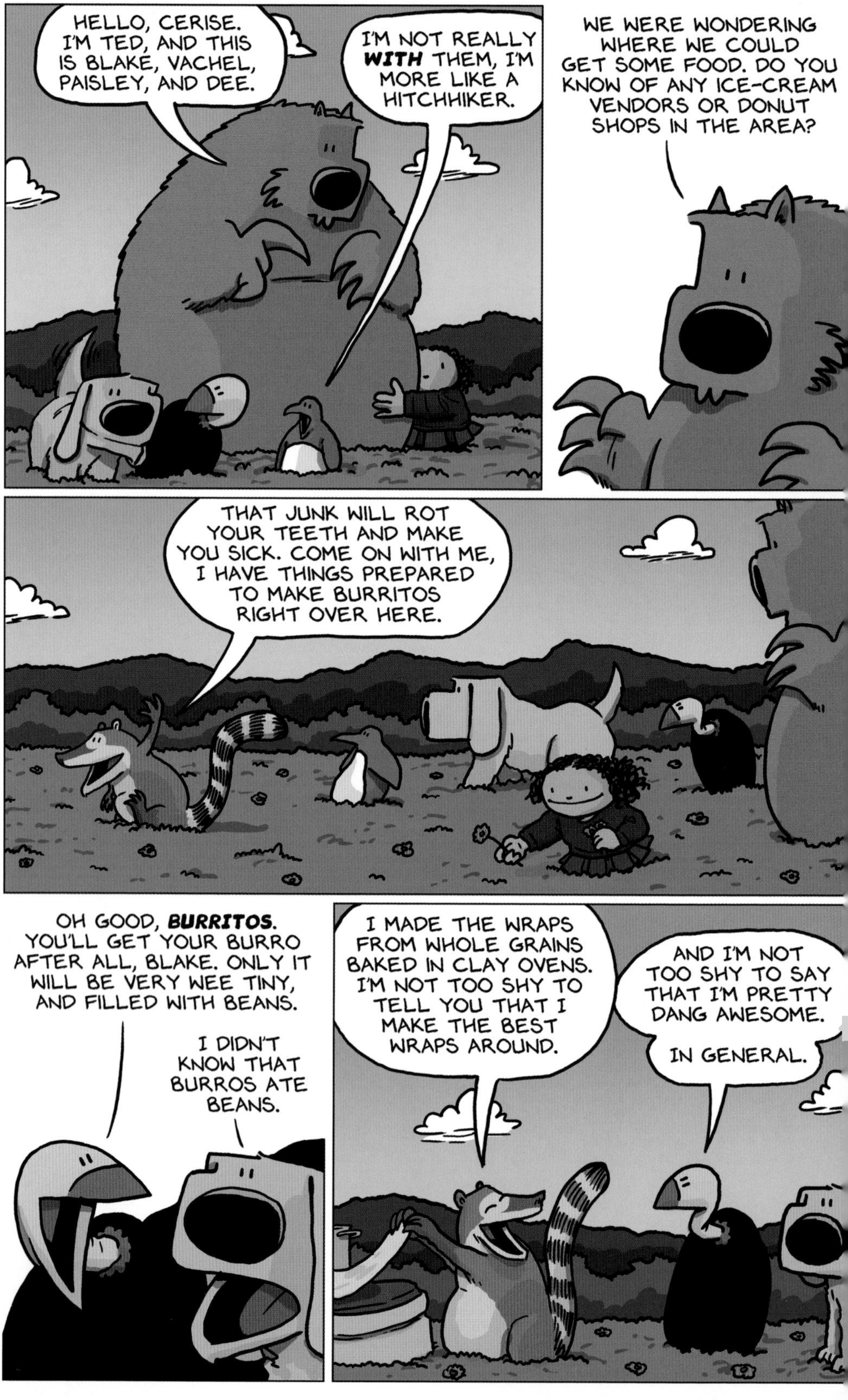
HELLO, CERISE. I'M TED, AND THIS IS BLAKE, VACHEL, PAISLEY, AND DEE.
I'M NOT REALLY **WITH** THEM, I'M MORE LIKE A HITCHHIKER.
WE WERE WONDERING WHERE WE COULD GET SOME FOOD. DO YOU KNOW OF ANY ICE-CREAM VENDORS OR DONUT SHOPS IN THE AREA?
THAT JUNK WILL ROT YOUR TEETH AND MAKE YOU SICK. COME ON WITH ME, I HAVE THINGS PREPARED TO MAKE BURRITOS RIGHT OVER HERE.
OH GOOD, **BURRITOS**. YOU'LL GET YOUR BURRO AFTER ALL, BLAKE. ONLY IT WILL BE VERY WEE TINY, AND FILLED WITH BEANS.
I DIDN'T KNOW THAT BURROS ATE BEANS.
I MADE THE WRAPS FROM WHOLE GRAINS BAKED IN CLAY OVENS. I'M NOT TOO SHY TO TELL YOU THAT I MAKE THE BEST WRAPS AROUND.
AND I'M NOT TOO SHY TO SAY THAT I'M PRETTY DANG AWESOME.
IN GENERAL.

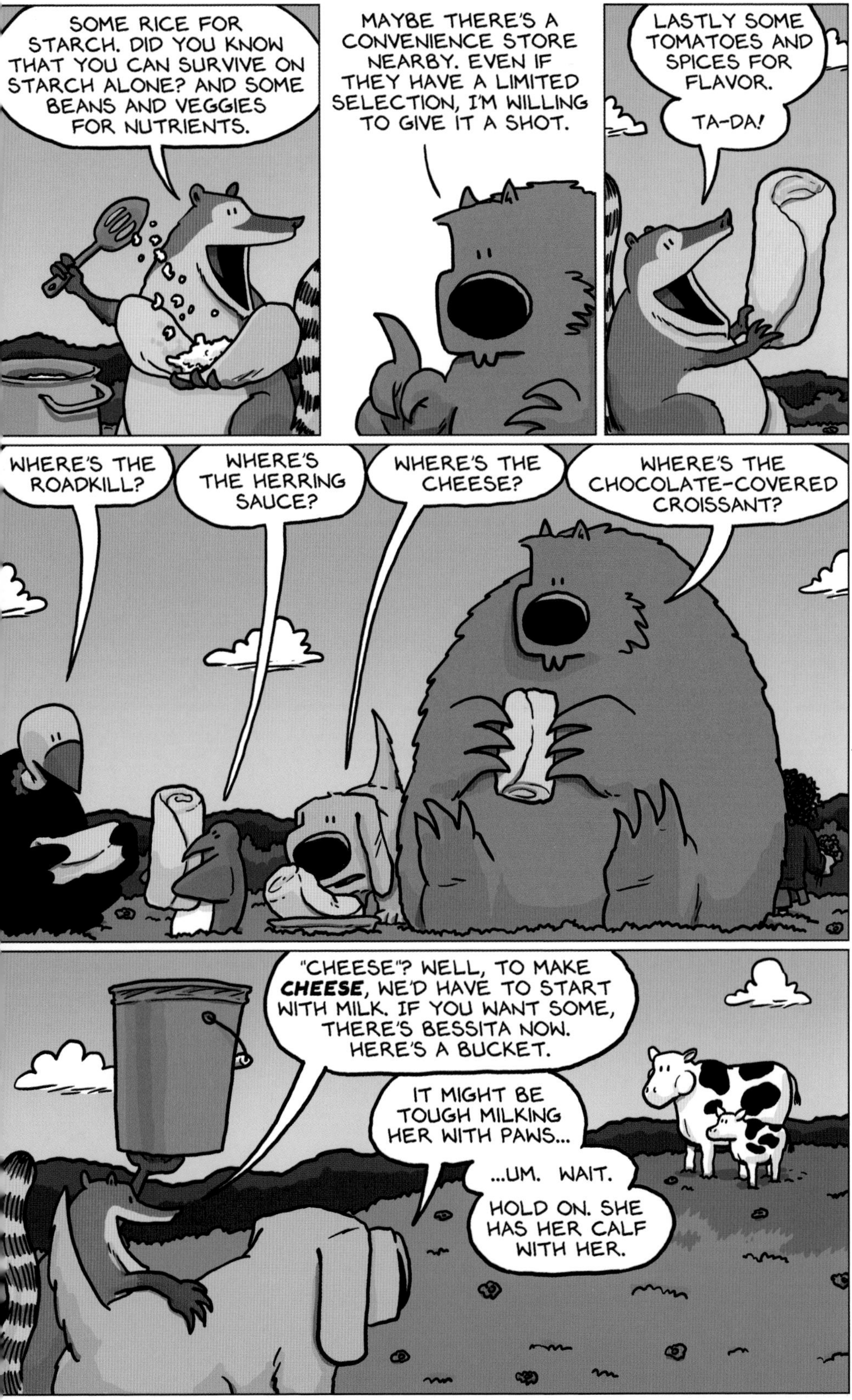
SOME RICE FOR STARCH. DID YOU KNOW THAT YOU CAN SURVIVE ON STARCH ALONE? AND SOME BEANS AND VEGGIES FOR NUTRIENTS.
MAYBE THERE'S A CONVENIENCE STORE NEARBY. EVEN IF THEY HAVE A LIMITED SELECTION, I'M WILLING TO GIVE IT A SHOT.
LASTLY SOME TOMATOES AND SPICES FOR FLAVOR.
TA-DA!
WHERE'S THE ROADKILL?
WHERE'S THE HERRING SAUCE?
WHERE'S THE CHEESE?
WHERE'S THE CHOCOLATE-COVERED CROISSANT?
"CHEESE"? WELL, TO MAKE **CHEESE**, WE'D HAVE TO START WITH MILK. IF YOU WANT SOME, THERE'S BESSITA NOW. HERE'S A BUCKET.
IT MIGHT BE TOUGH MILKING HER WITH PAWS...
...UM. WAIT.
HOLD ON. SHE HAS HER CALF WITH HER.

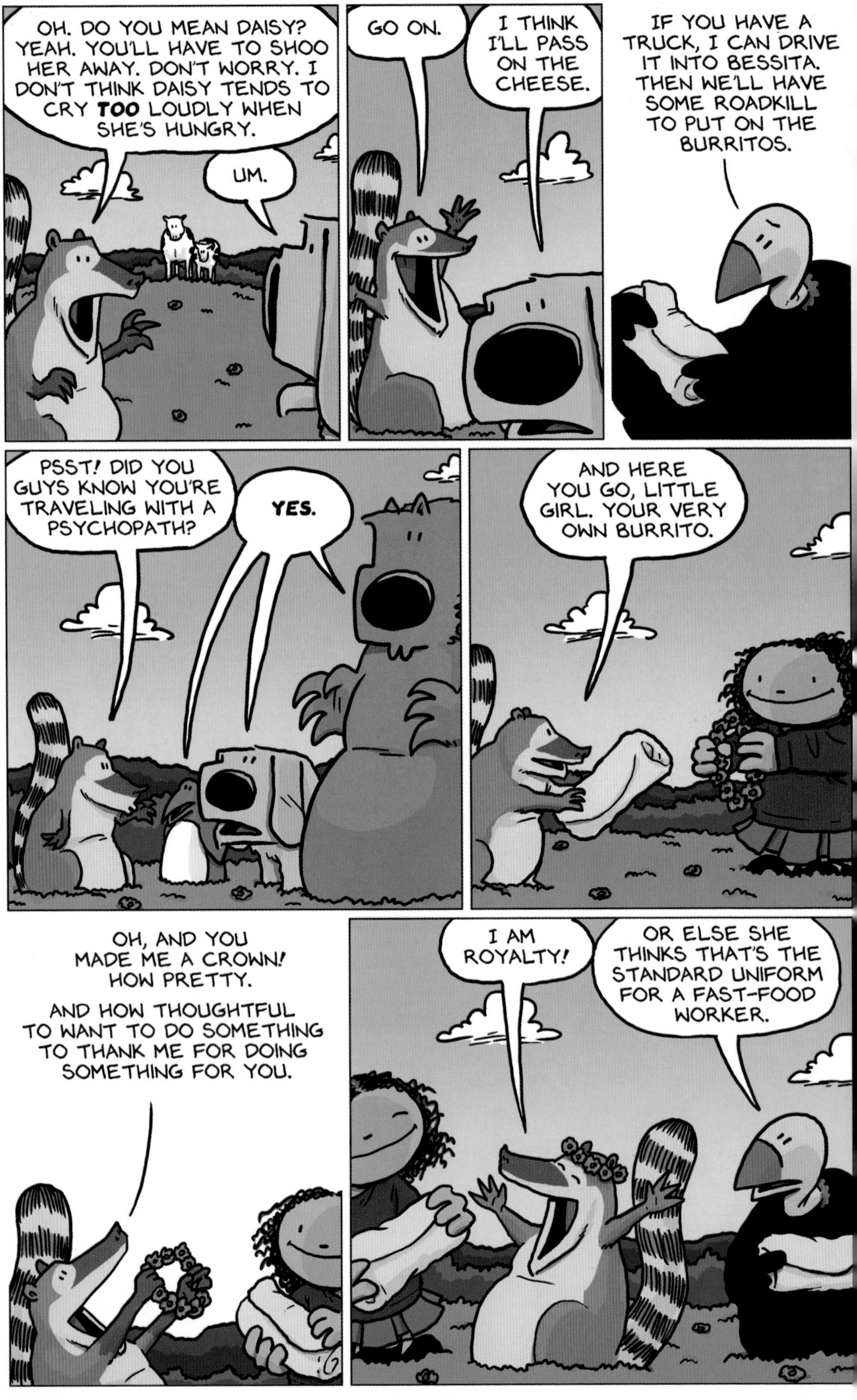
OH. DO YOU MEAN DAISY? YEAH. YOU'LL HAVE TO SHOO HER AWAY. DON'T WORRY. I DON'T THINK DAISY TENDS TO CRY **TOO** LOUDLY WHEN SHE'S HUNGRY.
UM.
GO ON.
I THINK I'LL PASS ON THE CHEESE.
IF YOU HAVE A TRUCK, I CAN DRIVE IT INTO BESSITA. THEN WE'LL HAVE SOME ROADKILL TO PUT ON THE BURRITOS.
PSST! DID YOU GUYS KNOW YOU'RE TRAVELING WITH A PSYCHOPATH?
YES.
AND HERE YOU GO, LITTLE GIRL. YOUR VERY OWN BURRITO.
OH, AND YOU MADE ME A CROWN! HOW PRETTY.
AND HOW THOUGHTFUL TO WANT TO DO SOMETHING TO THANK ME FOR DOING SOMETHING FOR YOU.
I AM ROYALTY!
OR ELSE SHE THINKS THAT'S THE STANDARD UNIFORM FOR A FAST-FOOD WORKER.

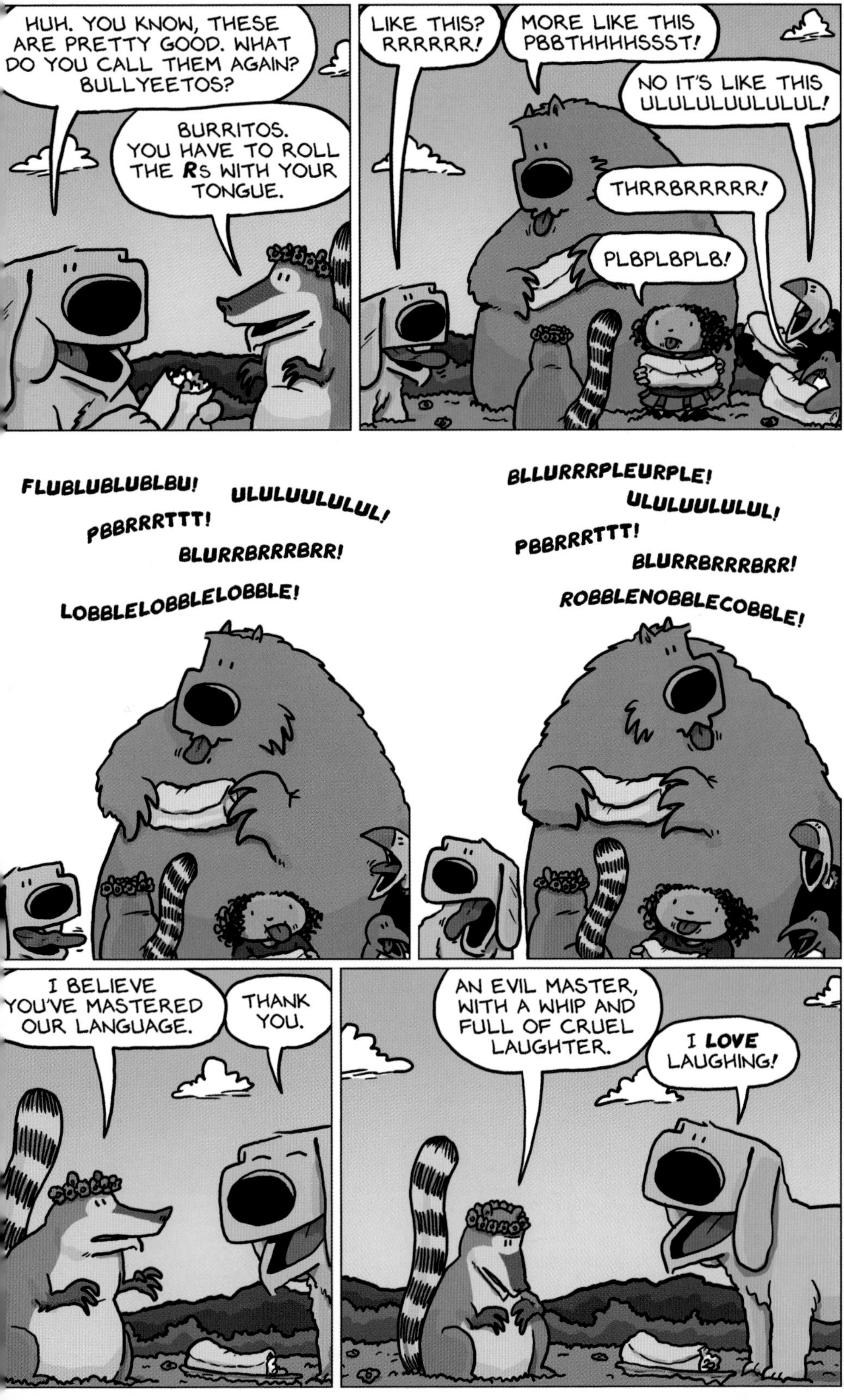
HUH. YOU KNOW, THESE ARE PRETTY GOOD. WHAT DO YOU CALL THEM AGAIN? BULLYEETOS?
BURRITOS. YOU HAVE TO ROLL THE **R**S WITH YOUR TONGUE.
LIKE THIS? RRRRRR!
MORE LIKE THIS PBBTHHHHSSST!
NO IT'S LIKE THIS ULULULUULULUL!
THRRBRRRRR!
PLBPLBPLB!
FLUBLUBLUBLBU!
ULULUULULUL!
PBBRRRTTT!
BLURRBRRRBRR!
LOBBLELOBBLELOBBLE!
BLLURRRPLEURPLE!
ULULUULULUL!
PBBRRRTTT!
BLURRBRRRBRR!
ROBBLENOBBLECOBBLE!
I BELIEVE YOU'VE MASTERED OUR LANGUAGE.
THANK YOU.
AN EVIL MASTER, WITH A WHIP AND FULL OF CRUEL LAUGHTER.
I **LOVE** LAUGHING!

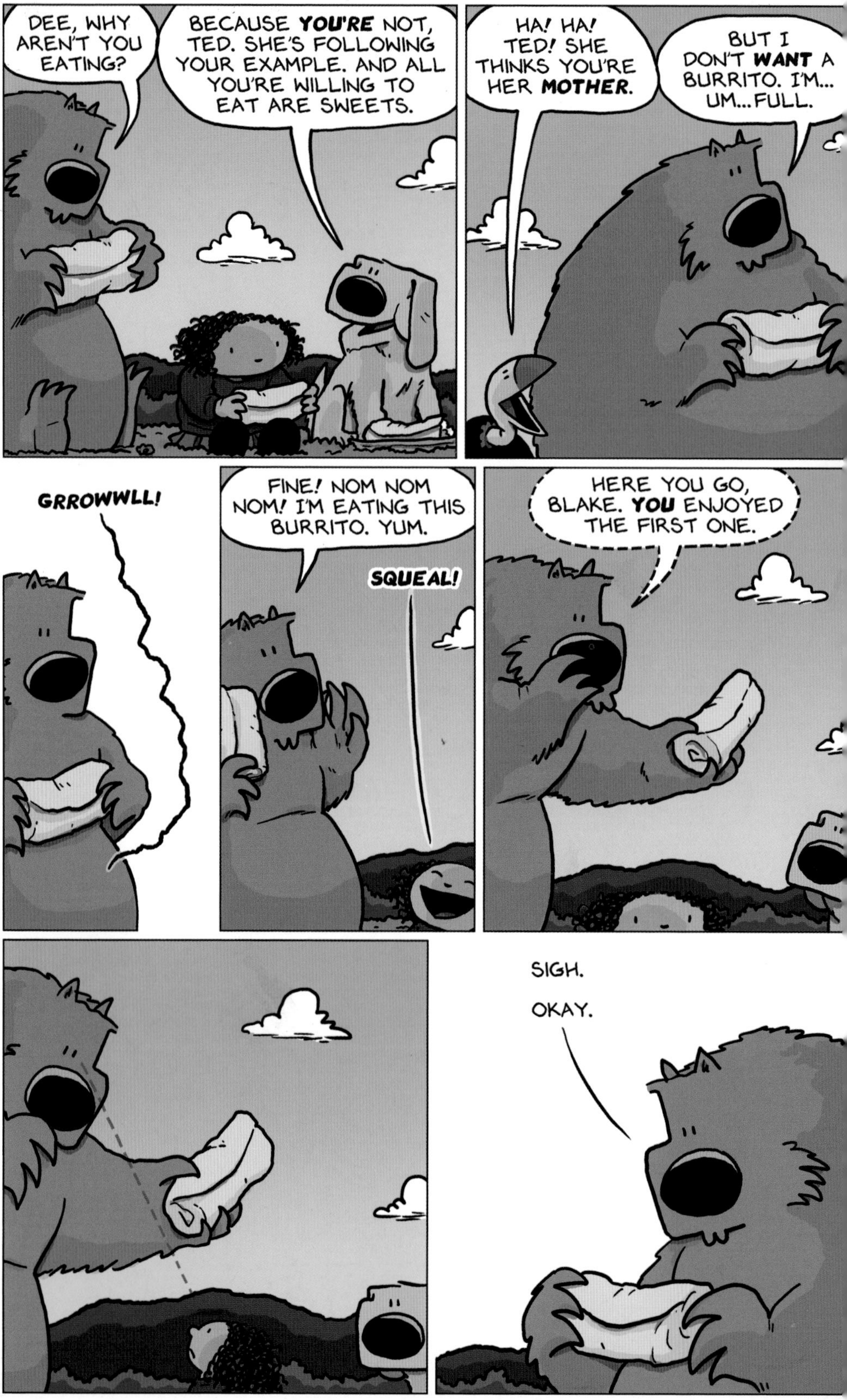
DEE, WHY AREN'T YOU EATING?
BECAUSE **YOU'RE** NOT, TED. SHE'S FOLLOWING YOUR EXAMPLE. AND ALL YOU'RE WILLING TO EAT ARE SWEETS.
HA! HA! TED! SHE THINKS YOU'RE HER **MOTHER**.
BUT I DON'T **WANT** A BURRITO. I'M... UM...FULL.
GRROWWLL!
FINE! NOM NOM NOM! I'M EATING THIS BURRITO. YUM.
SQUEAL!
HERE YOU GO, BLAKE. **YOU** ENJOYED THE FIRST ONE.
SIGH.
OKAY.

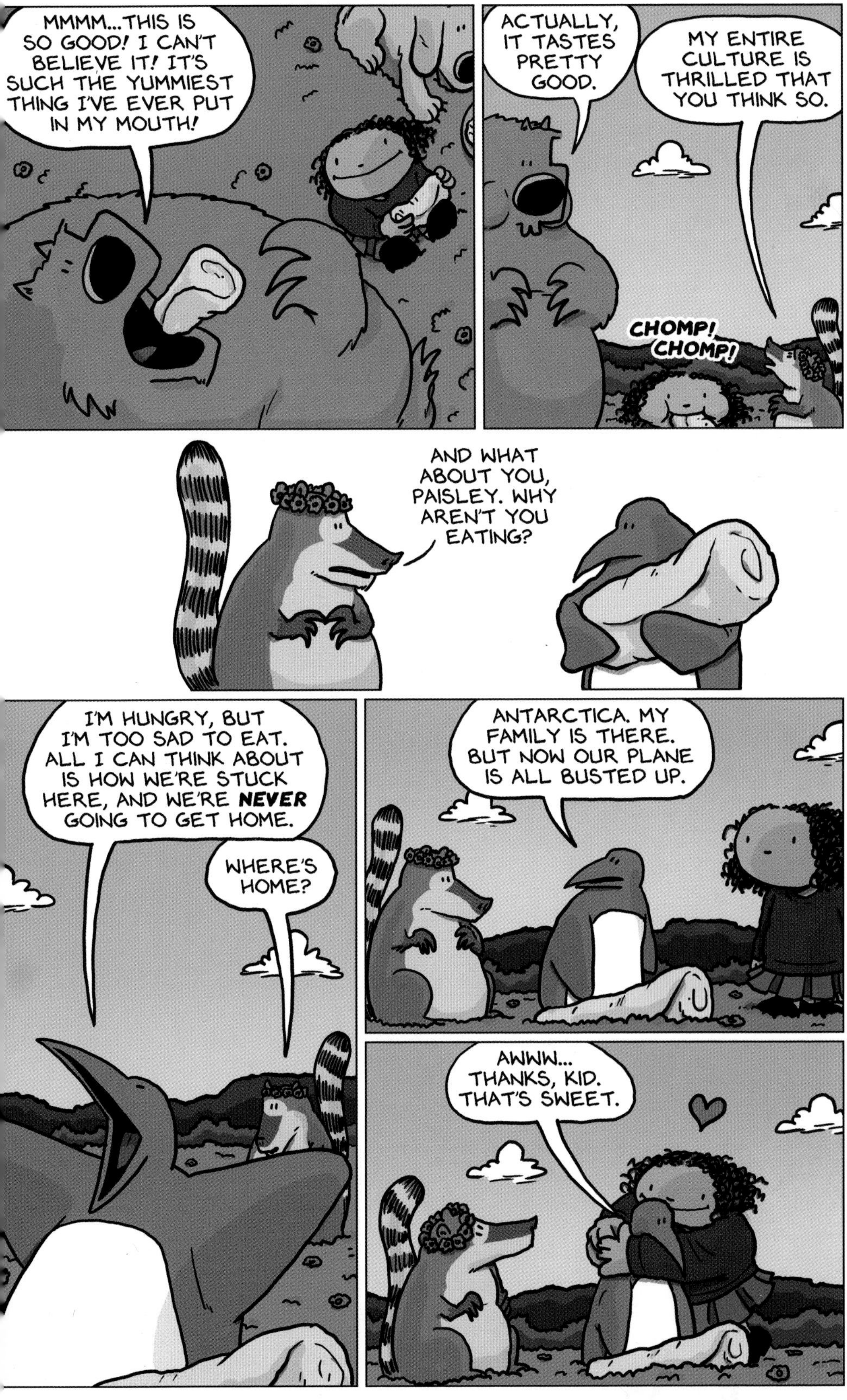
MMMM...THIS IS SO GOOD! I CAN'T BELIEVE IT! IT'S SUCH THE YUMMIEST THING I'VE EVER PUT IN MY MOUTH!
ACTUALLY, IT TASTES PRETTY GOOD.
MY ENTIRE CULTURE IS THRILLED THAT YOU THINK SO.
CHOMP! CHOMP!
AND WHAT ABOUT YOU, PAISLEY. WHY AREN'T YOU EATING?
I'M HUNGRY, BUT I'M TOO SAD TO EAT. ALL I CAN THINK ABOUT IS HOW WE'RE STUCK HERE, AND WE'RE **NEVER** GOING TO GET HOME.
WHERE'S HOME?
ANTARCTICA. MY FAMILY IS THERE. BUT NOW OUR PLANE IS ALL BUSTED UP.
AWWW... THANKS, KID. THAT'S SWEET.

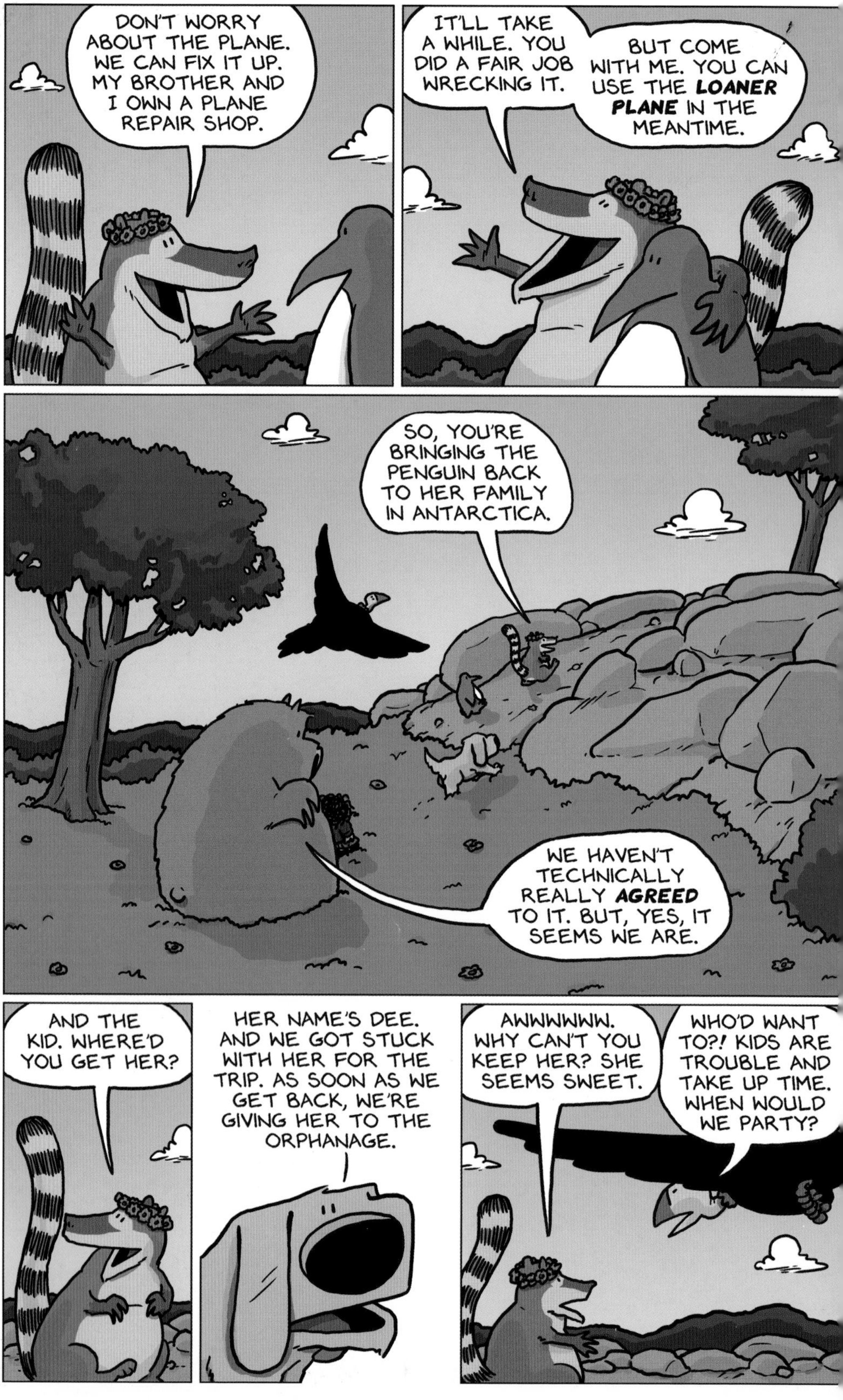
DON'T WORRY ABOUT THE PLANE. WE CAN FIX IT UP. MY BROTHER AND I OWN A PLANE REPAIR SHOP.
IT'LL TAKE A WHILE. YOU DID A FAIR JOB WRECKING IT.
BUT COME WITH ME. YOU CAN USE THE **LOANER PLANE** IN THE MEANTIME.
SO, YOU'RE BRINGING THE PENGUIN BACK TO HER FAMILY IN ANTARCTICA.
WE HAVEN'T TECHNICALLY REALLY **AGREED** TO IT. BUT, YES, IT SEEMS WE ARE.
AND THE KID. WHERE'D YOU GET HER?
HER NAME'S DEE. AND WE GOT STUCK WITH HER FOR THE TRIP. AS SOON AS WE GET BACK, WE'RE GIVING HER TO THE ORPHANAGE.
AWWWWWW. WHY CAN'T YOU KEEP HER? SHE SEEMS SWEET.
WHO'D WANT TO?! KIDS ARE TROUBLE AND TAKE UP TIME. WHEN WOULD WE PARTY?

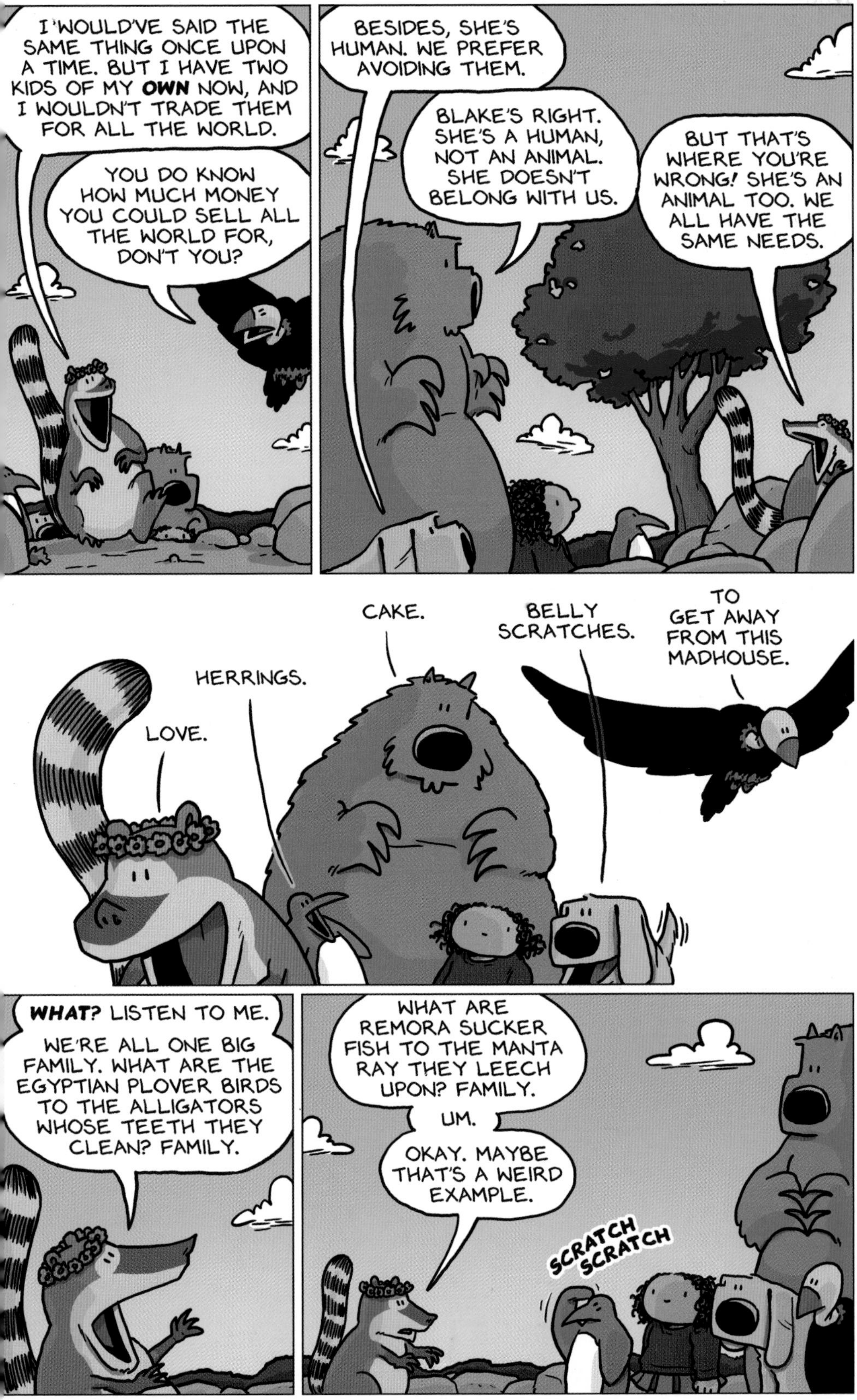
I WOULD'VE SAID THE SAME THING ONCE UPON A TIME. BUT I HAVE TWO KIDS OF MY **OWN** NOW, AND I WOULDN'T TRADE THEM FOR ALL THE WORLD.
YOU DO KNOW HOW MUCH MONEY YOU COULD SELL ALL THE WORLD FOR, DON'T YOU?
BESIDES, SHE'S HUMAN. WE PREFER AVOIDING THEM.
BLAKE'S RIGHT. SHE'S A HUMAN, NOT AN ANIMAL. SHE DOESN'T BELONG WITH US.
BUT THAT'S WHERE YOU'RE WRONG! SHE'S AN ANIMAL TOO. WE ALL HAVE THE SAME NEEDS.
LOVE.
HERRINGS.
CAKE.
BELLY SCRATCHES.
TO GET AWAY FROM THIS MADHOUSE.
WHAT? LISTEN TO ME.
WE'RE ALL ONE BIG FAMILY. WHAT ARE THE EGYPTIAN PLOVER BIRDS TO THE ALLIGATORS WHOSE TEETH THEY CLEAN? FAMILY.
WHAT ARE REMORA SUCKER FISH TO THE MANTA RAY THEY LEECH UPON? FAMILY.
UM.
OKAY. MAYBE THAT'S A WEIRD EXAMPLE.
SCRATCH SCRATCH

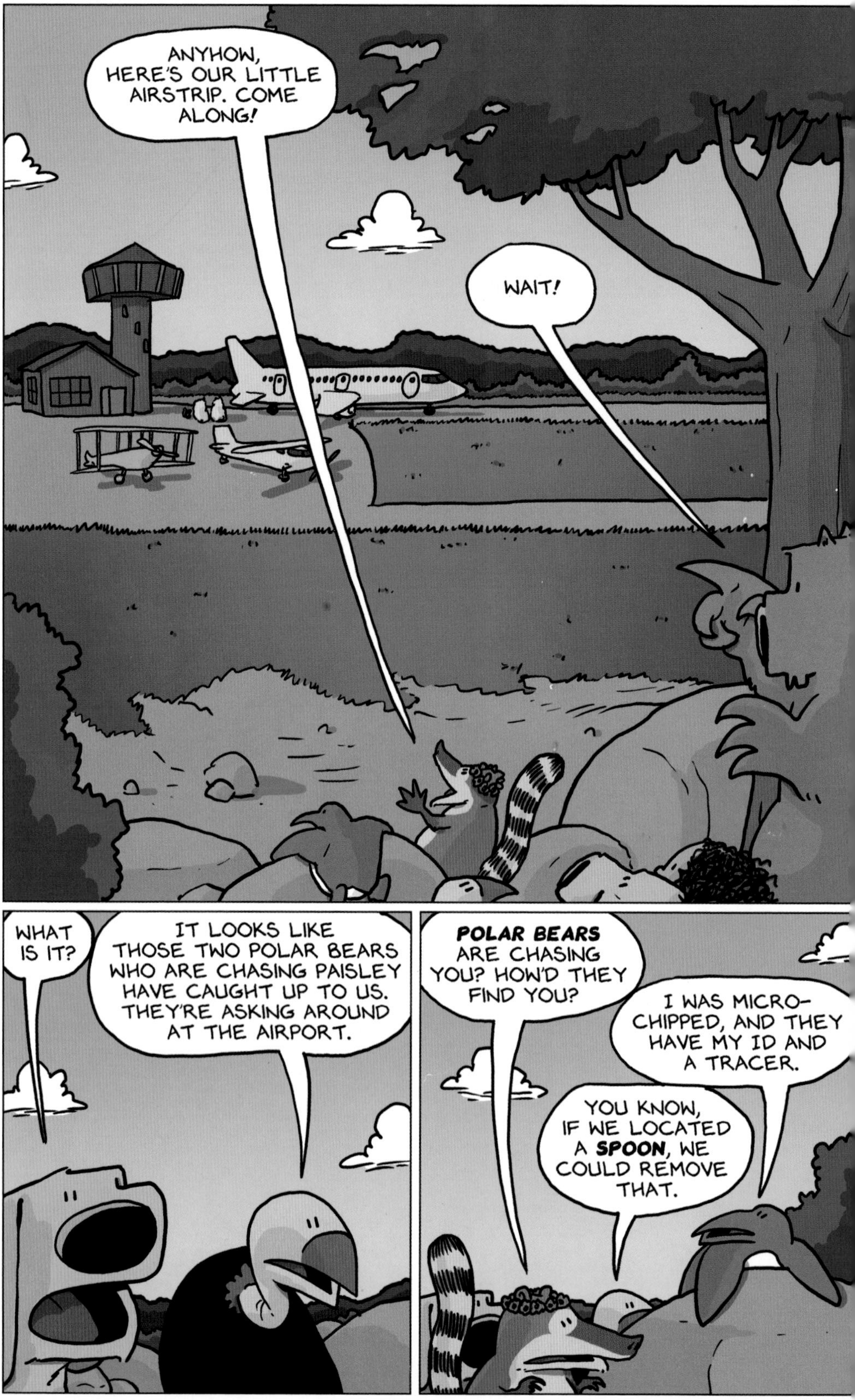
ANYHOW, HERE'S OUR LITTLE AIRSTRIP. COME ALONG!
WAIT!
WHAT IS IT?
IT LOOKS LIKE THOSE TWO POLAR BEARS WHO ARE CHASING PAISLEY HAVE CAUGHT UP TO US. THEY'RE ASKING AROUND AT THE AIRPORT.
POLAR BEARS ARE CHASING YOU? HOW'D THEY FIND YOU?
I WAS MICRO-CHIPPED, AND THEY HAVE MY ID AND A TRACER.
YOU KNOW, IF WE LOCATED A **SPOON**, WE COULD REMOVE THAT.

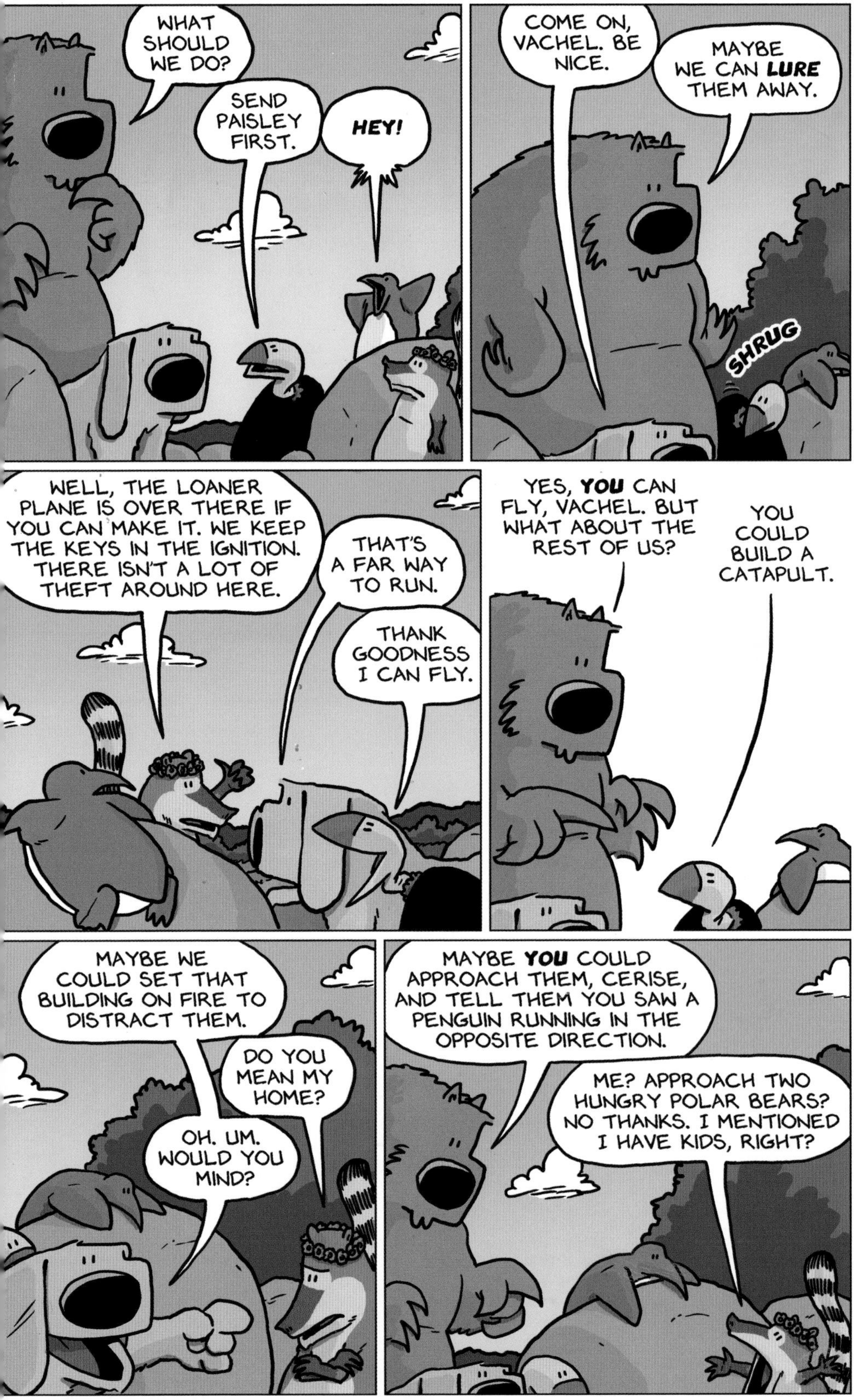
WHAT SHOULD WE DO?
SEND PAISLEY FIRST.
HEY!
COME ON, VACHEL. BE NICE.
MAYBE WE CAN **LURE** THEM AWAY.
SHRUG
WELL, THE LOANER PLANE IS OVER THERE IF YOU CAN MAKE IT. WE KEEP THE KEYS IN THE IGNITION. THERE ISN'T A LOT OF THEFT AROUND HERE.
THAT'S A FAR WAY TO RUN.
THANK GOODNESS I CAN FLY.
YES, **YOU** CAN FLY, VACHEL. BUT WHAT ABOUT THE REST OF US?
YOU COULD BUILD A CATAPULT.
MAYBE WE COULD SET THAT BUILDING ON FIRE TO DISTRACT THEM.
DO YOU MEAN MY HOME?
OH. UM. WOULD YOU MIND?
MAYBE **YOU** COULD APPROACH THEM, CERISE, AND TELL THEM YOU SAW A PENGUIN RUNNING IN THE OPPOSITE DIRECTION.
ME? APPROACH TWO HUNGRY POLAR BEARS? NO THANKS. I MENTIONED I HAVE KIDS, RIGHT?

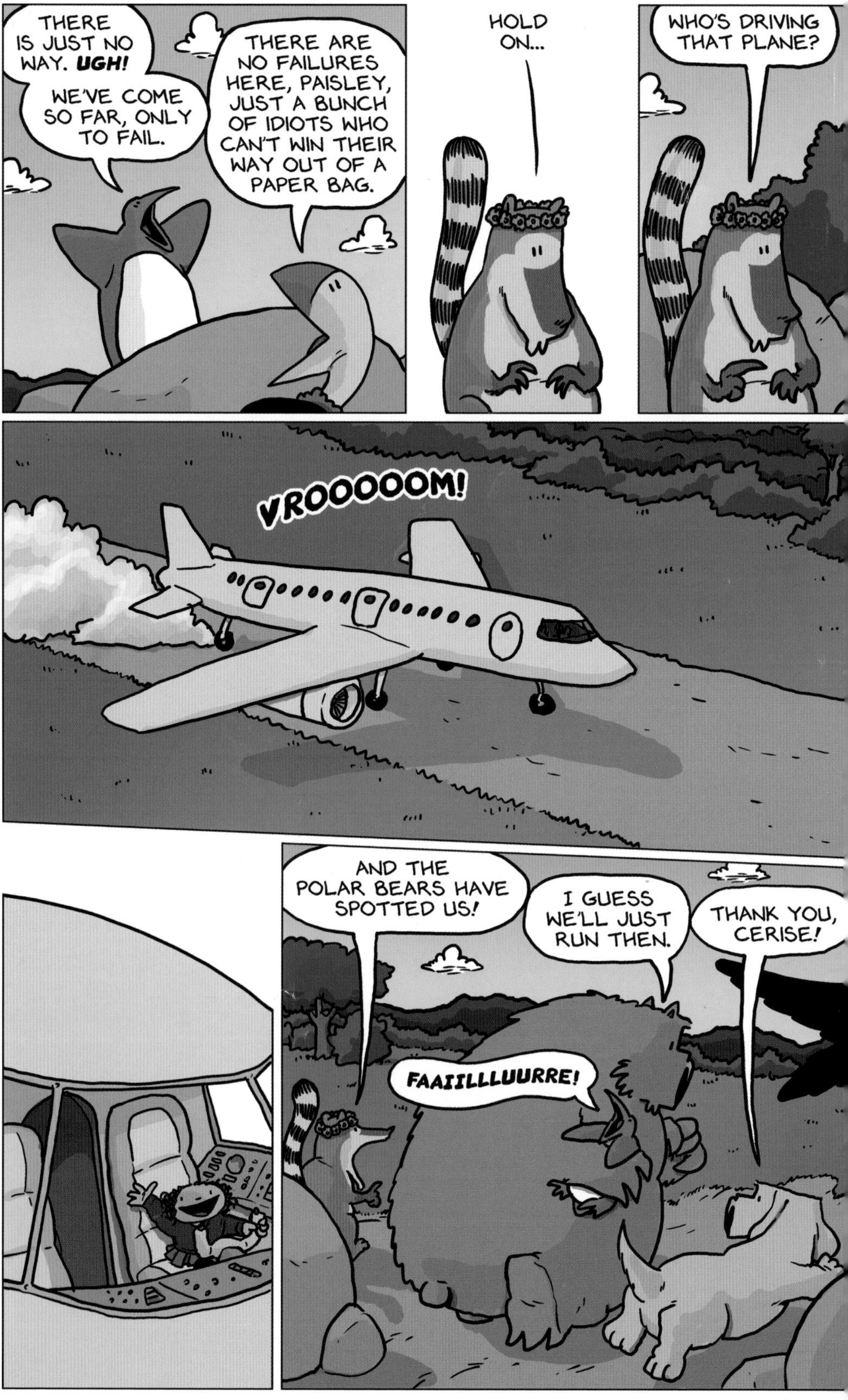
THERE IS JUST NO WAY. UGH!
WE'VE COME SO FAR, ONLY TO FAIL.
THERE ARE NO FAILURES HERE, PAISLEY, JUST A BUNCH OF IDIOTS WHO CAN'T WIN THEIR WAY OUT OF A PAPER BAG.
HOLD ON...
WHO'S DRIVING THAT PLANE?
VROOOOOM!
AND THE POLAR BEARS HAVE SPOTTED US!
I GUESS WE'LL JUST RUN THEN.
THANK YOU, CERISE!
FAAIILLLUURRE!

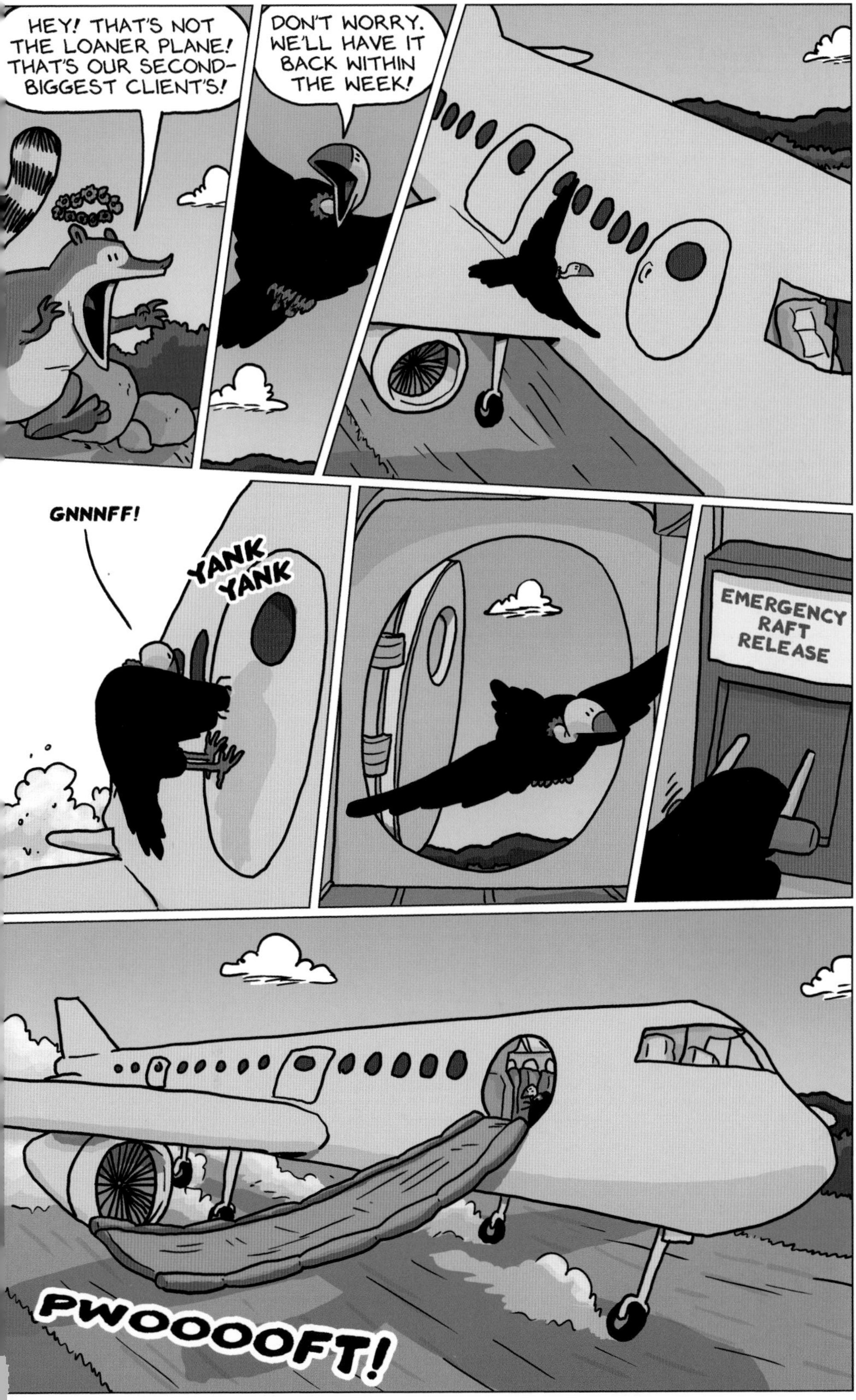
HEY! THAT'S NOT THE LOANER PLANE! THAT'S OUR SECOND-BIGGEST CLIENT'S!
DON'T WORRY. WE'LL HAVE IT BACK WITHIN THE WEEK!
GNNNFF!
YANK YANK
EMERGENCY RAFT RELEASE
PWOOOOOFT!

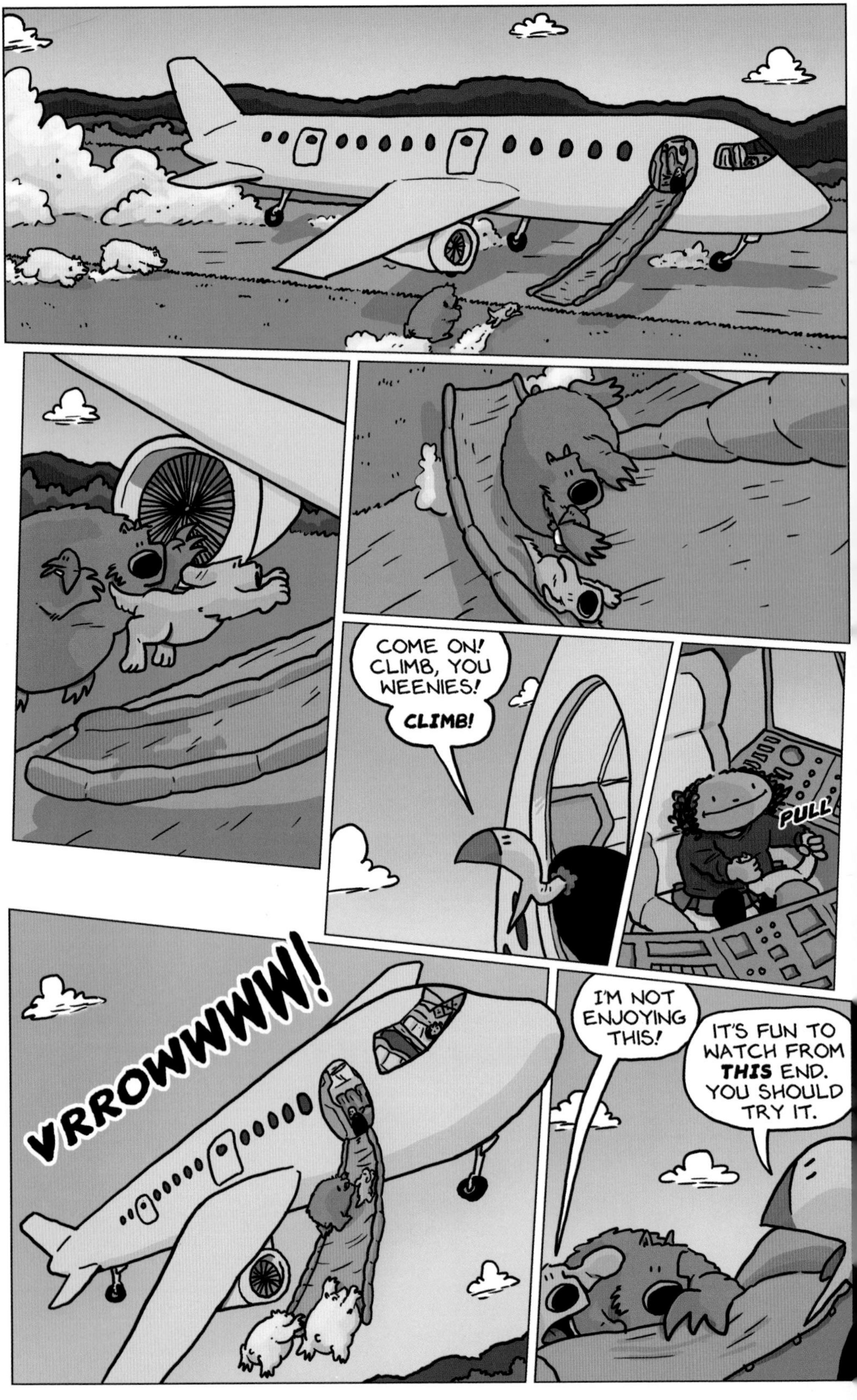
COME ON! CLIMB, YOU WEENIES!
CLIMB!
PULL
VRROWWWW!
I'M NOT ENJOYING THIS!
IT'S FUN TO WATCH FROM THIS END. YOU SHOULD TRY IT.

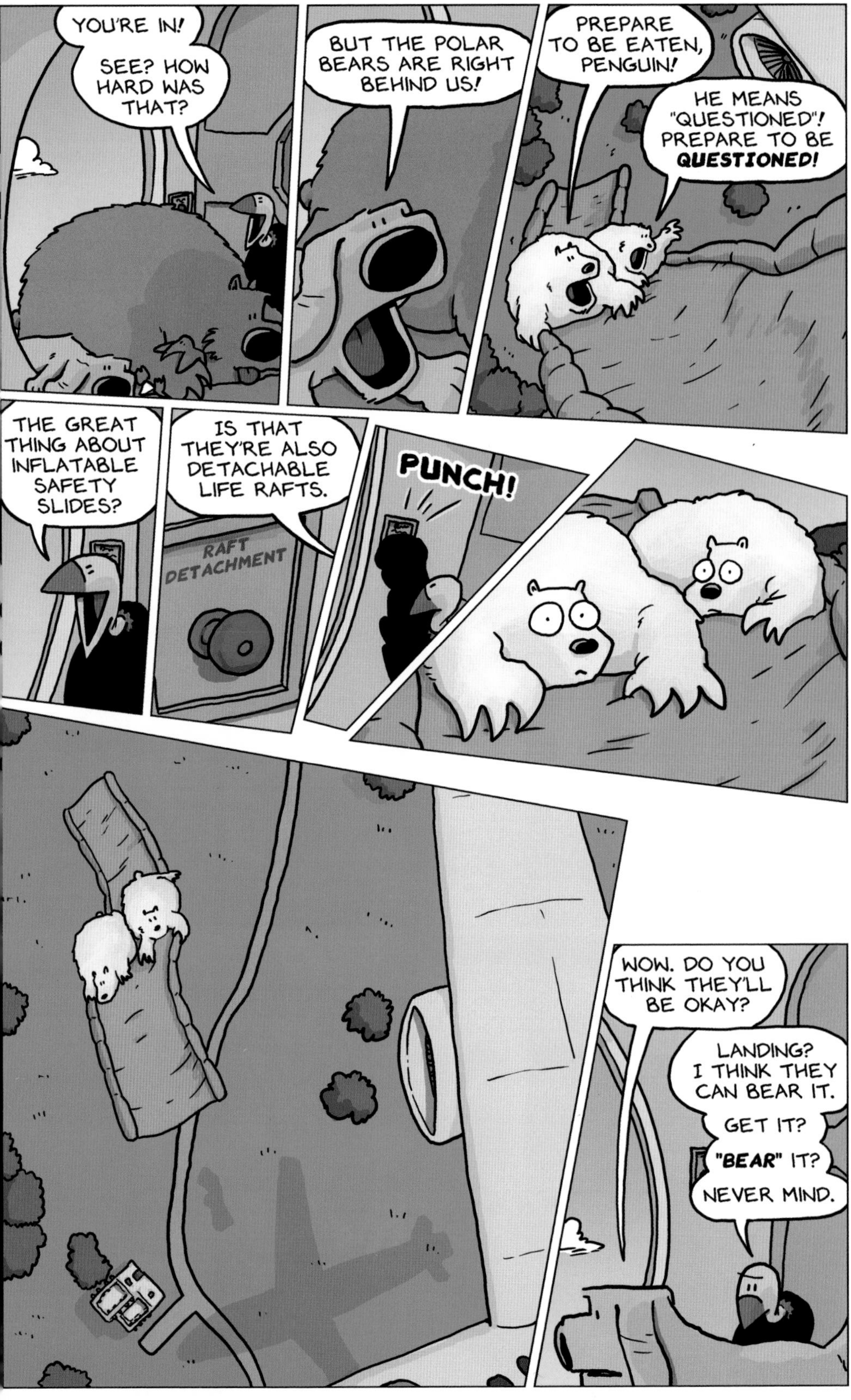
YOU'RE IN!
SEE? HOW HARD WAS THAT?
BUT THE POLAR BEARS ARE RIGHT BEHIND US!
PREPARE TO BE EATEN, PENGUIN!
HE MEANS "QUESTIONED"! PREPARE TO BE **QUESTIONED!**
THE GREAT THING ABOUT INFLATABLE SAFETY SLIDES?
IS THAT THEY'RE ALSO DETACHABLE LIFE RAFTS.
RAFT DETACHMENT
PUNCH!
WOW. DO YOU THINK THEY'LL BE OKAY?
LANDING? I THINK THEY CAN BEAR IT.
GET IT?
"**BEAR**" IT?
NEVER MIND.

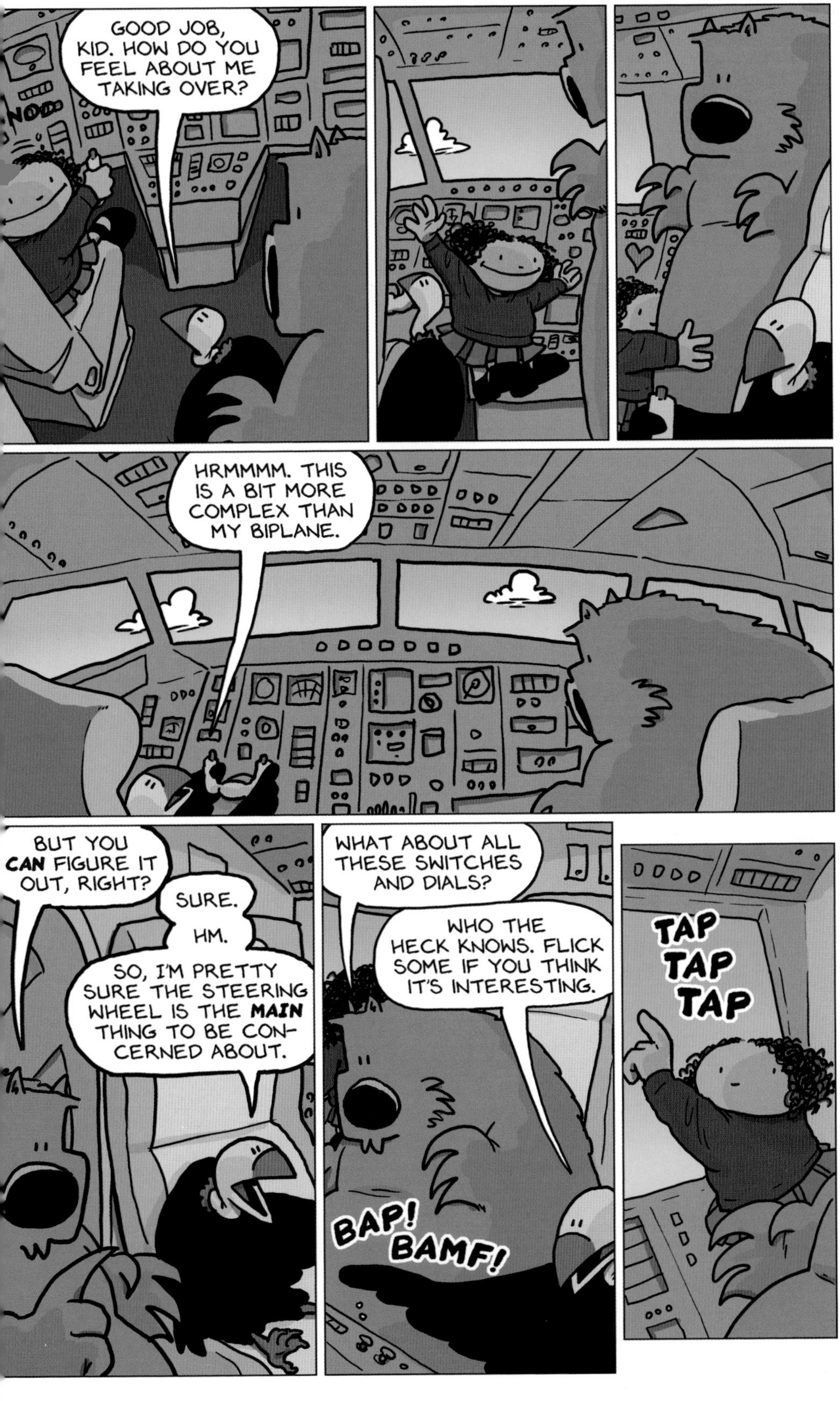

GOOD JOB, KID. HOW DO YOU FEEL ABOUT ME TAKING OVER?
NOD
HRMMMM. THIS IS A BIT MORE COMPLEX THAN MY BIPLANE.
BUT YOU **CAN** FIGURE IT OUT, RIGHT?
SURE.
HM.
SO, I'M PRETTY SURE THE STEERING WHEEL IS THE **MAIN** THING TO BE CONCERNED ABOUT.
WHAT ABOUT ALL THESE SWITCHES AND DIALS?
WHO THE HECK KNOWS. FLICK SOME IF YOU THINK IT'S INTERESTING.
BAP! BAMF!
TAP TAP TAP

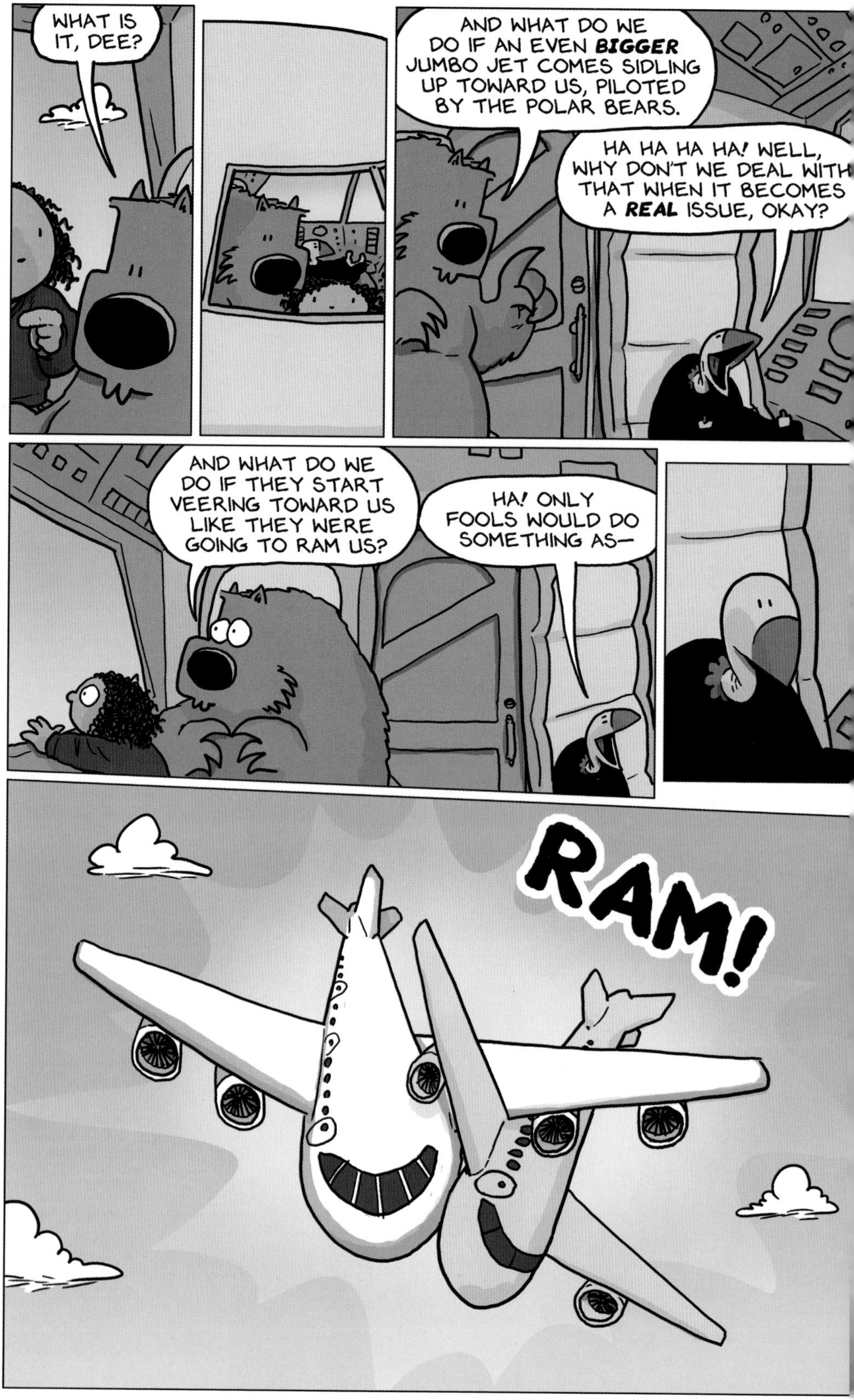
WHAT IS IT, DEE?
AND WHAT DO WE DO IF AN EVEN **BIGGER** JUMBO JET COMES SIDLING UP TOWARD US, PILOTED BY THE POLAR BEARS.
HA HA HA HA! WELL, WHY DON'T WE DEAL WITH THAT WHEN IT BECOMES A **REAL** ISSUE, OKAY?
AND WHAT DO WE DO IF THEY START VEERING TOWARD US LIKE THEY WERE GOING TO RAM US?
HA! ONLY FOOLS WOULD DO SOMETHING AS—
RAM!

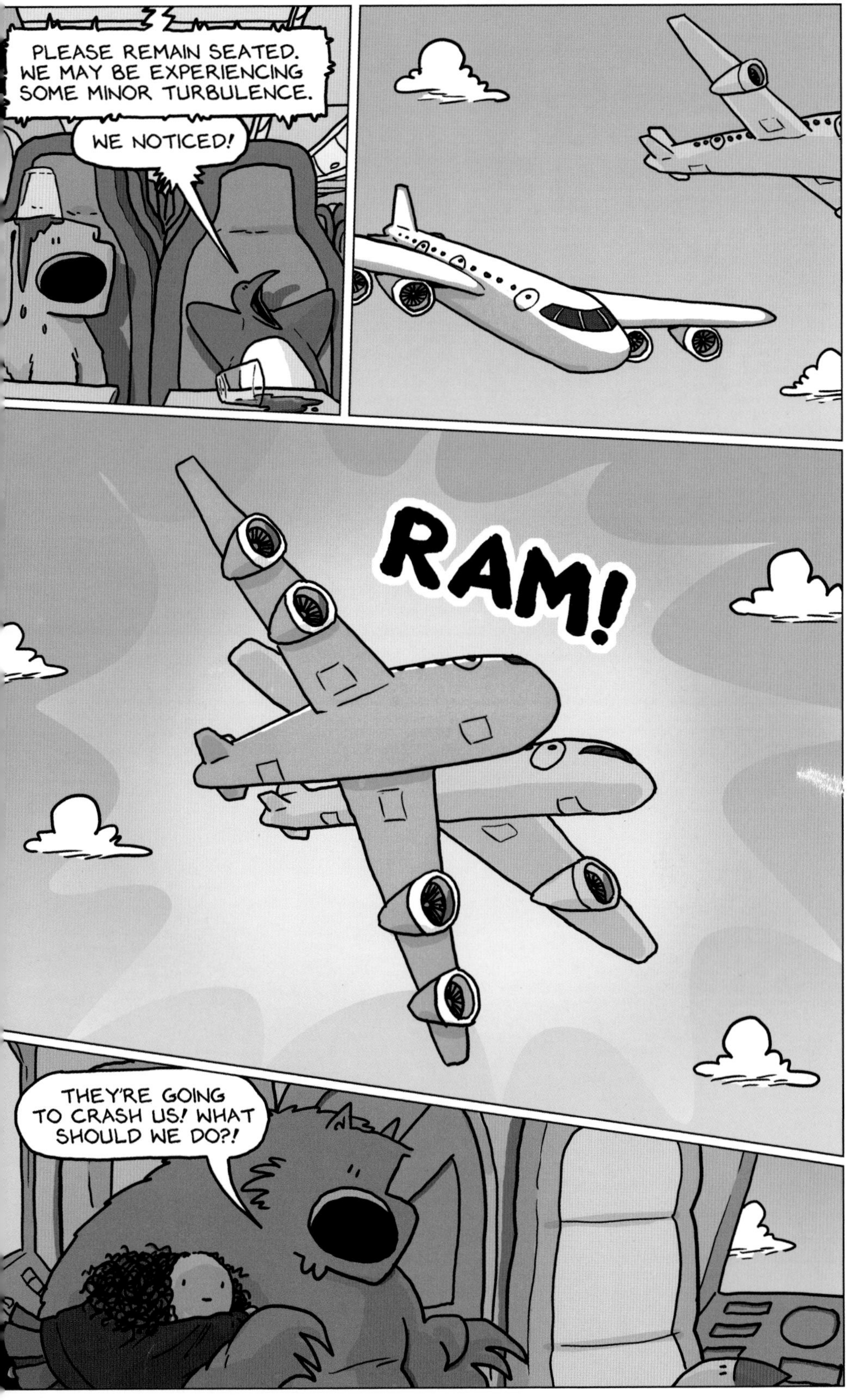
PLEASE REMAIN SEATED. WE MAY BE EXPERIENCING SOME MINOR TURBULENCE.
WE NOTICED!
RAM!
THEY'RE GOING TO CRASH US! WHAT SHOULD WE DO?!

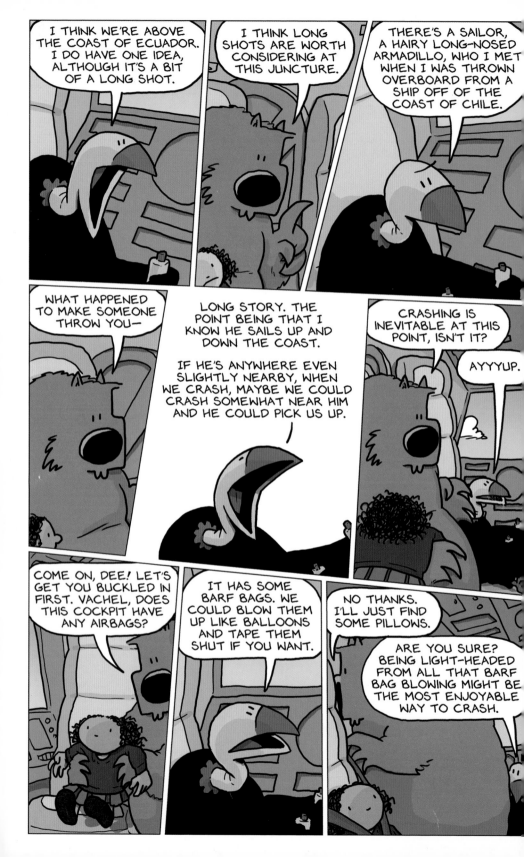

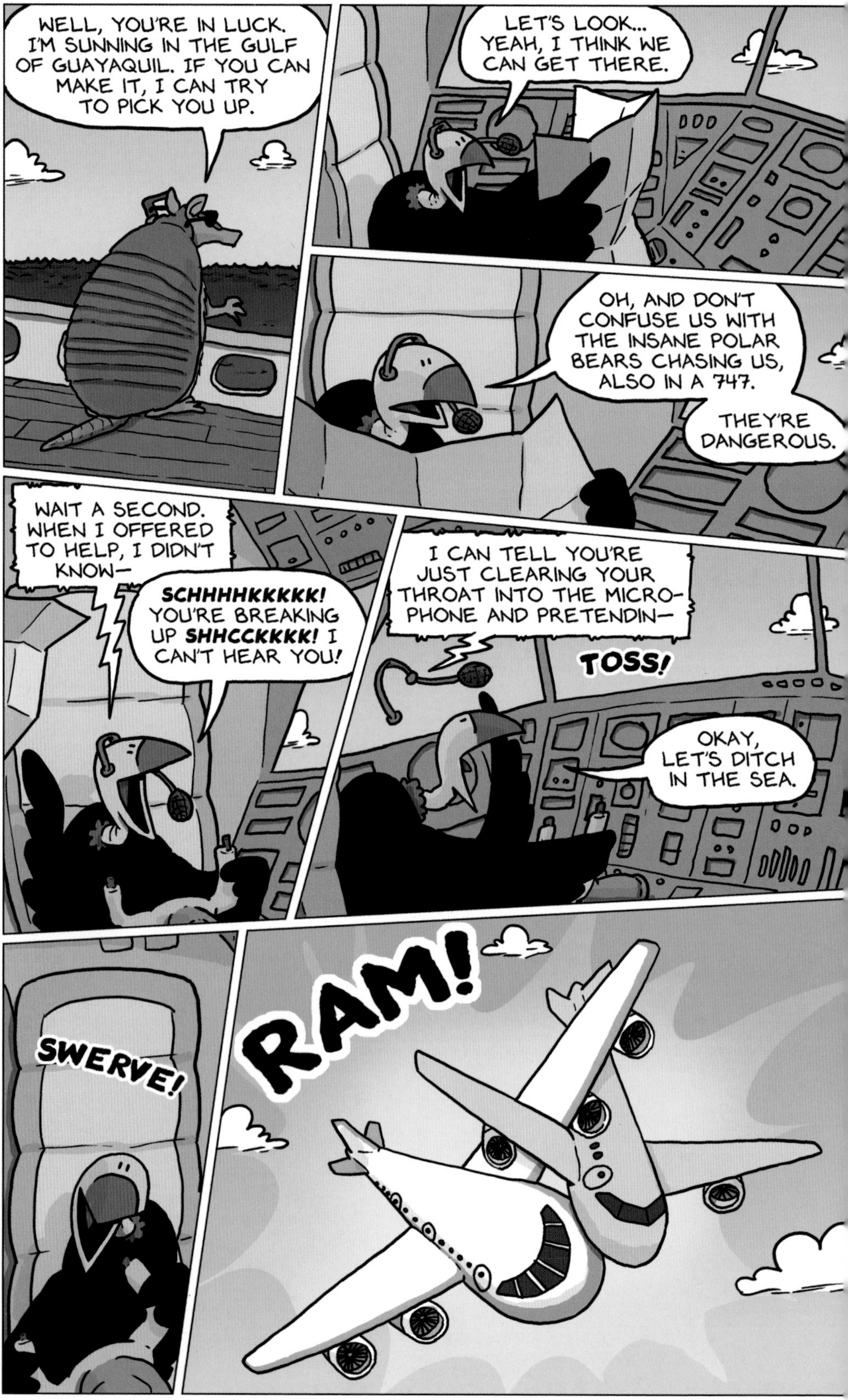
WELL, YOU'RE IN LUCK. I'M SUNNING IN THE GULF OF GUAYAQUIL. IF YOU CAN MAKE IT, I CAN TRY TO PICK YOU UP.
LET'S LOOK... YEAH, I THINK WE CAN GET THERE.
OH, AND DON'T CONFUSE US WITH THE INSANE POLAR BEARS CHASING US, ALSO IN A 747.
THEY'RE DANGEROUS.
WAIT A SECOND. WHEN I OFFERED TO HELP, I DIDN'T KNOW—
SCHHHHKKKKK! YOU'RE BREAKING UP SHHCCKKKK! I CAN'T HEAR YOU!
I CAN TELL YOU'RE JUST CLEARING YOUR THROAT INTO THE MICRO-PHONE AND PRETENDIN—
TOSS!
OKAY, LET'S DITCH IN THE SEA.
SWERVE!
RAM!

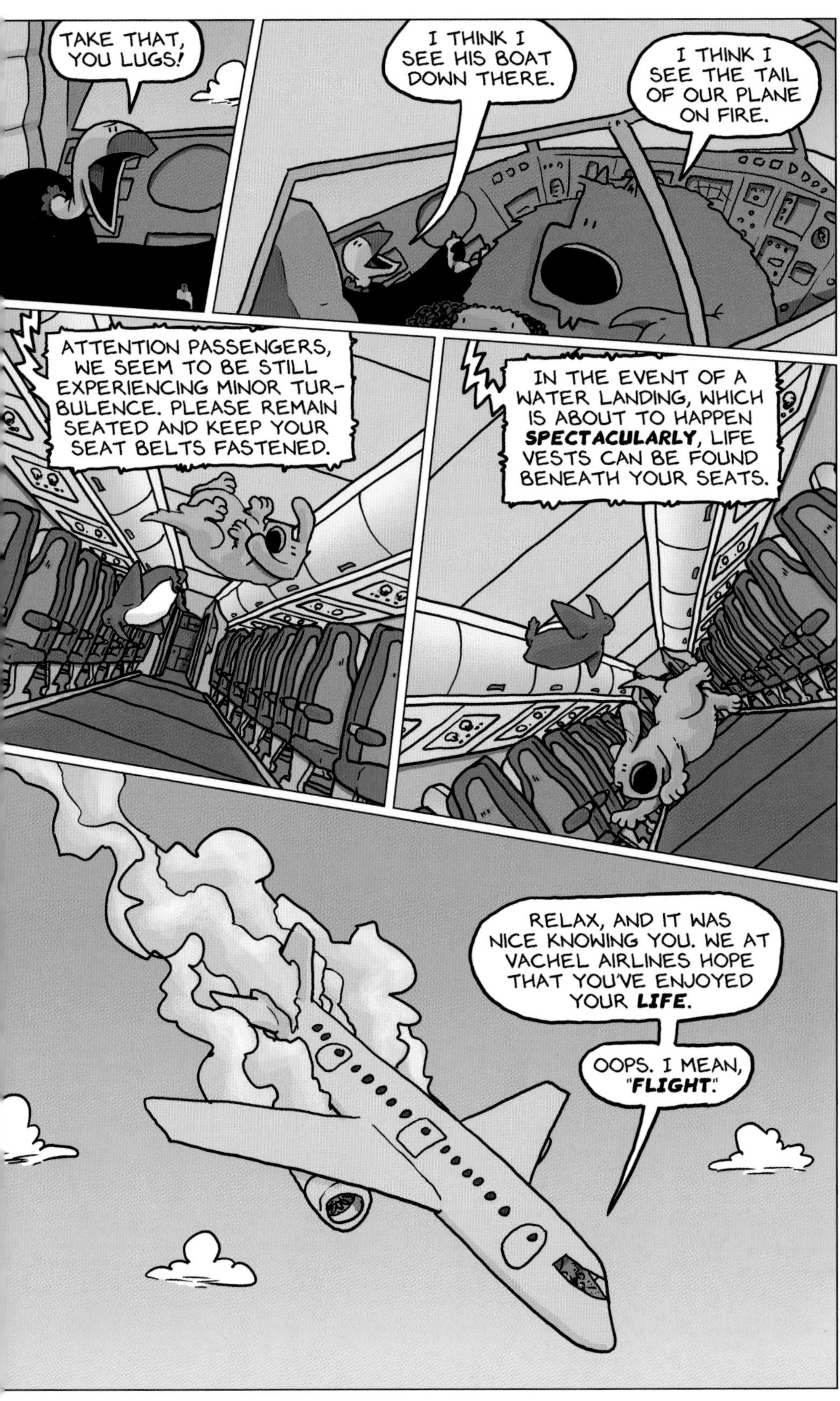
TAKE THAT, YOU LUGS!
I THINK I SEE HIS BOAT DOWN THERE.
I THINK I SEE THE TAIL OF OUR PLANE ON FIRE.
ATTENTION PASSENGERS, WE SEEM TO BE STILL EXPERIENCING MINOR TUR-BULENCE. PLEASE REMAIN SEATED AND KEEP YOUR SEAT BELTS FASTENED.
IN THE EVENT OF A WATER LANDING, WHICH IS ABOUT TO HAPPEN **SPECTACULARLY**, LIFE VESTS CAN BE FOUND BENEATH YOUR SEATS.
RELAX, AND IT WAS NICE KNOWING YOU. WE AT VACHEL AIRLINES HOPE THAT YOU'VE ENJOYED YOUR **LIFE**.
OOPS. I MEAN, "**FLIGHT**."

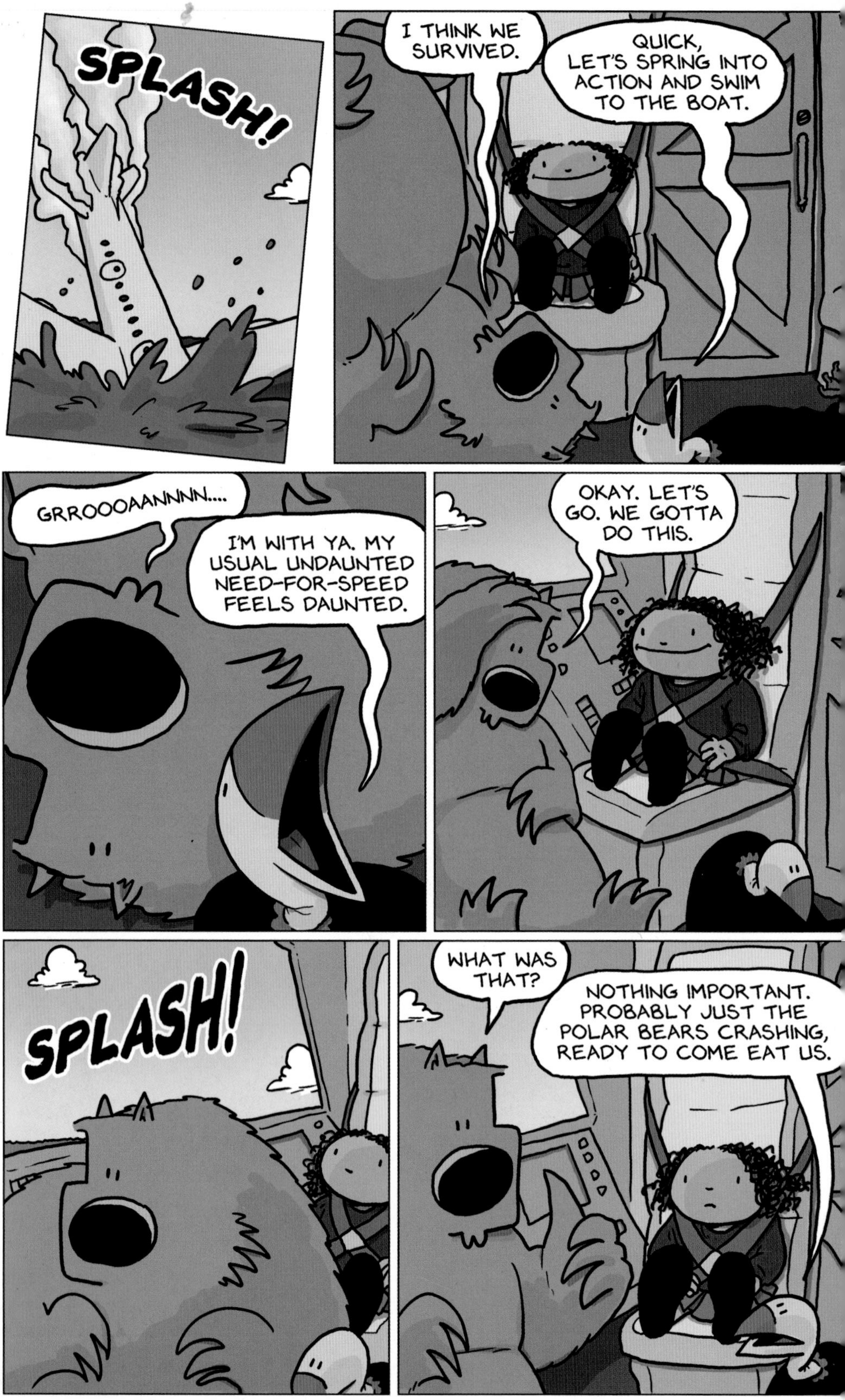
SPLASH!
I THINK WE SURVIVED.
QUICK, LET'S SPRING INTO ACTION AND SWIM TO THE BOAT.
GRROOOAANNNN....
I'M WITH YA. MY USUAL UNDAUNTED NEED-FOR-SPEED FEELS DAUNTED.
OKAY. LET'S GO. WE GOTTA DO THIS.
SPLASH!
WHAT WAS THAT?
NOTHING IMPORTANT. PROBABLY JUST THE POLAR BEARS CRASHING, READY TO COME EAT US.

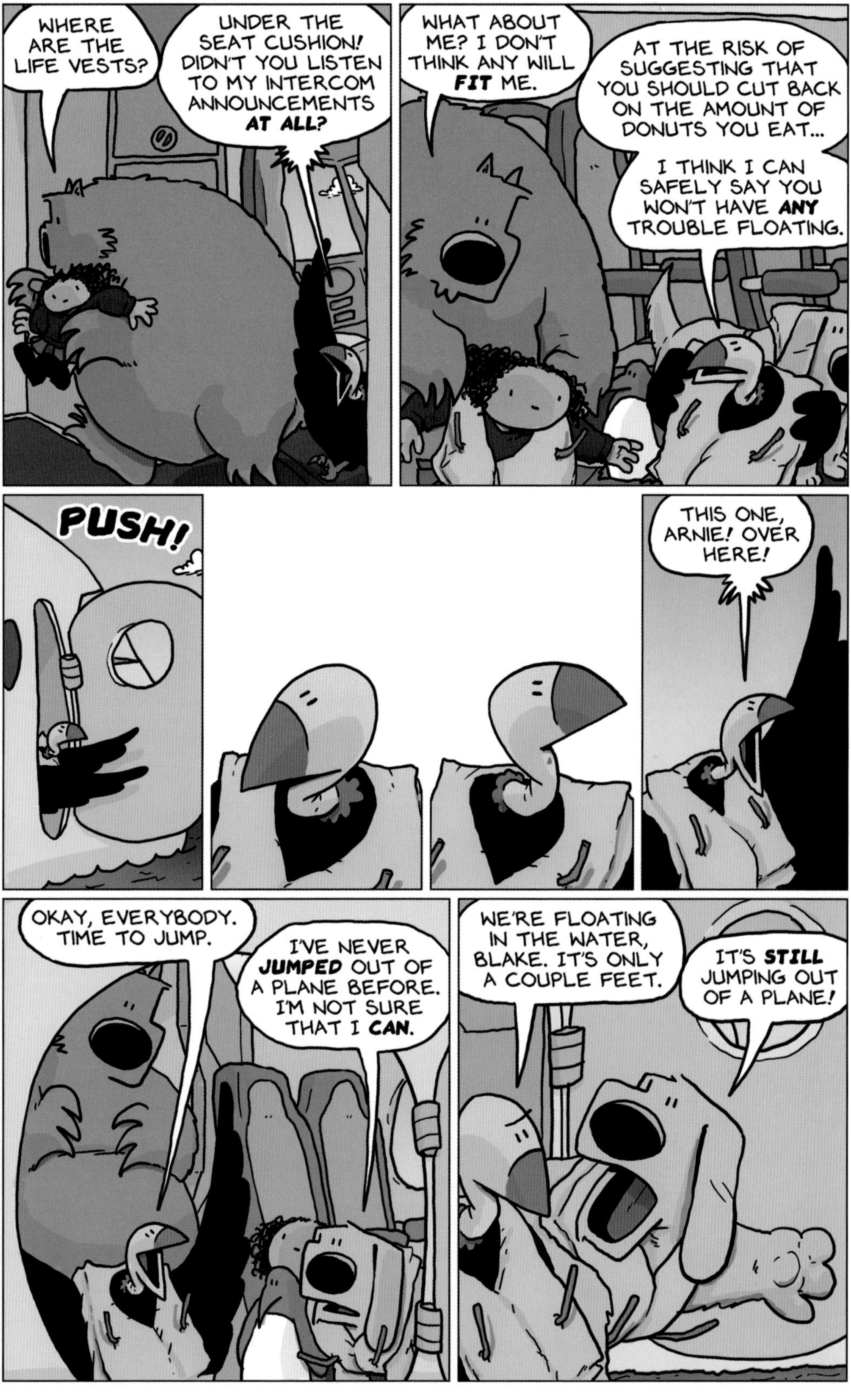
WHERE ARE THE LIFE VESTS?
UNDER THE SEAT CUSHION! DIDN'T YOU LISTEN TO MY INTERCOM ANNOUNCEMENTS AT ALL?
WHAT ABOUT ME? I DON'T THINK ANY WILL FIT ME.
AT THE RISK OF SUGGESTING THAT YOU SHOULD CUT BACK ON THE AMOUNT OF DONUTS YOU EAT...
I THINK I CAN SAFELY SAY YOU WON'T HAVE ANY TROUBLE FLOATING.
PUSH!
THIS ONE, ARNIE! OVER HERE!
OKAY, EVERYBODY. TIME TO JUMP.
I'VE NEVER JUMPED OUT OF A PLANE BEFORE. I'M NOT SURE THAT I CAN.
WE'RE FLOATING IN THE WATER, BLAKE. IT'S ONLY A COUPLE FEET.
IT'S STILL JUMPING OUT OF A PLANE!

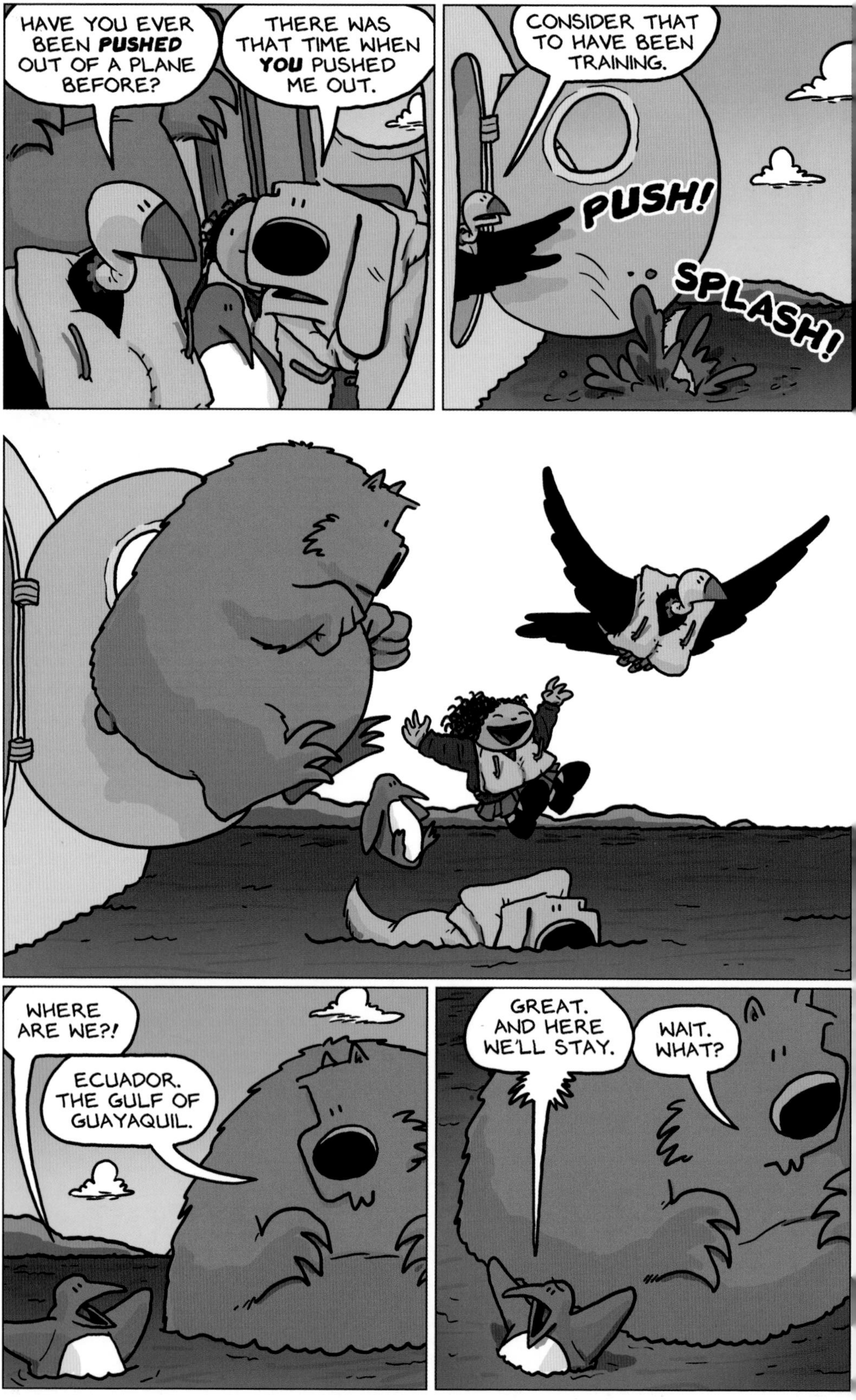
HAVE YOU EVER BEEN **PUSHED** OUT OF A PLANE BEFORE?
THERE WAS THAT TIME WHEN **YOU** PUSHED ME OUT.
CONSIDER THAT TO HAVE BEEN TRAINING.
PUSH!
SPLASH!
WHERE ARE WE?!
ECUADOR. THE GULF OF GUAYAQUIL.
GREAT. AND HERE WE'LL STAY.
WAIT. WHAT?

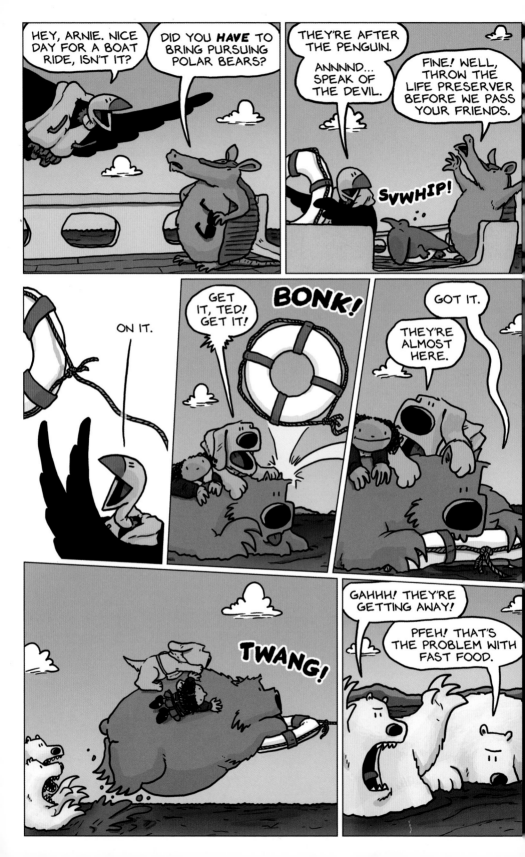

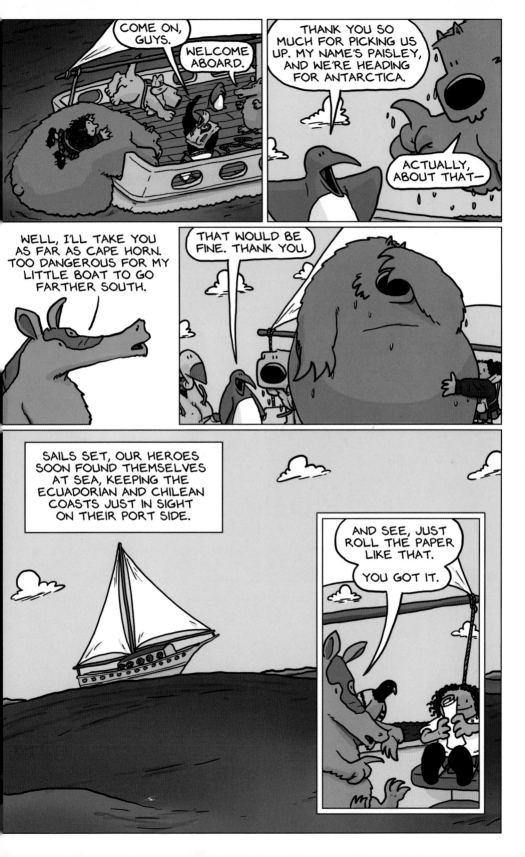

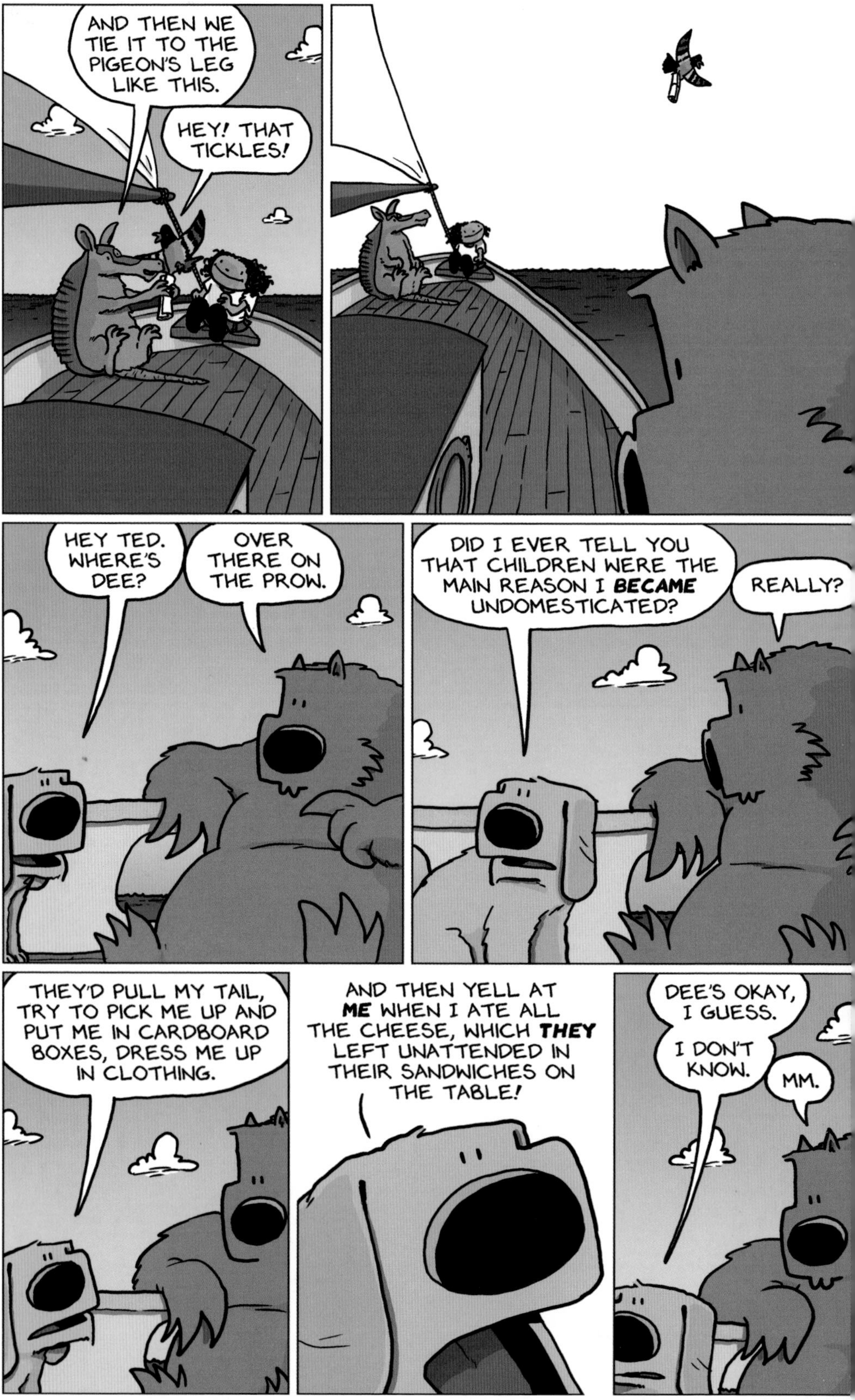
AND THEN WE TIE IT TO THE PIGEON'S LEG LIKE THIS.
HEY! THAT TICKLES!
HEY TED. WHERE'S DEE?
OVER THERE ON THE PROW.
DID I EVER TELL YOU THAT CHILDREN WERE THE MAIN REASON I **BECAME** UNDOMESTICATED?
REALLY?
THEY'D PULL MY TAIL, TRY TO PICK ME UP AND PUT ME IN CARDBOARD BOXES, DRESS ME UP IN CLOTHING.
AND THEN YELL AT **ME** WHEN I ATE ALL THE CHEESE, WHICH **THEY** LEFT UNATTENDED IN THEIR SANDWICHES ON THE TABLE!
DEE'S OKAY, I GUESS.
I DON'T KNOW.
MM.

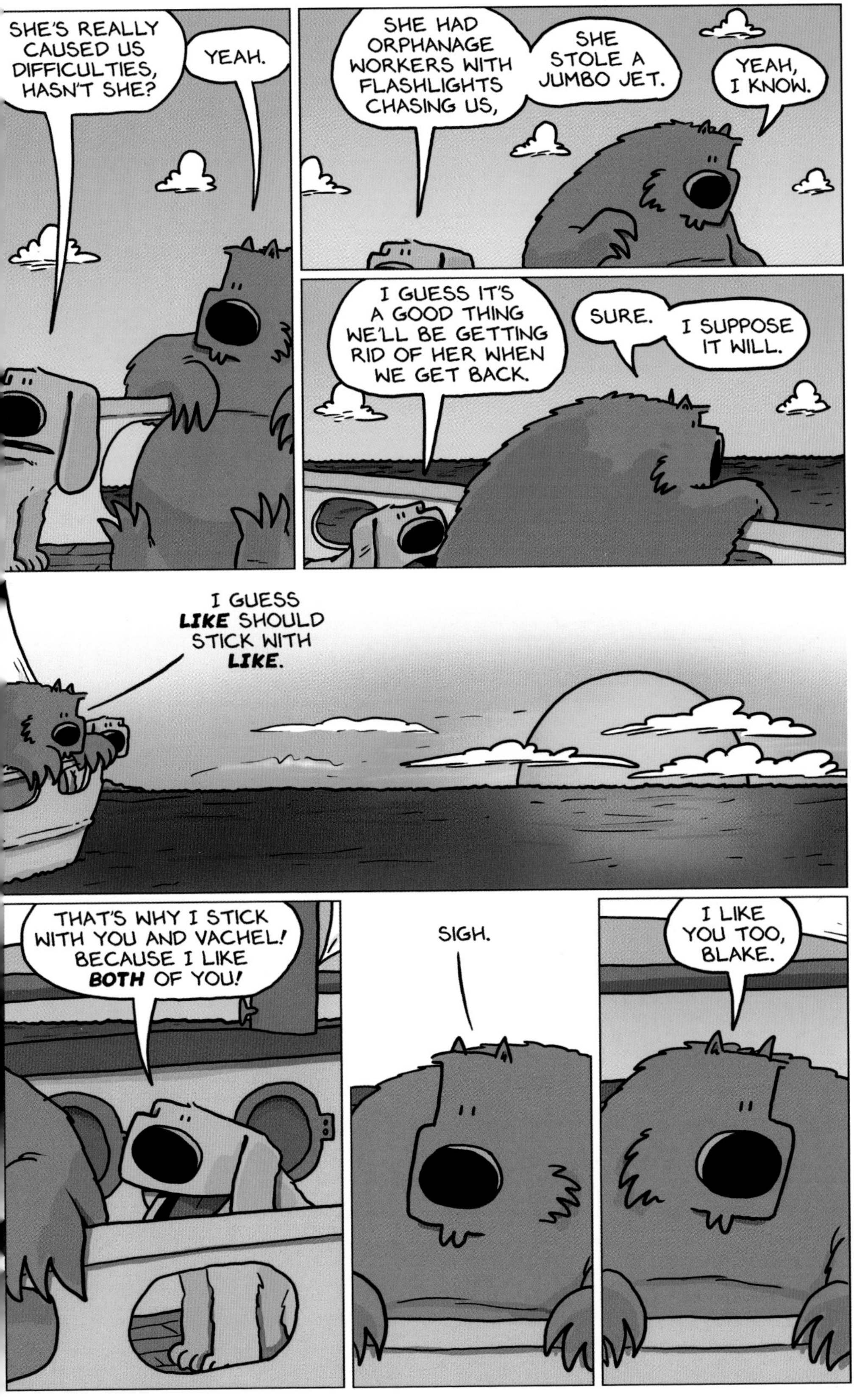
SHE'S REALLY CAUSED US DIFFICULTIES, HASN'T SHE?
YEAH.
SHE HAD ORPHANAGE WORKERS WITH FLASHLIGHTS CHASING US,
SHE STOLE A JUMBO JET.
YEAH, I KNOW.
I GUESS IT'S A GOOD THING WE'LL BE GETTING RID OF HER WHEN WE GET BACK.
SURE.
I SUPPOSE IT WILL.
I GUESS **LIKE** SHOULD STICK WITH **LIKE**.
THAT'S WHY I STICK WITH YOU AND VACHEL! BECAUSE I LIKE **BOTH** OF YOU!
SIGH.
I LIKE YOU TOO, BLAKE.

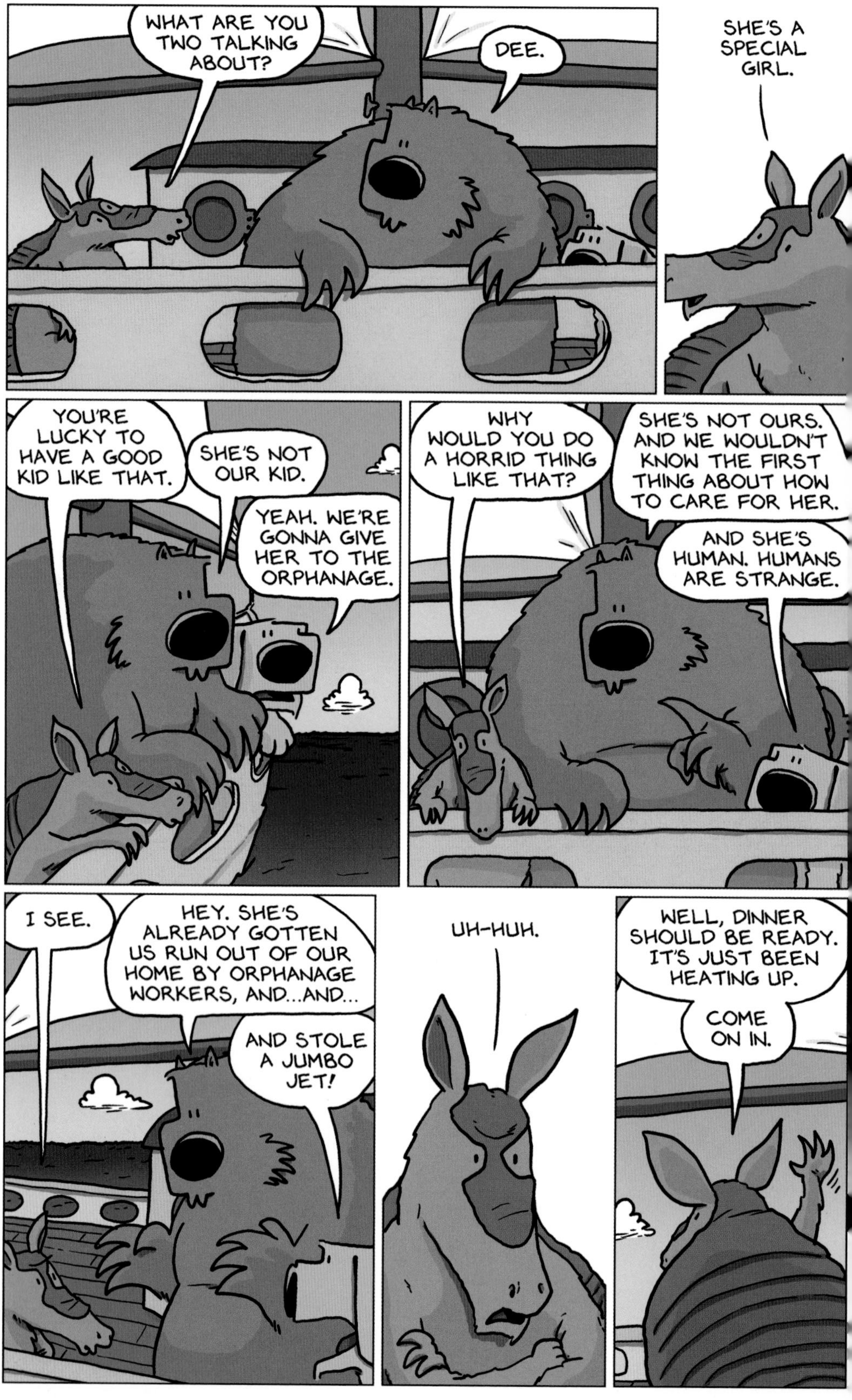
WHAT ARE YOU TWO TALKING ABOUT?
DEE.
SHE'S A SPECIAL GIRL.
YOU'RE LUCKY TO HAVE A GOOD KID LIKE THAT.
SHE'S NOT OUR KID.
YEAH. WE'RE GONNA GIVE HER TO THE ORPHANAGE.
WHY WOULD YOU DO A HORRID THING LIKE THAT?
SHE'S NOT OURS. AND WE WOULDN'T KNOW THE FIRST THING ABOUT HOW TO CARE FOR HER.
AND SHE'S HUMAN. HUMANS ARE STRANGE.
I SEE.
HEY. SHE'S ALREADY GOTTEN US RUN OUT OF OUR HOME BY ORPHANAGE WORKERS, AND...AND...
AND STOLE A JUMBO JET!
UH-HUH.
WELL, DINNER SHOULD BE READY. IT'S JUST BEEN HEATING UP.
COME ON IN.

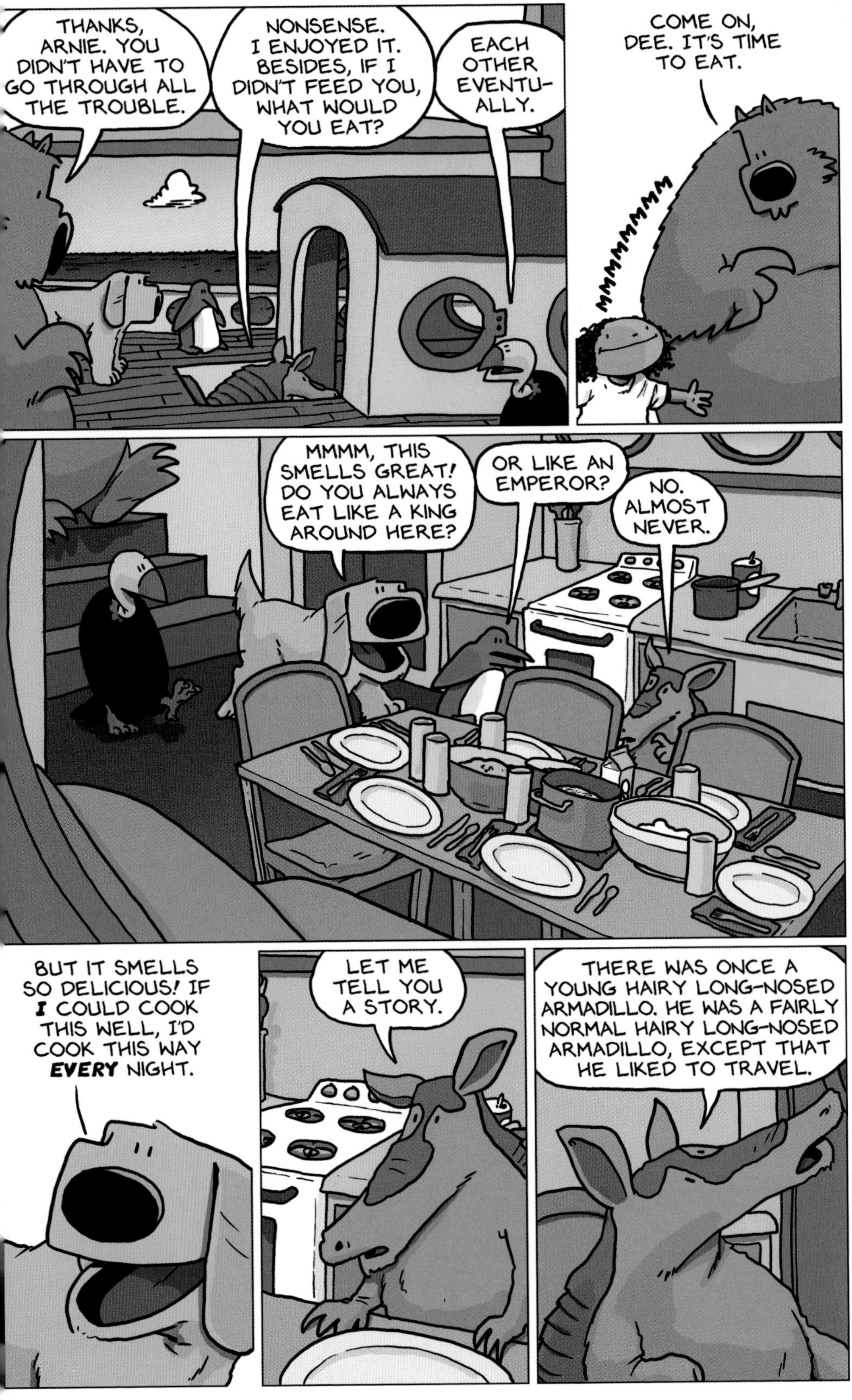
THANKS, ARNIE. YOU DIDN'T HAVE TO GO THROUGH ALL THE TROUBLE.
NONSENSE. I ENJOYED IT. BESIDES, IF I DIDN'T FEED YOU, WHAT WOULD YOU EAT?
EACH OTHER EVENTU-ALLY.
COME ON, DEE. IT'S TIME TO EAT.
MMMMMMMMMM
MMMM, THIS SMELLS GREAT! DO YOU ALWAYS EAT LIKE A KING AROUND HERE?
OR LIKE AN EMPEROR?
NO. ALMOST NEVER.
BUT IT SMELLS SO DELICIOUS! IF *I* COULD COOK THIS WELL, I'D COOK THIS WAY **EVERY** NIGHT.
LET ME TELL YOU A STORY.
THERE WAS ONCE A YOUNG HAIRY LONG-NOSED ARMADILLO. HE WAS A FAIRLY NORMAL HAIRY LONG-NOSED ARMADILLO, EXCEPT THAT HE LIKED TO TRAVEL.

USUALLY A YOUNG ARMADILLO FINDS A GOOD EIGHT ACRES AND SETTLES DOWN WITH FRIENDS AND FAMILY, BUT HE HAD THE ITCH TO SEE THE WORLD.

I COULDA TOLD YOU THAT! LEAVING HOME IS NOTHING BUT TROUBLE.

SO THIS ARMADILLO WENT OUT TO SEA, TRAVELING AND VISITING EVERY BEAUTIFUL CITY ALONG THE COAST OF ECUADOR, PERU, AND CHILE.

ECUADOR!
GUAYAQUIL! PERU!
CHIMBOTE!
LIMA!
ICA! ARICA! CHILE!
ANTOFAGASTA!
SANTIAGO!
CONCEPCION!
PUERTO MONTT!
PUNTA ARENAS!

BUT AFTER TIME, HE FELT HIS LIFE HAD BECOME POINTLESS.

ALL CITIES LOOKED THE SAME, ALL FACES WERE STRANGERS, AND HE LONGED FOR THE DAYS IN THE PRAIRIE GRASS WITH HIS FAMILY.

BUT WHEN HE WENT HOME, HE DIDN'T KNOW ANYONE. THEY'D ALL MOVED AWAY.

AND SO HE SAILED AWAY AGAIN. ALONE. AND HE'S FELT LONELY EVER SINCE.

HE SOUNDS LIKE A TOTAL LOSER. IF HE HAD ANY BACKBONE, ANY ENDURANCE, HE'D STILL BE TRAVELING AND HAVING A GREAT TIME.

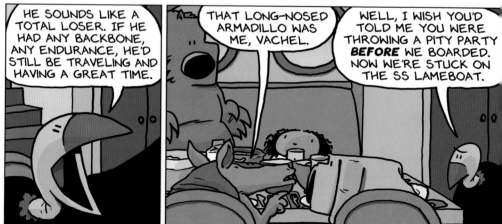

THAT LONG-NOSED ARMADILLO WAS ME, VACHEL.

WELL, I WISH YOU'D TOLD ME YOU WERE THROWING A PITY PARTY *BEFORE* WE BOARDED. NOW WE'RE STUCK ON THE SS LAMEBOAT.

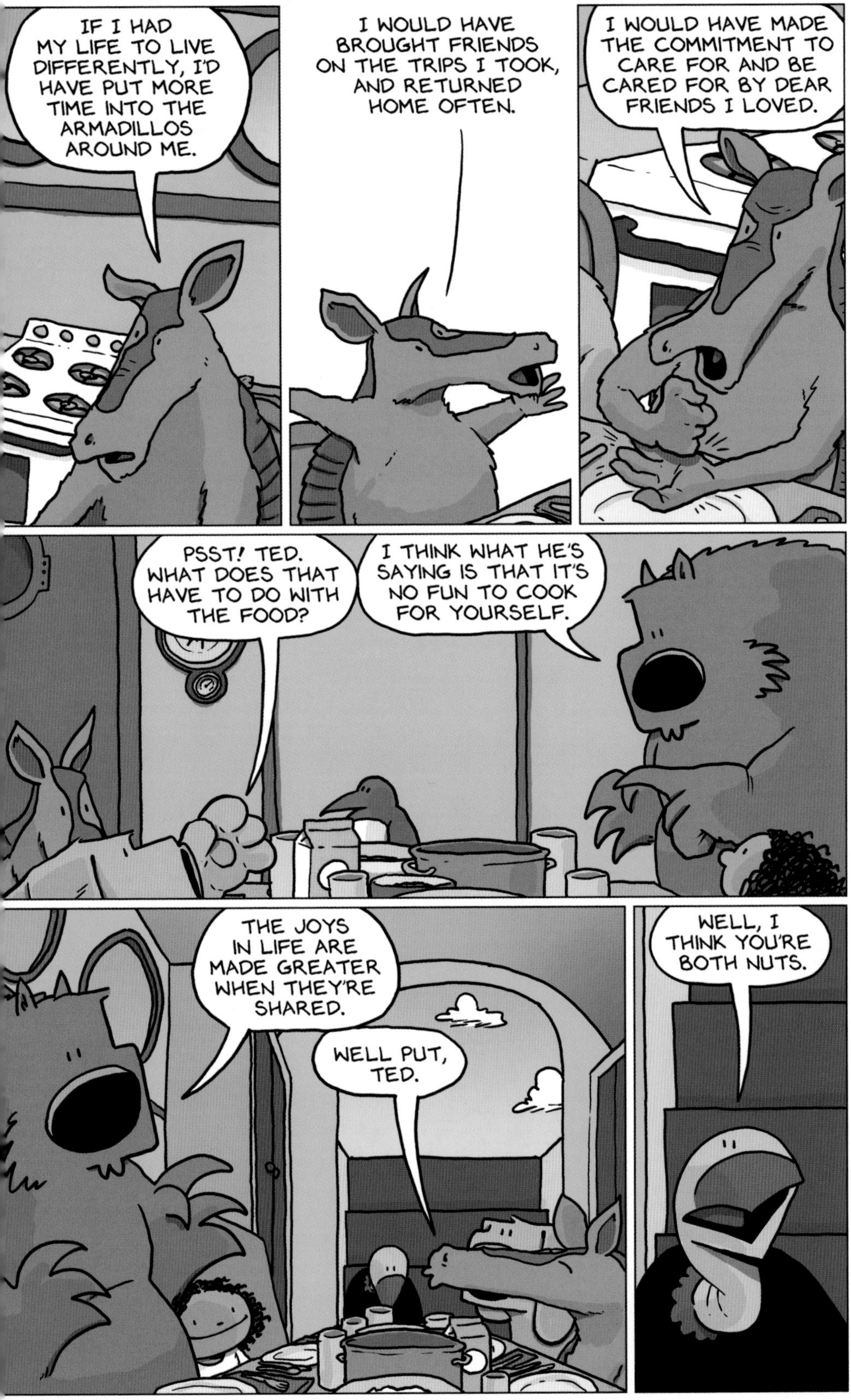
IF I HAD MY LIFE TO LIVE DIFFERENTLY, I'D HAVE PUT MORE TIME INTO THE ARMADILLOS AROUND ME.
I WOULD HAVE BROUGHT FRIENDS ON THE TRIPS I TOOK, AND RETURNED HOME OFTEN.
I WOULD HAVE MADE THE COMMITMENT TO CARE FOR AND BE CARED FOR BY DEAR FRIENDS I LOVED.
PSST! TED. WHAT DOES THAT HAVE TO DO WITH THE FOOD?
I THINK WHAT HE'S SAYING IS THAT IT'S NO FUN TO COOK FOR YOURSELF.
THE JOYS IN LIFE ARE MADE GREATER WHEN THEY'RE SHARED.
WELL PUT, TED.
WELL, I THINK YOU'RE BOTH NUTS.

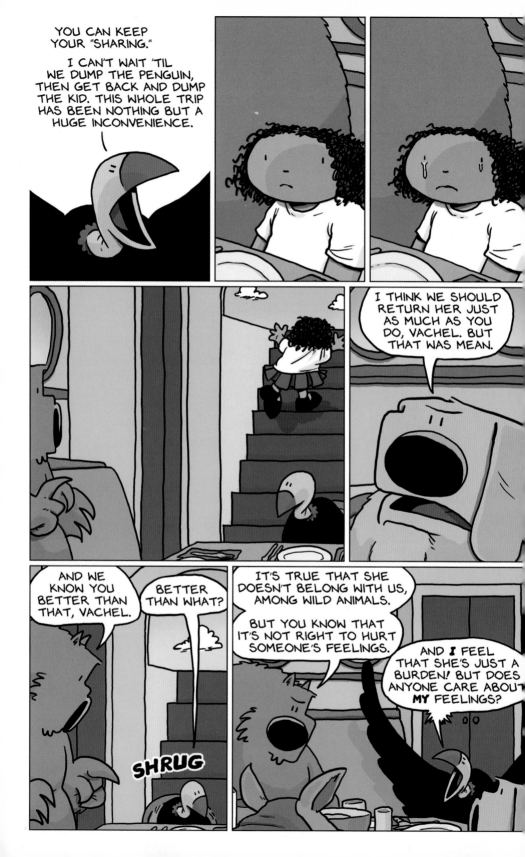

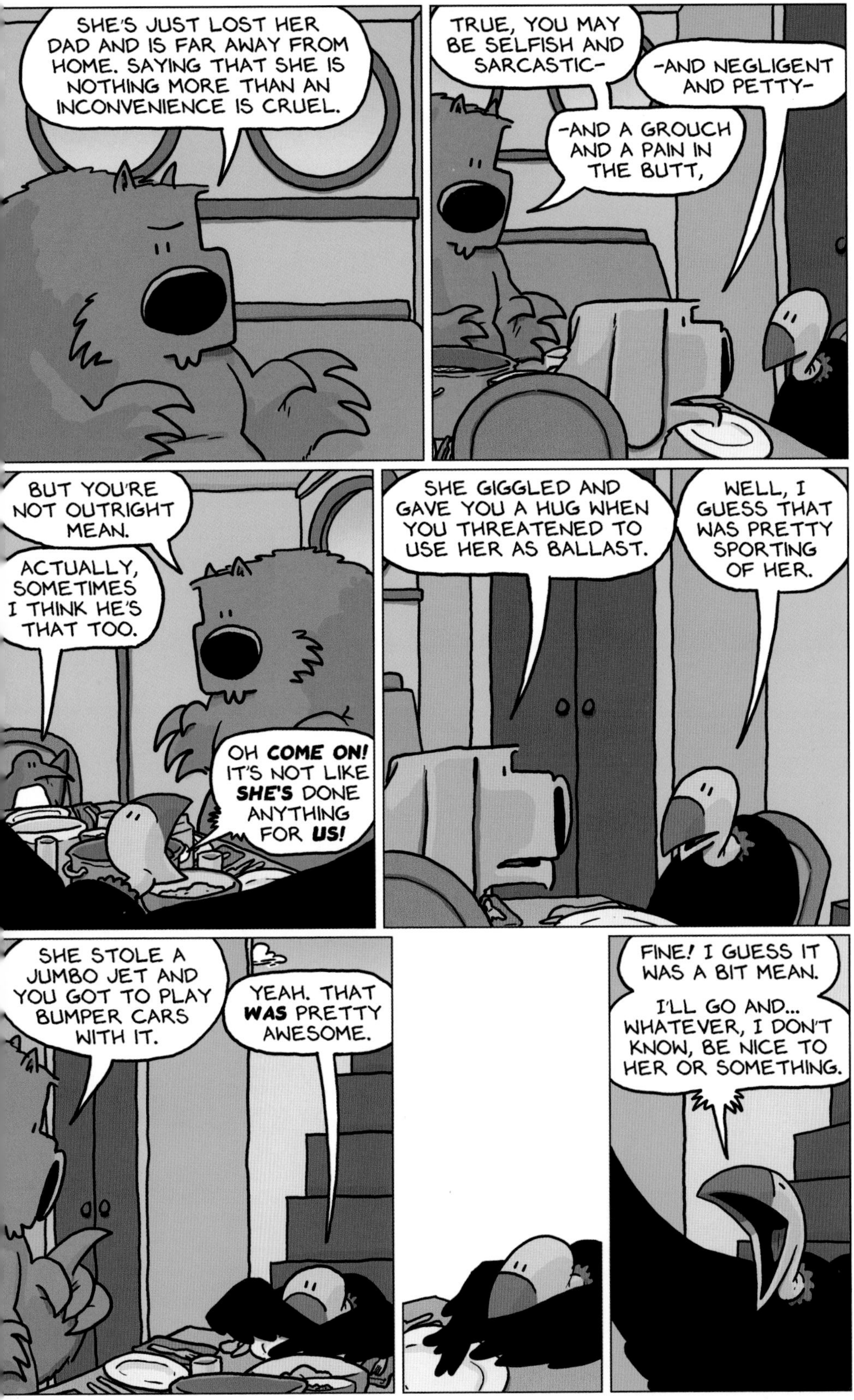
SHE'S JUST LOST HER DAD AND IS FAR AWAY FROM HOME. SAYING THAT SHE IS NOTHING MORE THAN AN INCONVENIENCE IS CRUEL.
TRUE, YOU MAY BE SELFISH AND SARCASTIC-
-AND NEGLIGENT AND PETTY-
-AND A GROUCH AND A PAIN IN THE BUTT,
BUT YOU'RE NOT OUTRIGHT MEAN.
ACTUALLY, SOMETIMES I THINK HE'S THAT TOO.
OH COME ON! IT'S NOT LIKE SHE'S DONE ANYTHING FOR US!
SHE GIGGLED AND GAVE YOU A HUG WHEN YOU THREATENED TO USE HER AS BALLAST.
WELL, I GUESS THAT WAS PRETTY SPORTING OF HER.
SHE STOLE A JUMBO JET AND YOU GOT TO PLAY BUMPER CARS WITH IT.
YEAH. THAT WAS PRETTY AWESOME.
FINE! I GUESS IT WAS A BIT MEAN.
I'LL GO AND... WHATEVER, I DON'T KNOW, BE NICE TO HER OR SOMETHING.

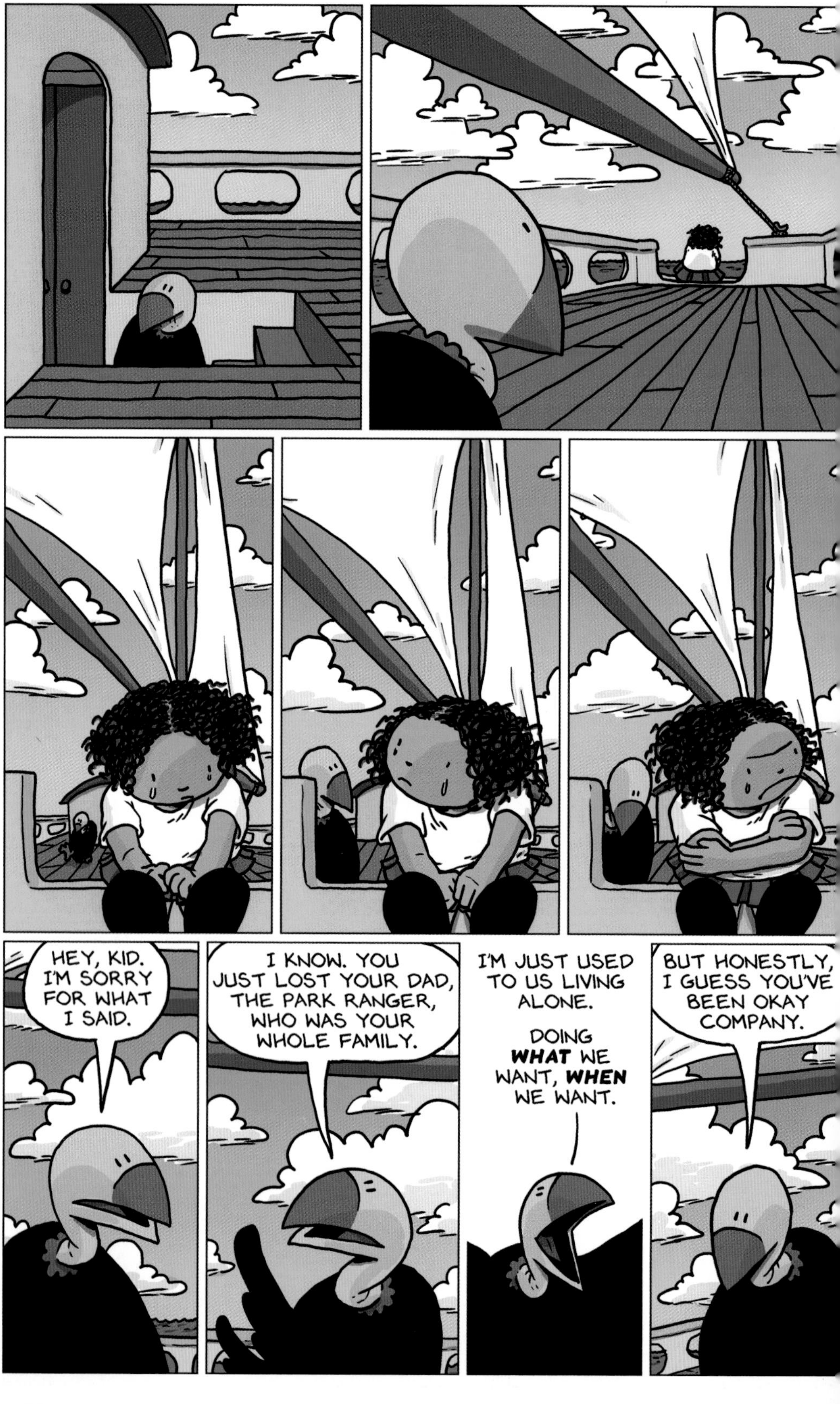
HEY, KID. I'M SORRY FOR WHAT I SAID.
I KNOW. YOU JUST LOST YOUR DAD, THE PARK RANGER, WHO WAS YOUR WHOLE FAMILY.
I'M JUST USED TO US LIVING ALONE.
DOING **WHAT** WE WANT, **WHEN** WE WANT.
BUT HONESTLY, I GUESS YOU'VE BEEN OKAY COMPANY.

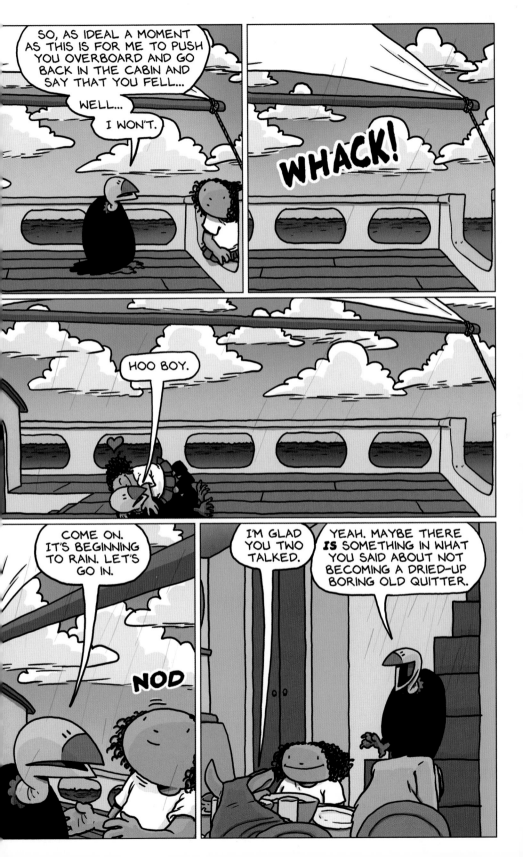

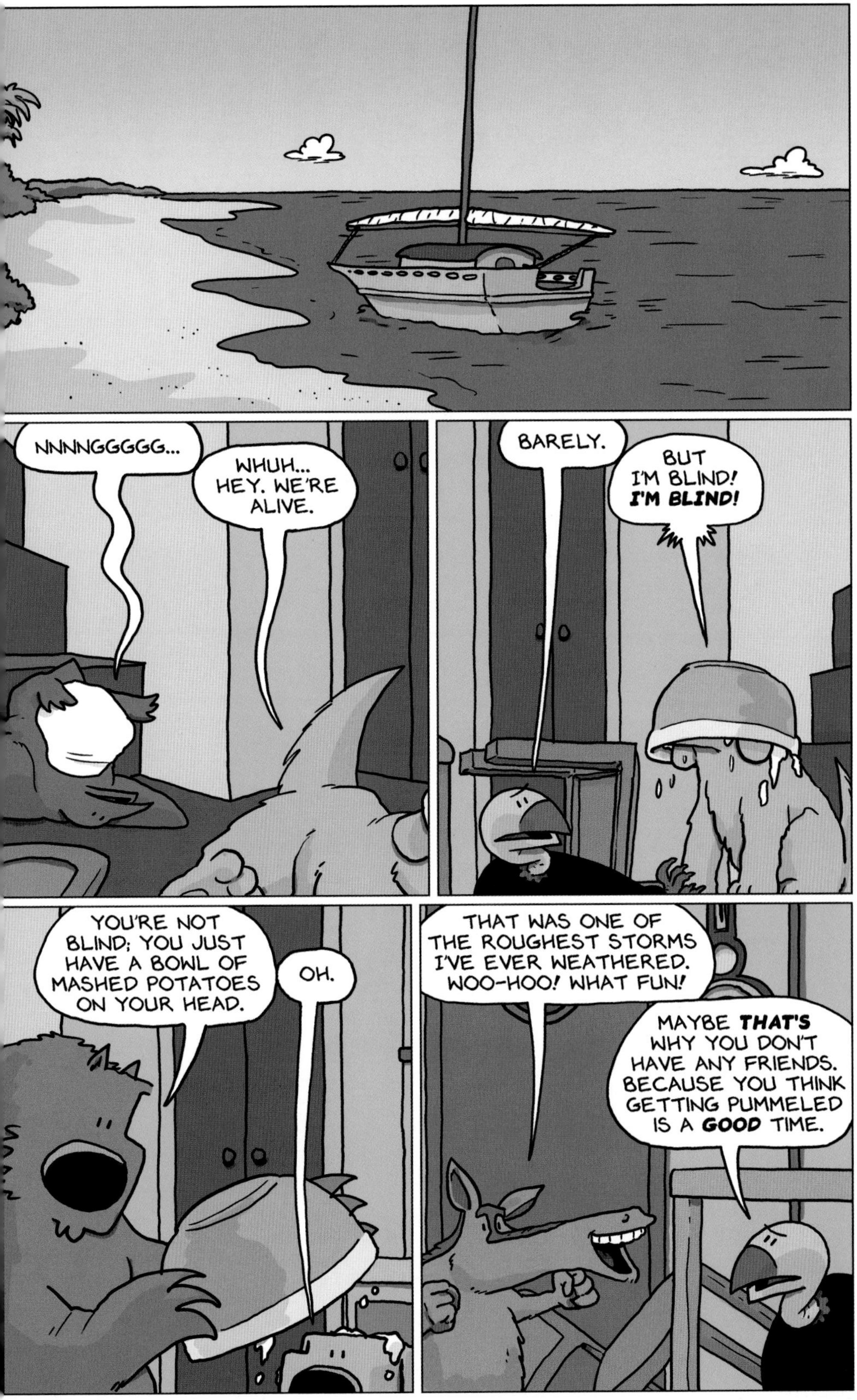
NNNNGGGGG...
WHUH... HEY. WE'RE ALIVE.
BARELY.
BUT I'M BLIND! **I'M BLIND!**
YOU'RE NOT BLIND; YOU JUST HAVE A BOWL OF MASHED POTATOES ON YOUR HEAD.
OH.
THAT WAS ONE OF THE ROUGHEST STORMS I'VE EVER WEATHERED. WOO-HOO! WHAT FUN!
MAYBE **THAT'S** WHY YOU DON'T HAVE ANY FRIENDS. BECAUSE YOU THINK GETTING PUMMELED IS A **GOOD** TIME.

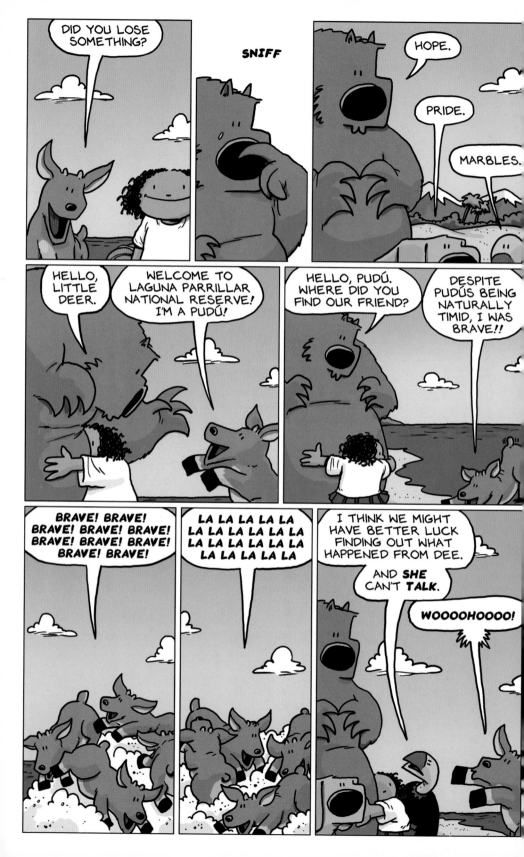

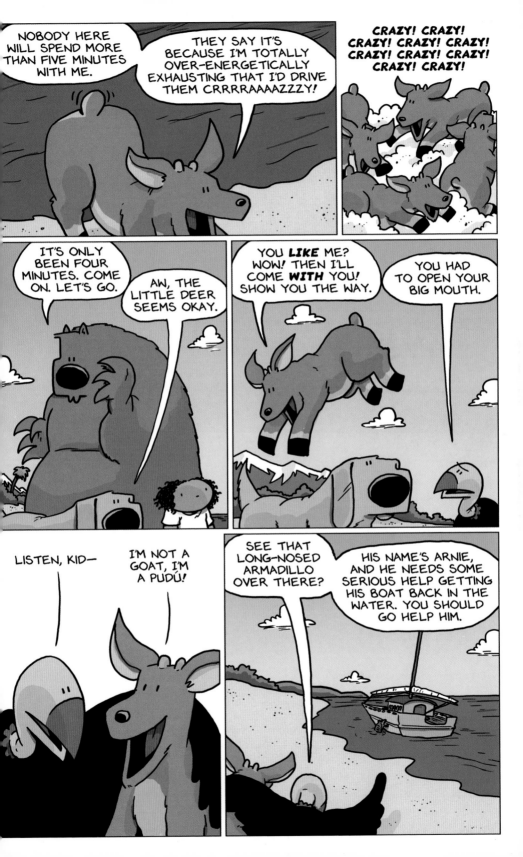

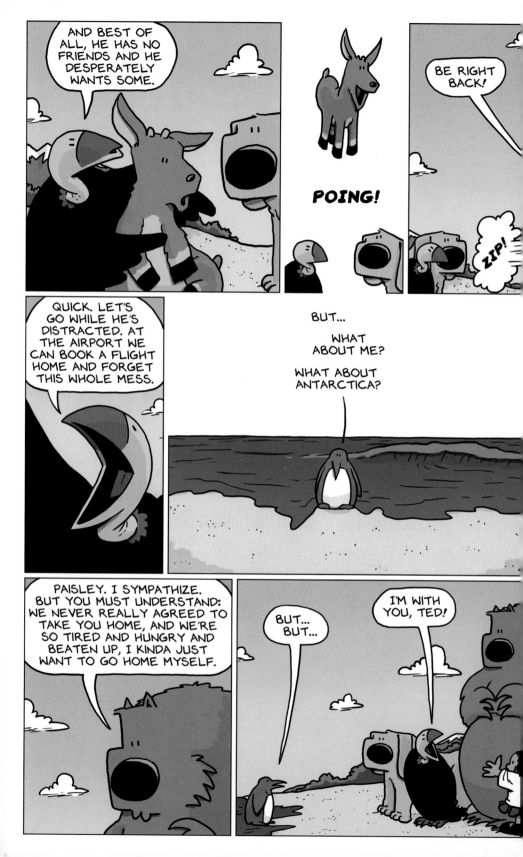

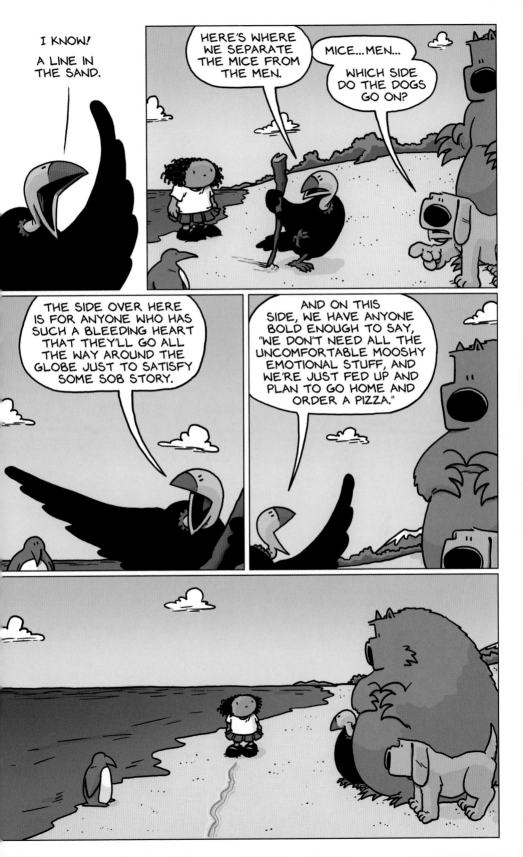

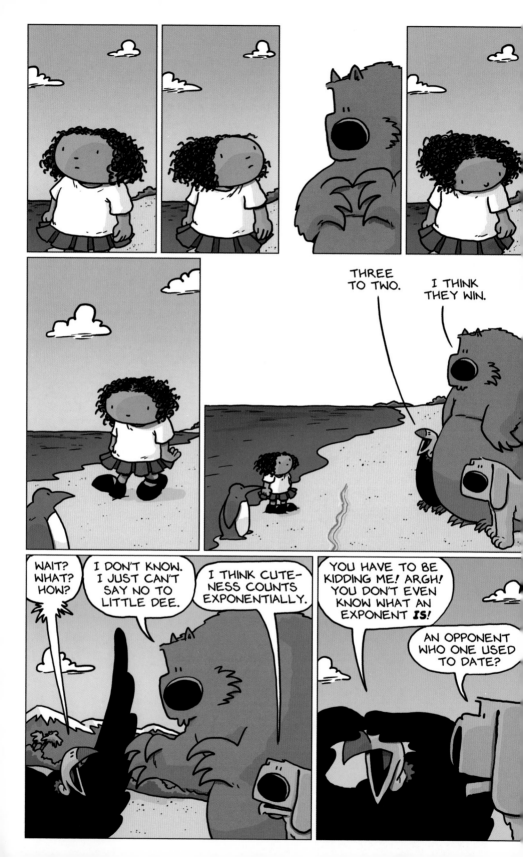

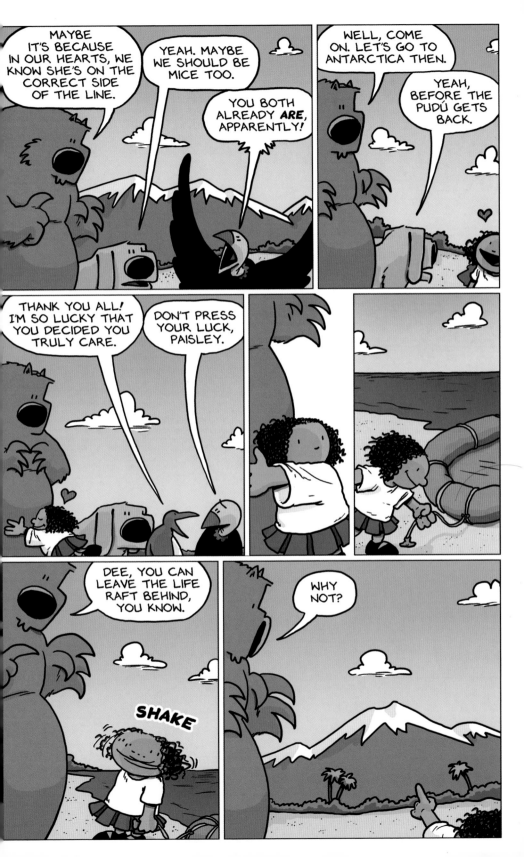

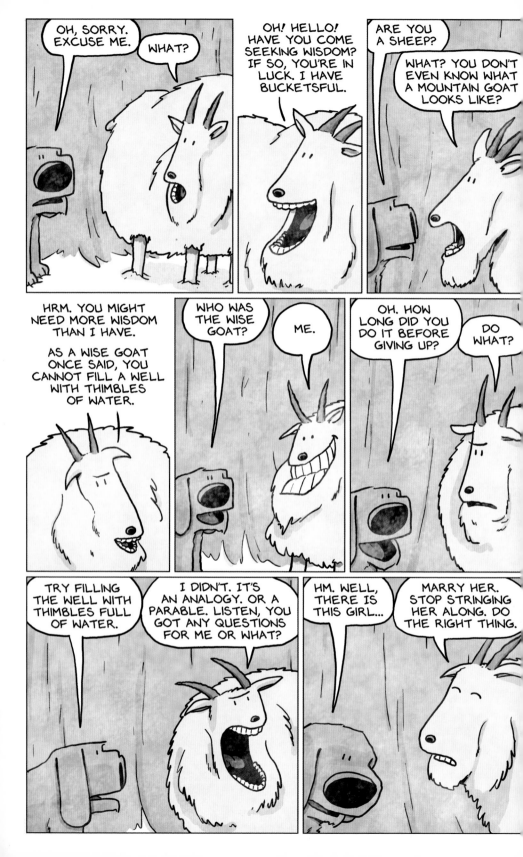

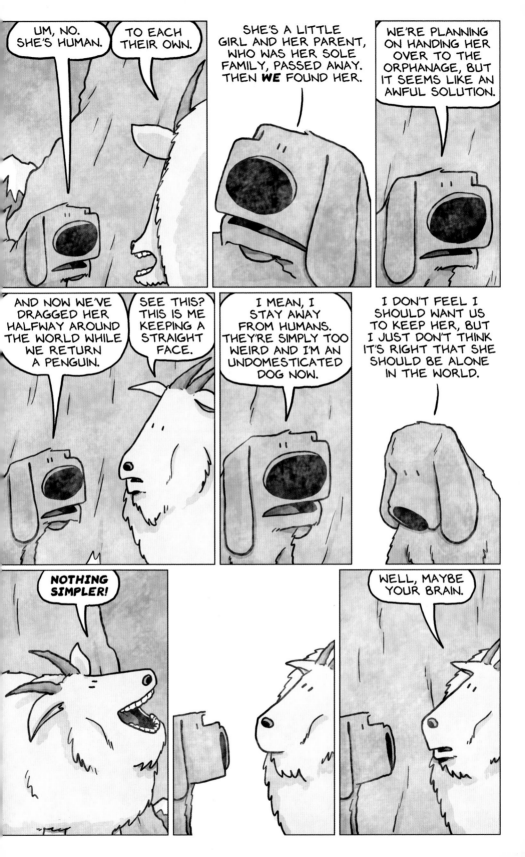

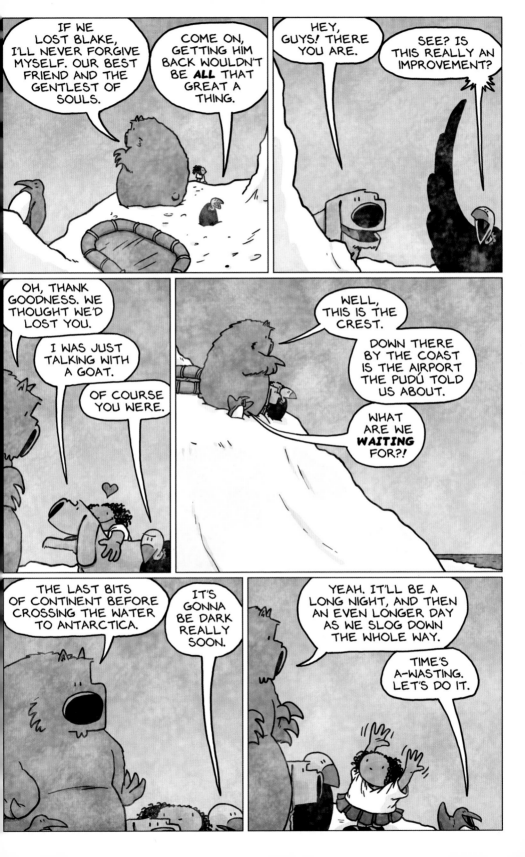

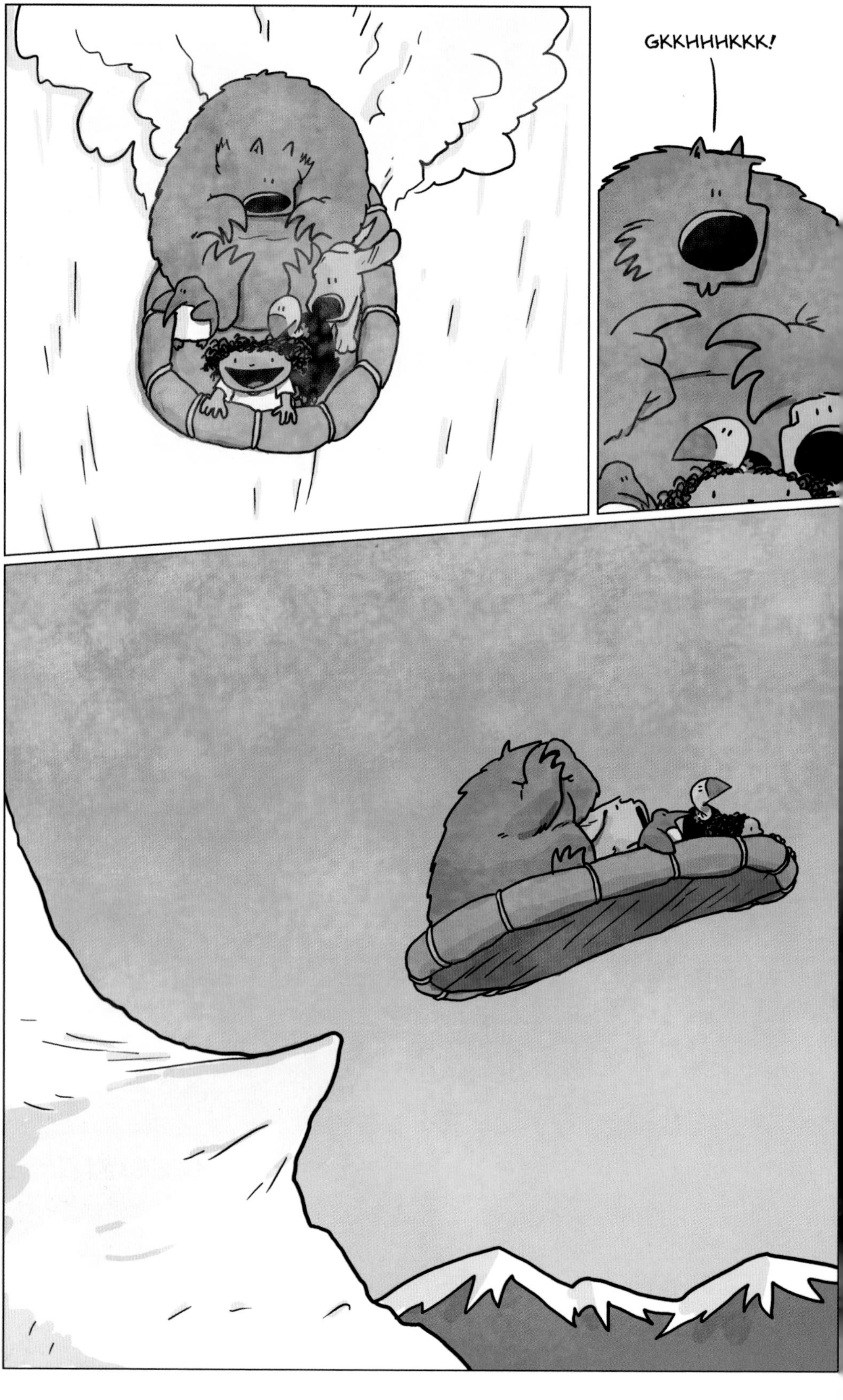
GKKHHHKKK!

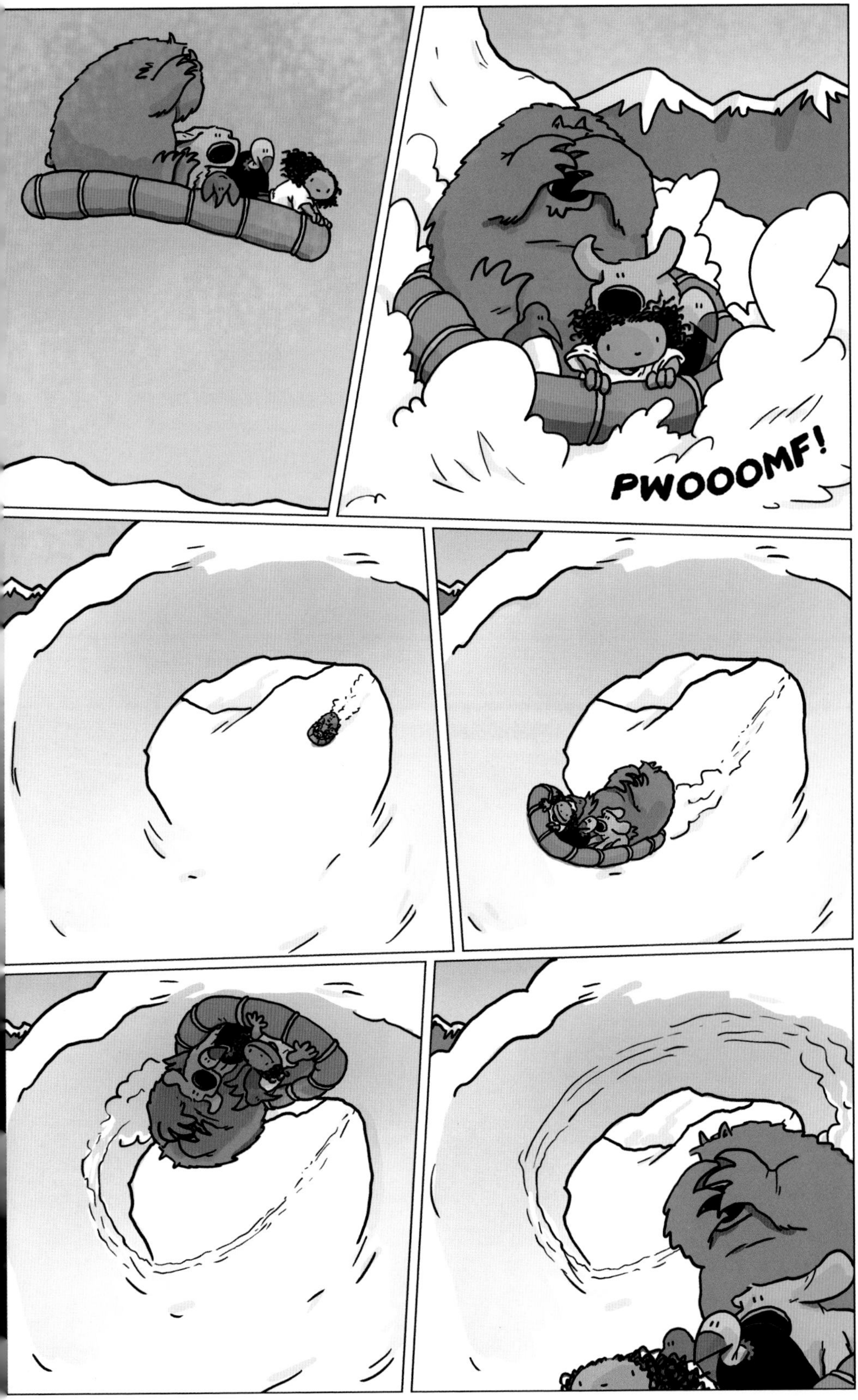
PWOOOMF!

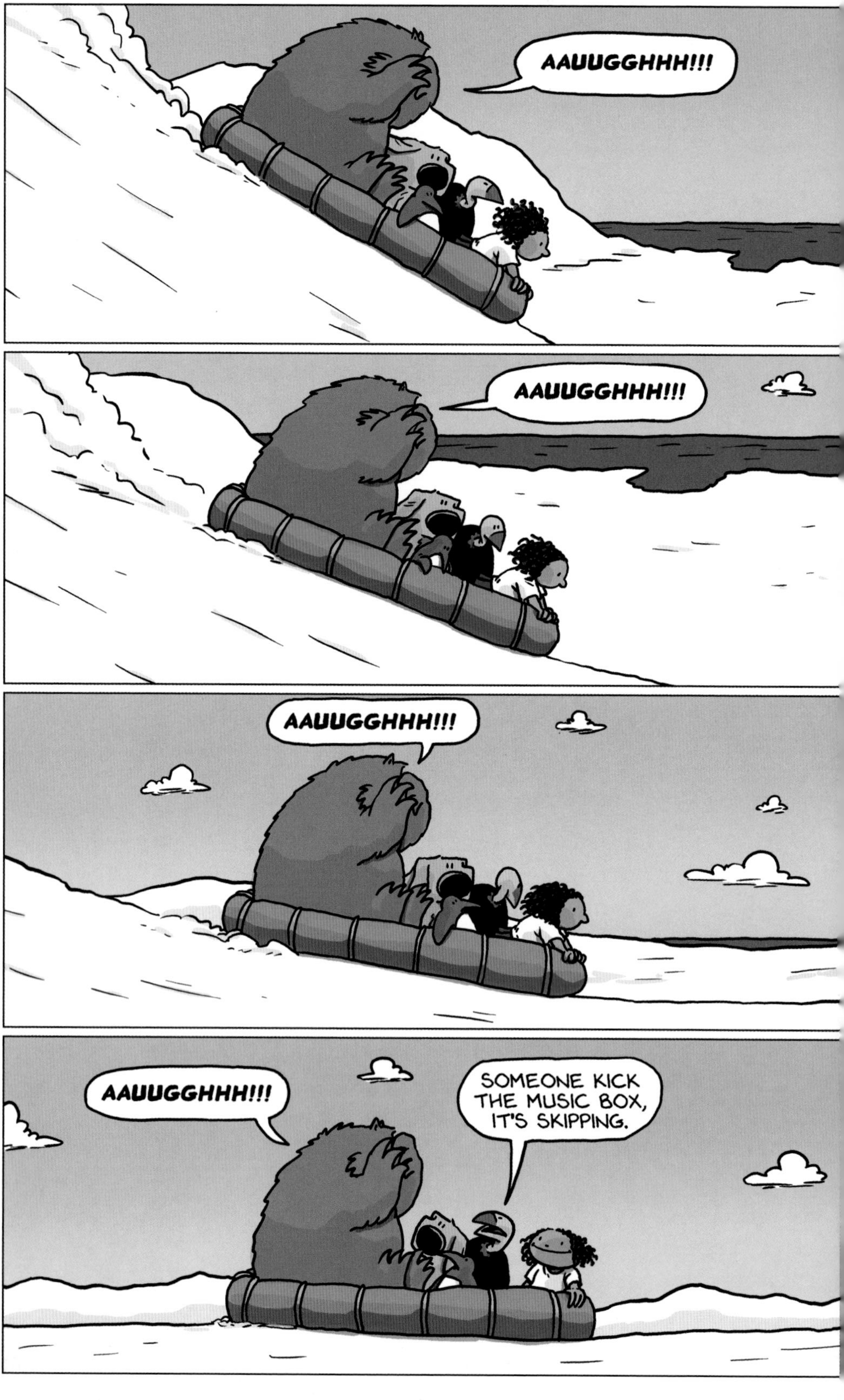
AAUUGGHHH!!!
AAUUGGHHH!!!
AAUUGGHHH!!!
AAUUGGHHH!!!
SOMEONE KICK THE MUSIC BOX, IT'S SKIPPING.

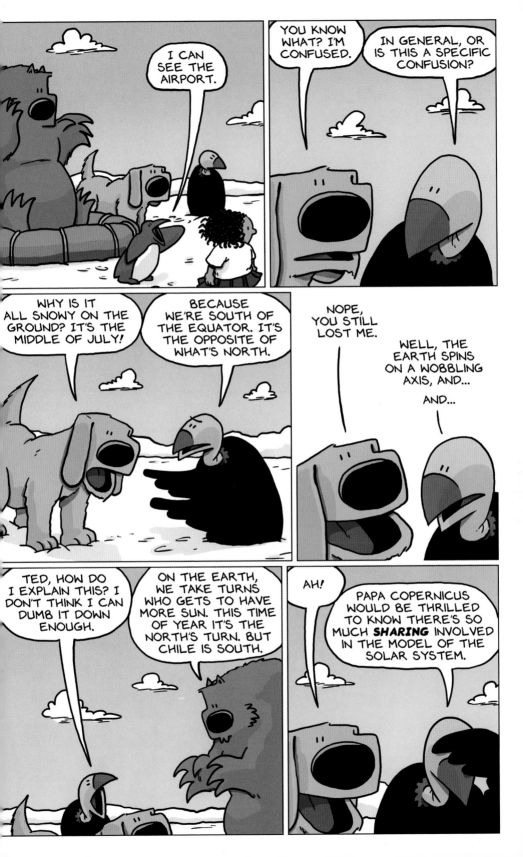

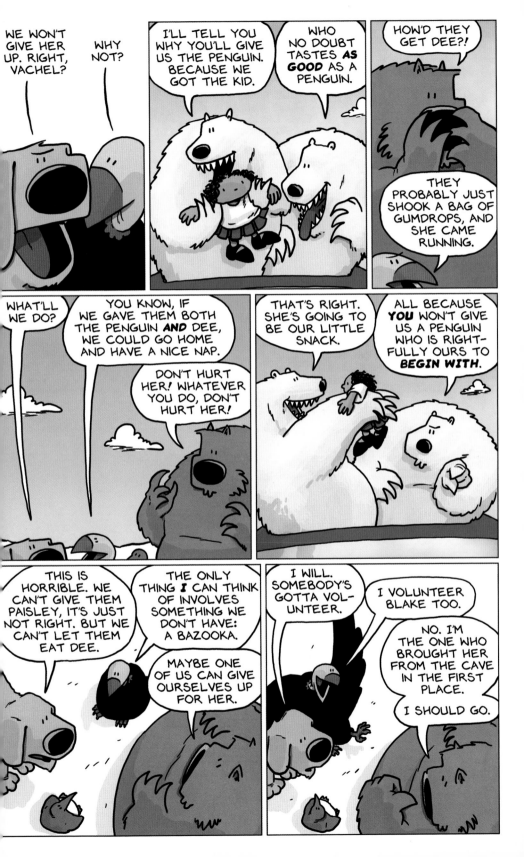

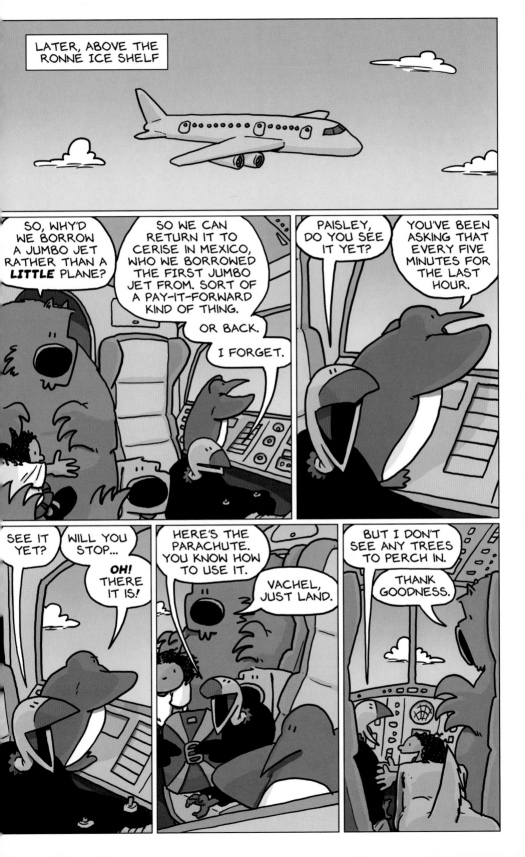

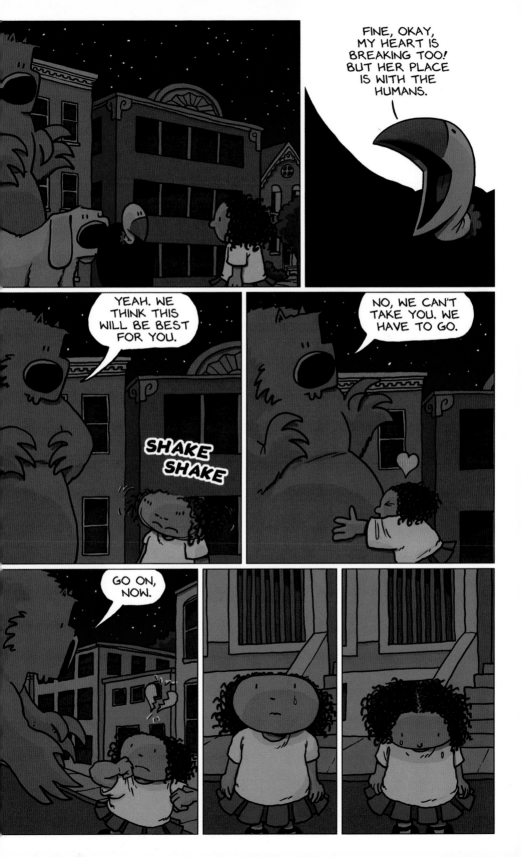

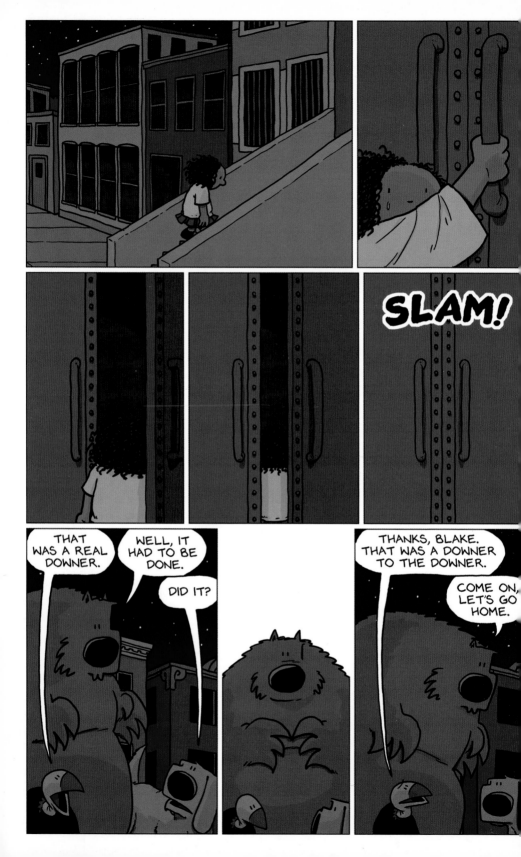

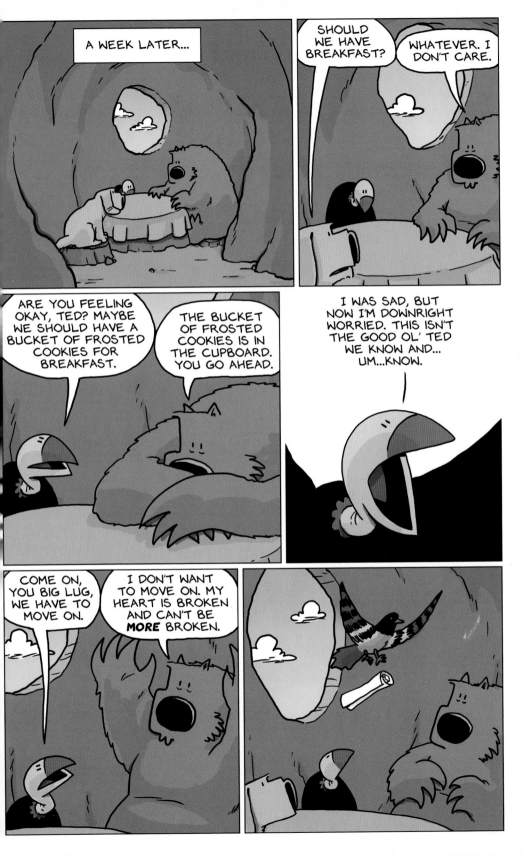

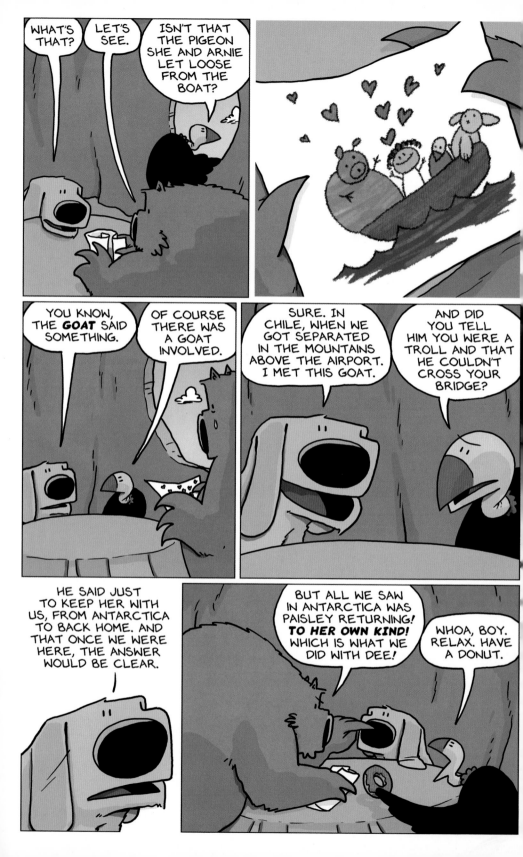

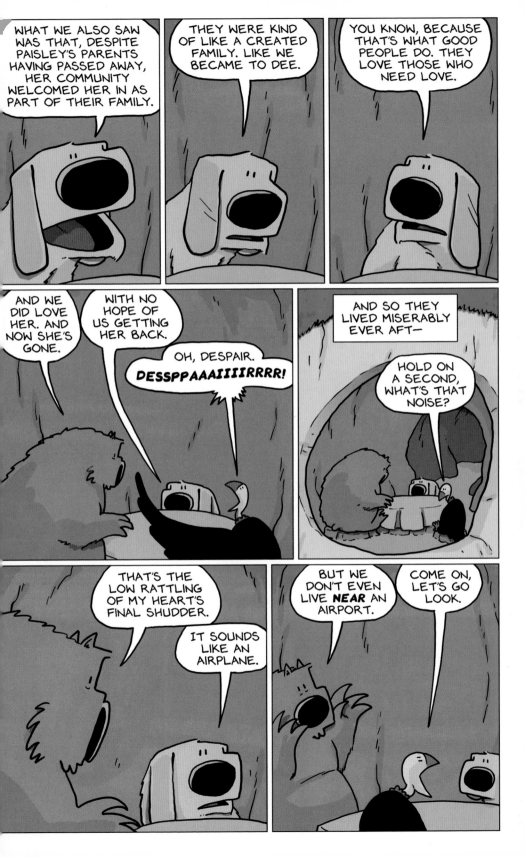

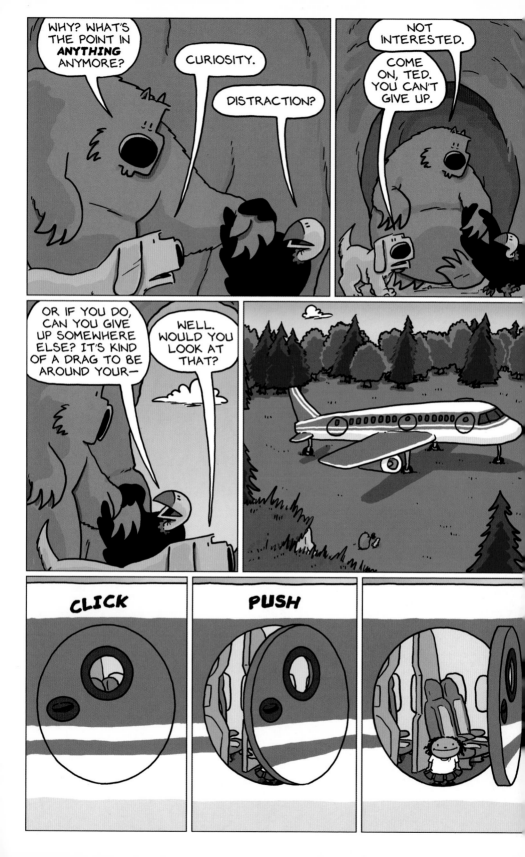

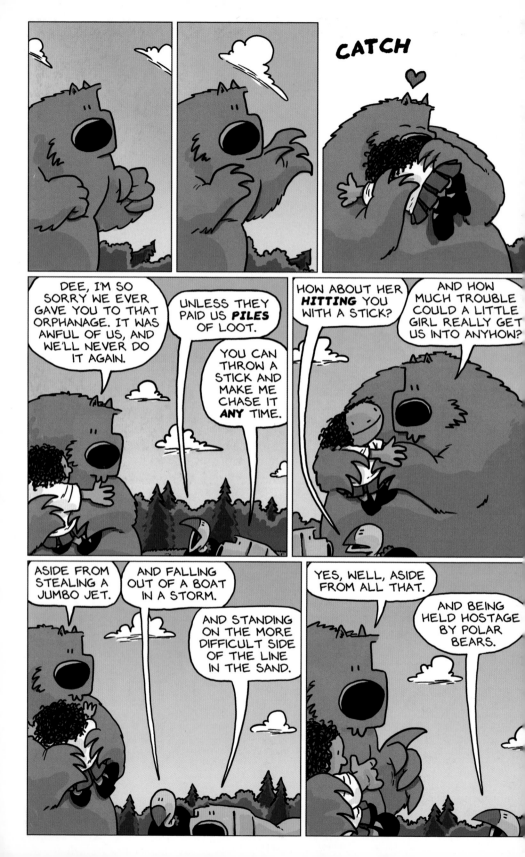

THE END